1962

Samantha Henthorn

For Dad, the best dad on two wheels.

Chapter 1: The Man Of The House

"*Our Father, who art in heaven*"
He had been waiting to communicate with God all week, it was his regular request for help and private contemplation.
"*Hallowed be thy name*" keeping his eyes closed so that his internal dialogue remained hidden.
"*Thy kingdom come*... God, dear God, it's me... Ernest Bradshaw" The vicar's watchfulness burned through the curtain of his eyelids. "*Thy will be done*... ME! Ernest Bradshaw! You know me... you know everyone according t'vicar"
 Ernest risked half a glance in front of him, and made a split-second decision to continue "*On earth as it is in heaven.* The thing is, I was wondering if you could see your way to getting rid of Mark Crosby, he goes to my school, he usually picks on Harold, but see, Harold has broken his ankle, but you probably know that. *And forgive us our trespasses*. See God, I don't trespass, it wasn't me, *as we forgive those who trespass against us* (apart from Mark Crosby) *And lead us not into temptation*... and now I reckon with Harold out of action, they're probably gonna pick on me, so if you could just see your way fit to getting rid of him, not permanent like... don't forget, God: Mark Crosby

his name is. I'd point him out, God but he isn't here, see he doesn't come to church, but I do. I come every Sunday with me mother and Uncle Billy. You know God, do your 'works in mysterious ways' thing, God... *Ahhhh-men*... Oh God! I mean *Amen* I didn't mean to miss the end of *Our Father*" Creaky church pews and coughing fits infected the congregation. "Who are you talking to?" Ernest's mother mouthed, without making a sound.

"Our Father" Agreed Father Dunn, his sing-song prayer voice herding his obedient flock. "Let us pray today for the sons of our church, that they will fear you, Lord, please take our sons into your loving and holy hands as they become men. Joshua in verses 1-9 reads: *'Have I not commanded you? Be strong and courageous. Do not be frightened, and do not be dismayed for the Lord your God is with you wherever you go'* we pray that the Lord God is with our sons"

The finishing prayer's message caught by the congregation, before the finishing hymn.
"So I'm on me own then? As long as I am not frightened, and go wherever I am going?" Ernest's private prayer continued. He took a sideways glance at his mother.

"Oh no! I didn't mean to forget, God, please help me mother, in anything that she needs help with, like maybe don't let her see I've made a hole in me sock, she hates it if anything like that happens... That's me mother, God: ROSE BRADSHAW, you've known her longer than I have"

Ernest was now sure that he had covered everything he needed to in his prayers.

His mother sort of sighed, secretly asking God if Father Dunn was inventing subliminal messages for his sermon.

"Dear God, it's me, Rose Bradshaw. I know 'Vicar just said we should pray for our sons, as they become men, but I need to make sure - he didn't mean before they become soldiers, did he? I was listening God, but the word 'courageous' threw me It's like twenty odd years ago all over again in the news, and our Ernest, well he's only fourteen, and I know I didn't have him christened, but you know why God, and I prayed like mad for forgiveness, you know that God, You were there... I know life's not meant to be fair, but does Father Dunn know summat I don't God? Me nerves won't take much more... Amen" Mother and son stood side by side talking to God without making a sound, next to Uncle Billy, who only ever spoke without making a sound, ever.

"*All things bright and beautiful, all creatures great and small*" Father Dunn sang with his sing-song hymn voice "*All things bright and beautiful*, including my Ernest, who is both great, and small" Rose Bradshaw made doe-eyed loving admiration at her forward facing

son, who was singing without making a sound "*The Lord God made them all*, that's right Mrs Sidebottom you can keep your sideways glances at me and our Ernest every Sunday... *the Lord God made them all*"

Ernest looked at Uncle Billy, he had forgotten him in his prayers but decided against bothering God for the third time; because Uncle Billy appeared to be at it himself. Eyes firmly shut, Billy risked opening one of them. The second he noticed Father Dunn's mouth begin to move, his eye was expertly closed again. Hands clenched in a knuckle-baring prayer pose, Uncle Billy appeared to be having a good chat with God, his deafness excused him from painful hymn singing every Sunday. The Bradshaw family left the house of forgiveness and its occupying hypocrites. Coins in the collection plate, donated by those with a man's wage to share. Queuing up to be judged, Father Dunn shook the hands of each and every one.

"Mrs Bradshaw" he patted her hand, she did not correct him with 'Miss'

"And young man" The Vicar shook Ernest's hand, who did not correct him because he was a 'man' the sermon had said so, a man without dismay and plenty of courage. There seemed to be hesitation, as Father Dunn took Uncle Billy's hand "Peace be with you" He said.

"Hmm," Uncle Billy corrected him because that was all he could say.

This Sunday's supply of welcome was withdrawn by two wooden church doors. Father Dunn looked at the collection plate. Someone

had donated a mint humbug. It was February,
 and 1962 had not spent many of its Sundays.
There would be fifty-two in total, all of them
quiet because God said so. All speaking a
different sermon, because God said so. All of
 them lacking open amenities, because God said

so. The silence of the church allowed Father Dunn to enjoy his direct hotline to God. Every Sunday, he would dip his finger into the bible and pick out a reading at random. With failing eyesight and tiny newspaper print, he was no more in touch with current affairs than he was with his congregation's silent pleading. There was work to be done, God had said so, and Father Dunn would preach week in, week out. Guiding the way, which he would not correct because God said so. During the fifty-two Sundays of 1962, God was to put faith in people - mankind. Not only that they would *do* the right thing, but that they would also *pray* for the right thing. As for Ernest's prayers about the bullies, he would have to make do with a quick fix, a reading about courage, picked at random by Father Dunn, because God said so.

Later that same day, when the Sunday roast had been cleared away, and hours had
passed with nothing to do and nothing to say. Ernest, his mother and Uncle Billy took the weekly bus journey to Auntie Marigold and
 Uncle Norman's house.   Marigold Bradshaw was always going to do well for herself in life.
 This was obvious on the Bradshaw family photograph, captured in sepia when Marigold was fourteen and Rose was age nine. Marigold, imposing and impressive on the back row, shoulders straight, hair behaving itself, brand
 new dress. The centre of the photograph, the centre of attention, her proudly positioned head articulated 'I plan to marry well'. Marigold stood
 above her little sister Rose, perched upon a

three-legged stool underneath Marigold. Head bowed, small and shy with her hair in her eyes, and a hand me down dress. Rose had no plan, but in life, received a surprise. Marigold pitied her little sister, but it was not her job to pass judgement; not on a Sunday.

And now, in 1962, Marigold Schofield nee Bradshaw wore gardening gloves and a pinafore apron. She lived in a detached house with a full-length bay window. Her three grown-up sons all married and moved on. It was just Marigold, Rusty the Red Setter and Norman, putting on appearances in the front garden. Marigold had already received two compliments from passing strangers that afternoon. Even in February, the rose bushes were taking over the garden, as bossy as the woman who planted them. Her sister Rose, nephew Ernest, and Uncle Billy were expected for tea; high tea. Marigold spotted her guests entering the scene and excused herself from her rose bush admirers. For the second time that day, the Bradshaw family queued up to be judged.

"Rose! Ernest, aww Billy love" Marigold, embracing with her outside voice, she stopped pretending to garden. Marigold had been pushing a garden hoe around, whilst Norman, who was not pretending, swept up intruding rubbish from the main road. It was still early in the year, but Marigold insisted on portraying a perfect exterior at all times. There was no hesitation when Marigold said hello to Uncle Billy. It had been Rose's turn to take him in, and then it had been Rose's turn again. Marigold had assumed that Rose needed a 'man about the

house' including the extra lodging money. It was Marigold's job to assume because her husband Norman lent Rose money for a bathroom fitting.
"Hello Rose, how's our Ernest?" without waiting for Ernest's reply, Norman turned to
Billy, he never knew the correct way to say hello, so he forcefully shook his hand.
"Rose, I've been thinking, you've not done anything with that shelter in't back 'ave you? You know, for when't bomb goes off" Norman adopted Rose as an ally.

"Norman! Outside voices, please!" Auntie Marigold chastised her husband, her own voice gradually disappearing into a hiss "Don't come with any of that bomb talk in front of our Ernest"
"Only, I've saved the paper for you, it's got summat in the headlines... about America and Russia" Uncle Norman ignored his wife, then his own voice disappeared into a whisper. After a few shifty glances, Auntie Marigold tried to divert Ernest
"How would you like this, Ernest love? Tell you what, when I die, I'll leave it to you in my will"
"A family heirloom?" Ernest's boredom brightened.
"What on earth is our Ernest going to want with a flippin' garden hoe? There's nowt but that shelter in the back yard, we've no need for gardening tackle!"
"Are you dying, Auntie Marigold?" Ernest had rewound the conversation in his mind, with shifty glances and grown up talk, he fathomed

something was wrong.

Perhaps he should have extended his prayers to everyone he knew - or blood relatives at least.

"Oh no! You daft apeth Ernest. Come on inside now, time for tea" Auntie Marigold said in her best outside voice, she guided her sister into the kitchen by her elbow, where they enjoyed small sandwiches in a kitchen that smelled of celery. Ernest always worried that Auntie Marigold's high-tea would never fill him up, but it always did.

"Why are we not allowed int' dining room today, or the front room?" Ernest slightly picked up on Auntie Marigold's vanity. There was no need to banish him really, Ernest had been brought up by his mother, who would never allow any faults or flaws.

"It's Rusty, he had an accident, it wasn't his fault" Uncle Norman had been married to Auntie Marigold for the majority of his adult life, and so knew all about faults and flaws.

"In the parlour, there was .." Auntie Marigold hesitated to find the right word "He left some... poop" Auntie Marigold's voice disappeared into a whisper, even though she was inside.

Ernest laughed, then Uncle Billy laughed because Ernest laughed. Rose breathed a sigh of relief. Today's faults and flaws would not be produced from her portion of the family "Is that why none of your lot are here today?"

"Well, I can't let Richard's wife know I allowed dog dirt on my Winchester rug!" Auntie Marigold did manage a smile, but she was the only one in the room who failed to see the funny side.

 "Ernest, young man, will you take your uncle to the pub?" Uncle Norman confused Ernest with his invitation.
"Uncle Billy?"
"No, I meant me!" Uncle Norman did not know how to invite Uncle Billy, so the invitation remained unspoken.
"He's asleep int' chair anyway, and me mother and Auntie Marigold are having one of their chats" Ernest's voice disappeared into a mimicking whisper.
"Right you are then lad, you know the way"
 Ernest insisted on taking the garden hoe, his new family heirloom to the pub. Happy in himself, God had been listening to him because Auntie Marigold's front room meant shoes off, and of course, that would reveal the hidden hole in his sock. Thank goodness for dog dirt.
Uncle and nephew walked over the field towards The Brown Cow. Ernest using the garden hoe as some sort of oversized walking stick, Rusty obediently plodding at the side of
Norman. The journey to the pub was a bit on the long side for Rusty's liking, still, he had the Winchester rug in the parlour to look forward to.
The February sun started to shine on the cold ground, Uncle Norman spotted a cyclist rolling along ahead, something to do on a Sunday in the second year of the decade with
 new possibilities. And was the cyclist a girl? Norman was sure he saw mousey brown hair protruding from under a bobble hat. He looked ahead at Ernest who was now stretching his new

toy as far as it would go and then stretching his leg as far as he could, thrilled to bits with a garden implement. Ernest had not even noticed the girl. Norman thought of his own grown-up sons, he could not remember them being as childlike when they were fourteen and now, of course, they were thrilled to bits with their executive pay packets from his company, 'Schofield and Sons'. The girl cycled towards Norman and Rusty, passing Ernest first, who still did not look up.

"That boy needs a hobby," Uncle Norman said to Rusty, who of course could not answer, but understood completely.

The Brown Cow was home to migrating men-folk from various Victorian terraces and pre-fabricated council homes, enjoying silent Sunday evenings, supping their pints. The seats outside were dry enough to sit on, Uncle Norman treated Ernest to a cordial. Rusty was admiring his own reflection in a puddle, his red beard dangling into the rainwater.

"How old are you, Ernest?" Uncle Norman knew everything but had to start the conversation somewhere.

"Fourteen"

"Fourteen, soon to be fifteen?"

"Not really, I'm not even fourteen and a half"

"Still, you're the man of the house, have you thought about getting a Sat'day job? Help your mother out?"

"Well, she reckons she's asked Old Potts but he's a bit stingy like" Ernest was scraping the mud from in between the cobbles with the gardening tool. Uncle Norman jumped on the mention of Old Potts "Old? How old?"

"Err well, not as old as you, but older than me mother I think, why?" Ernest squinted up at his uncle.

"Oh, nothing I thought your mother's works was owned by an older man, a man and his son? So is Old Potts the son? Or the older man?"

Ernest shrugged.

"He has his finger in lots of pies has Old Potts, so I believe... Not just a greengrocer or distribution warehouse, his business has grown right from the market stalls he still has up Smithfield"

"You're gettin' Old Potts mixed up with his dad, Even Older Potts. And he's not a baker, Uncle" all Ernest had heard was 'pies'.

"Have you ever been on a bicycle, lad? Do you know how to ride one?" Uncle Norman changed the subject.

"Yeah, course I do!" Ernest shook his head at Uncle Norman, mother always said he was a 'know it all' but he had plenty of questions today.

"I found this on't notice board inside, thought it might be something you could get into" Uncle Norman put a flyer in Ernest's hand.

'THE EAST LANCASHIRE INTERNATIONAL CYCLING CLUB' - *club runs and beginner's rides most Sundays and every Wednesday evening*. Ernest's face lit up, and then screwed up, Uncle Norman may be a business man, but he had not figured this one out. "I've no bike, Uncle Norman!"

"I know! But if you get fixed up with that delivery boy job, a bike'll come with it!" Uncle Norman had it figured out after all.

"Right come on then, sup up, tell your mother I'll have a word with Old Potts if she likes"
"Oh, I don't think you'll need to, me mother knows how to boss people. And anyway t'other day she said that the Russians are going to blow us all up. Then ever since, she keeps switching the wireless off just before I come downstairs. One day I'm gettin' up before her to find out what's happening, I'm a man now, God said so in church this morning, so I should know what's going on. D'you reckon that's why Old Potts said he didn't need a delivery boy? Because of the Russians?" Ernest had never spoken so many words all at once before, but he certainly did not expect Uncle Norman's response, he burst out laughing, picked up Rusty's lead and finished his pint.
"No! Ha! No that's not the reason Ernest, but don't you worry about anything, just carry on regardless, do your best at school, but no,
 don't worry about those Russians, we've got that shelter in your back yard to hide in, and there might even be room for a bicycle!"

Chapter 2: Belief In Oneself.

Bullying and teasing were considered a 'rite of passage' in 1962, celebrating the transition from adolescence to adulthood. There was nothing right about it, but it was a fact of life, no one could be trusted, bullies were around every corner, and they came in all shapes and sizes. Bullying is fuelled by new and interesting information. Any information that put the bully above the victim was indeed new and interesting and must be acted on as soon as possible, this kept the bully on top. Nobody was safe, some were not even safe in their own homes, the tradition of bullying passed from one generation to another. Those who had the misfortune to learn about bullying from their own parents would often be the most skilled at it. After all, they had to learn it from somewhere. The most skilful bullies would form gangs, there is protection in numbers. 'A bully' (singular), became 'the bullies' (plural), and so on. In return, those bullies in the gang did have to accept a fair amount of 'light teasing' to keep their place; that is how it worked.

Ernest Bradshaw did not live with any such bullies, and so had not learnt the full set of rules. Neither had he been much of a target up until now, but with the new information about Harold being off school with a broken ankle, Ernest's position with Mark Crosby was about to change.

Minding his own business on his way to school, with spring in his step and renewed vigour in his mind, Ernest turned the corner. The sheer size of the three thick set boys stepping out in front of him blocked his sunlight and path.

"Hi-ya Ernest, we've been waiting for you" Mark Crosby feigned friendship for Ernest. "My mum tells me your mum is getting you in with Old Potts as a delivery boy. My mum told me, said Old Potts wouldn't take me on, on account of me record. Whereas you, Ernest Bradshaw, the golden boy is getting straight in there. We don't think that's fair do we?" Mark Crosby addressed his henchmen behind him.

The only thing unfair about this scenario is that Mark Crosby's mother works at the same place as Ernest's own mother. Gleaning and sharing information like she had read it in a newspaper. Ernest could not say anything. His thoughts turned to Father Dunn's words.

'Be courageous wherever you are going', but Ernest was trapped. Unable to *go* anywhere, impossible to squeeze past these three laughing Luddites.

"So we'll be needing a cut of the delivery money. Won't we boys?"

"Err I haven't actually got the job, me Mother has only *asked* Potts, Old Potts. Apparently, he's thinking about it" Ernest practised his courage.

"*APPARENTLY*!" The three boys exploded into laughter as though Ernest had said something hilarious. Then Mark Crosby stopped laughing and fixed his stare at Ernest. Expertly referring to the twins behind him, whilst his mouth was moving for Ernest's benefit. This was it, the new information that Mark Crosby really wanted to tease Ernest about.

"Why doesn't your Dad get you a job then? You know, instead of leaving it all to your mother?" Mark Crosby's sickly sweet sarcasm prickled Ernest's innocent soul.

"I haven't got a Dad" Ernest blushed, although he was not sure why. Continuing his steep learning curve, he cottoned on to Mark

Crosby's disingenuous method of guessing and confirming.
 Ernest was proud of his mother. She deserved a bloody medal, but Mark Crosby was about to touch a nerve.
Ernest summoned his courage. And Mark Crosby smelt it like he had been trained for it. A scuffle broke out, the bullies soon got the better of Ernest. One of the Benson twins shoved him in the chest, pushing him back into the hedge. Fortunately, Ernest's prayers were about to turn that same corner.
"Stop right there lads" Mr Cooley roared, his briefcase at his side. His long thin teacher's nose met with Mark Crosby's forehead.
"What's going on here? Benson! Crosby! Get inside, both of you... All three of you!" Mr Cooley's tall, thin frame conducted the boys.
"Bradshaw.... my office now, before assembly"
Ernest opened his mouth to protest his innocence but thought better of it
"You're for it now *Braaaadshaw*" Mark Crosby teased in a sing-song voice
"I said inside - you" Mr Cooley pointed and pushed Mark Crosby "And a 'yes sir' wouldn't go amiss"
"Yes sir" the three bullies chorused in uncharacteristic quiet voices.
Ernest said "Yes Sir" but was out of sync with the others. He followed Mr Cooley to his office. He was forced to explain what happened with the three bullies, whilst Mr Cooley found Ernest's file in the big metal drawers. He paced up and down, reciting

a lecture about being in his office before the first school bell. Ernest's file was a thin A4 folder containing information about his address, next of kin, and nothing else because Ernest had never been in trouble.

"So last week they were trying to get you to trick Harold Goatshead - who by the way has a broken ankle, and you're telling me you told them you wanted no part of it, now you say they are bullying you?" Mr Cooley was towering over Ernest. "Yes...I"

"Did I say speak? Hmm?" Mr Cooley turned sharply towards Ernest. Was this a trick question? Ernest's eyes were all over the deputy head's office.

"NO, I did not! You've blathered on enough about Mark Crosby, 'then he did this, then he did that' you're becoming an adult now, so start acting like one!"

Ernest gasped, and the schoolmaster continued. "You're doing nothing but provoking these boys, and you can't expect the teaching staff to act as referees to your fights for the rest of term" Mr Cooley was waiting for a response "WELL"

"Yes Sir," Ernest said. Talk about victim blaming, he thought.

"So, they were picking on you because you don't have a father?" Mr Cooley investigated whilst stalking up and down

like a giraffe. Ernest decided against speaking, it was probably another trick question and the clock on the wall said it was nearly nine, he knew that Mr Cooley could not keep him in this uncomfortable conversation forever.

"Do you know what that makes you, do you know

why they're teasing you about your father, Bradshaw? Eh?" Mr Cooley had both hands on the desk, lurching towards Ernest.
This definitely must be a trick question, although Ernest was still not sure if he should answer, he sort of knew what Mr Cooley was getting at, but he wasn't about to say *that* in front of a teacher. Especially not Mr Cooley, he was as inconsistent as the weather. The students never knew where they stood with him, he kept them on edge, that was how teachers worked in 1962. Ernest was considering telling him all about his mother, who deserved a medal but Mr Cooley slammed a ruler down on the desk... "WELL"
Then the sound of the assembly bell rang... It was much louder in the teacher's office.
Ernest was dismissed, and despite the previous uncertainty of Mr Cooley's attitude, Ernest knew that the teacher had kept him in his office just long enough to make him feel like he was in trouble.
The lack of punishment for the scuffle with Mark Crosby would be their secret. He made his way into the assembly, met by faces that gave him a new kudos, he had just been in the teacher's office with Mr Cooley and this could only mean one thing...

A school assembly was usually for the announcing of general matters, the humble bragging of the school's cricket team and the shaming of naughty pupils. Followed by the compulsory singing of hymns, accompanied by the one-hundred-year-old music teacher, Mrs

Ogle and her standard piano on wheels.
This morning, the entire school had been
assembled in the hall. The pupils were living in
fear as Monday usually meant uniform
inspection. Thinking back to this morning's
rigmarole, Ernest started to worry. His mother
had got up like a shot out of the armchair and
rushed off to catch the bus, it all happened so
quickly, she had been asleep downstairs with the
newspaper that Uncle Norman had given her
covering her face, the headlines gently rising and
falling : "KENNEDY READY FOR SOVIET
SHOWDOWN ... *Britain behind U.S.*"
Ernest could not be sure if his mother was
dressed underneath her coat. Ernest had to get
himself ready, wearing that same sock with a hole
and doing his own tie. He had left Uncle Billy
wearing his flat cap and underpants, and
he now was sat in assembly. Ernest could not be
entirely sure if his shirt was tucked in but did
not look down because he knew this would draw
attention to himself. Mark Crosby was fighting
with one of the Benson twins in the corner. Mr
Cooley did not say a word. He picked Mark
Crosby up by the scruff of his neck and threw him
down on a seat next to Ernest. The sudden shock
of this made Mark Crosby tear up. This was not
hidden from Ernest, Mark Crosby had a new
respect for him after this morning's trip to Mr
Cooley's office.
"Good morning pupils" Mr Cooley cupped his
hand around his ear to receive the school's 'hello'.
"Good morning Mr Cooley" Teenagers and
teachers chorused in return.
"Today I want to talk to you about life"

Mrs Ogle, behind Mr Cooley on a piano stool, straightened her back and widened her eyes. She was not expecting this and started fussing and tut-tutting through the music sheets to find a hymn about 'life'.

"You, that is each and every one of you, have your entire life ahead of you. For those of you about to embark on your final year of school, that is those of you that are age fourteen now" Mr Cooley had lost most of the pupils at this point with his overuse of 'you'.

"Life is what you make of it, and now that it is 1962, you will have chances, opportunities ahead of you. Your children will have opportunities that even you won't have. As long as you believe in yourself" Mr Cooley stopped in his tracks and pulled his forelock. The silence caught the school's attention, Mrs Ogle was in a state of panic, all she had come up with was 'Abide With Me'. Positioned directly underneath Mr Cooley's armpit, Mrs Ogle cringed on the uncomfortable piano stool. In his office, Ernest had not noticed Mr Cooley's scruffiness, but at the front of the assembly hall, his unshaven appearance matched his unpredictable ramblings.

"Whatever you read in the news, just ignore it" This instigated coughing and protestation from Mr James, the Geography teacher "Well don't ignore it, but, what I'm trying to say is don't give up on life, whatever you do. You could be something. Each and every one of you has a talent" Mr Cooley looked at the back row of naughty boys, Mark Crosby was enough to induce stage fright in any teacher, but Mr Cooley pulled himself together to continue, without giving in to the temptation to say 'even you, Mark Crosby'. Mr Cooley wiped his brow. If only the school audience knew how closely Mr Cooley had been reading the newspapers.

"You are all talented, you just don't know it yet, that is what your own individual talent is, you know, what you are good at. But if you believe in yourself, It will bring out your talent, your skills, and then you'll be better prepared for life, the life you are about to live" Mr Cooley paused for the third time. Mrs Ogle took this as a cue to start playing the piano, her fingers instinctively fell on 'All Things Bright And Beautiful' but Mr Cooley started talking again, she jumped and the piano lid slammed shut on her fingers.

"If I had given up my ambition, just because of the war, then where would I be? I kept going, I believed I had found my skill, my talent and I wasn't going to give up teaching just because of a war!"

Every grown up, every adult in the room, and every adult that the pupils knew, parents, aunts, uncles, grandparents had all been affected by World War II. And now in 1962, the news was war coloured again. If only they knew the real ambition that Mr Cooley had sacrificed. The newsreaders had a special 'war-tone' in their voices. Some adults ignored it, protecting their children from the reminder, the unfortunate chance that this could happen all over again. But here was Mr Cooley commanding the assembly, scaring the children and angering the teachers. Mrs Ogle was a nervous wreck, she could not even muster a rendition of

'Chopsticks' on that piano now. The bell rang quieter in the school hall and it signalled the first lesson.

Later that same day, when Monday blues had been banished away. Hours of Chemistry, History and Mathematics had produced no talent or skills promised, Ernest had questions for his mother. "Mr Cooley said that everyone has a talent. He said that one day we will realise what our talent is, and it will be useful in life"
"Did he?"
"Yes, what's your talent Mother?"
Rose Bradshaw looked around her home, at her record player where an Edith Piaf LP was propped up on display. What would 'the little sparrow' say to her son's question about life? What skills, what talents could Rose tell him about? She looked at Ernest's expectant face. Her next mouthful of food punctuated her words. "Talent? Well, I suppose I'm quite organised at work. Potts has put his feelers out he wants to promote someone, and it might be me" Rose looked at Ernest, who did not appear to be satisfied with this answer, she searched again; 'No Regrets' crooned in Rose's head.
"And I suppose I am good at looking after you, making sure you've got everything you need, no holes in your clothes, that sort of thing. I don't want anyone thinking we are scruffy, because, y'know" Rose looked down. Ernest flinched, maybe it was time to confess about the hole in his sock. Rose took this as shame, but Ernest had a further question.

"Uncle Norman said that Old Potts has his fingers in all the pies or summat?"

Rose's coaster dropped from the bottom of her drinking glass.

"What was Uncle Norman talking about Old... That's Mr Potts to you, what was he talking about him for?" Rose steadied her hand holding the glass with the other hand, whilst Edith Piaf warbled in her mind.Uncle Billy stopped eating, he could not hear a word Ernest or Rose were saying but sat up to take notice.

"Oh about you getting me a delivery boy job, he said that I would get a bike with the round, then I can join a cycling club. And I'm wondering if that might be my talent, because if I had a bike, I could cycle away from anything, from any danger like Mark Crosby, or even the Russians. God spoke to me in the church, I said a prayer and then God made the vicar say summat like 'be courageous wherever you are going' so can you ask him, mum?" Ernest stuffed his mouth with whatever was on the end of his fork.

Rose started laughing and shook her head. Uncle Billy started eating again.

"Ask who? You've lost me!"

"Old Potts. Anyway, what's Uncle Billy's talent then?"

Rose looked at Uncle Billy, she had often been the only person to understand him.

"He is very good at communicating"

"What! He can't even talk!"

"Doesn't matter, Ernest, that's what he is good at,
and if that doesn't suit you, he's good with his
hands, he was a joiner's apprentice when he was
your age"
And with that, Uncle Billy, oblivious to the fact he
was being discussed finished eating first and
made a start on the washing up.
"Well I've decided, that's what my talent is going
to be," said Ernest.
"What's that then?" said Rose.
"Cycling, I'm going to win a cycle race!"

Chapter 3: Summer Ambition.

After much verbal manipulation during the early
months of 1962, Mr Potts the greengrocer finally
succumbed to Rose Bradshaw's persuasion.
"I suppose your lad can start that round for me, I
can't get the van up Lever Brew" He had said,
awkwardly invading Rose's space. Albeit a quiet
person, when it came to her son Ernest,
Rose would perpetually nest and nurture using a
skill that could rival any member of the animal
kingdom. In spring, the seeds she had sown
began to take root and her son, Ernest was now
to be employed by Mr Potts as the bicycle
 delivery boy at Potts' Greengrocers. The majority

of the deliveries were conveyed in his van, but
the cottages on Lever Brew had
 proven to be virtually inaccessible on four
wheels. As much as Mr Potts wanted to say no
 to Rose (he had his reasons) he eventually
 said yes to employing her son. Maybe this
summer things would be different.
Now, British summer time begins officially when
the clocks change at the end of March.
The weather, however, does not automatically
follow. Ernest Bradshaw set out on a wintry
March day, on the ancient low gravity Hercules
carrier bike he began to nurture his own set of
dreams. Dreams that would burst into blooming
bounty during June and July. The loaned cycle
was designed and fit for purpose, the front
wheel smaller to accommodate a basket. It was
 heavy, to begin with. Add to that Ernest's
fourteen-year-old body, basket and side pannier
bags filled with pounds upon pounds of potatoes,
and the Hercules bicycle became a herculean
challenge. Ernest, with his mother's determination
behind him, although wobbly at
first soon found he could manage. His little white
legs, white knuckles, jaw set, chin pointing
forwards pushed down the pedals. Round and
round, up and down, goods delivered, wages
pocketed. Ernest had never had money before
and did not know what to do
 with nearly a whole pound to himself every week.
April came and went, apple blossoms blew in his
face and stuck to his glasses. Youthful athleticism
on his side, Ernest's
 stamina grew and improved. He could not say he
had ever really noticed summer before. The dewy

scent of sunrise, the singing birds, the layers shed. When he started his round the sky was still dawn coloured, when he finished, it
was light. His mother, Rose awaited and anticipated summer every year.
"There's nowt better than a British summertime" She would say, for her, it was always over far too soon. However, for fourteen-year-old Ernest, long summer days
were about to become long summer months. Time enough to nurture his budding ambition. By May, Ernest's confidence began to vegetate. He had moved on from 'managing' the deliveries, to dispatching them with ease. His customers appeared impressed. Mrs Smith from one of the cottages teased him
"Eee Ernest! Ever thought of putting in for th'Olympic team on that bike?"
And that was all Ernest needed. His backbone fertilised, ambition soon flourished into dreams of winning imaginary cycle races. 'I'm getting good at this' he told himself, Mr Cooley was right! Everyone has a talent! The green grass, the green leaves, everything 1962's summer touched was about to blossom. By the time the bluebells started to nod, Mr Potts would tell Ernest:
" You're the fastest delivery boy on two wheels" Mr Brown, the butcher swilling out his bucket in the back entry overheard this and soon asked Ernest to deliver for him too.
Bacon and braising steak in brown paper. Like the tomato plant in one of the cottage's greenhouses, Ernest's round was about to branch off in several directions. His growing round now easily

managed. Ernest was proud of his abilities, a secret garden of success in his own mind. But one heady Sunday of early spring heat, at Auntie Marigold and Uncle
Norman's house, Ernest was asked what he planned to do when he left school. Drunk on homemade honey and elderflower cordial, Ernest blurted out :

"I'm going to join the Great Britain Olympic cycling team!"

The grown-ups laughter withered him, even Uncle Billy laughed.

"Ernest! Has that Mr Cooley put ideas into your head? You'll be getting a proper job, you didn't see your cousins having fanciful ideas about talent!" Rose blazed at her son. She breathed in, Auntie Marigold was just about to ask her to use her 'outside voice' when Rose whispered to her "That teacher's having a breakdown, not enough sleep since his wife gave birth to twins, that sort of thing" Rose silently mouthed the word 'breakdown' and Auntie Marigold whispered back 'My three went to the Grammar school'.

Later on, when the outside crockery had been cleared away, Auntie Marigold read something out from yesterday's newspaper, about the 'bay of pigs' that's how it started, and it was all still going on.

"No Rose, it doesn't say the world is going to blow up *as such*, but folk will have to make of it what they will. I mean, for goodness sake, I can't have the world blowing up, I need to
defend my title at the baking contest in the church hall next Sunday!" Auntie Marigold was not taking the threat of nuclear war as

seriously as her sister. Rose could then be overheard explaining that she had warned Ernest not to sing his own praises and that he 'had no right coming out with such fanciful ideas'. Uncle Norman approached Ernest who was pulling the petals off a poppy, hanging limp, defeated by the breeze.

"Ernest, if you're serious about cycling I can p'rhaps introduce you to a chap I know, Harry Hill the Olympian"

"Who?" Ernest asked. His mother always said that Uncle Norman is a 'know it all' but Ernest could not see the harm in knowing things.

"Yes, Harry Hill, He's a local hero! He won bronze, you know, cycling in't 1936 Olympics!"

"Well, I wasn't alive then Uncle" Perhaps Uncle Norman didn't know everything.

"I know lad, but that doesn't mean it didn't happen. I reckon if you get your training in for the rest of the summer, you'll be ready for one of those cycle races you see on Sundays in September. Bloody nuisance they are, have to take the car round a different way if the wife wants to visit your mother"

"Is he in that cycling club you gave me the leaflet for?"

"What leaflet?" Uncle Norman sometimes despaired for his nephew.

"When you took me for a walk to The Brown Cow, you bought me a cordial and gave me a leaflet about a cycling club. I've spent all of spring learning how to cycle at work, don't you remember?" Ernest sometimes despaired of Uncle Norman. He cannot even remember

encouraging Ernest to ride a bicycle, and now he says he knows a famous Olympian. And his mother! She had been cheering him on for fourteen years but now she was telling him not to have any ambition about the Olympics!
The Russians, Mark Crosby, Ernest's own mother, and Uncle Norman's name dropping conspired and colluded Ernest's determination to be 'courageous, wherever he was going'. The summer of 1962 began to nurture Ernest's cycling ambition. He pulled the last petal off the poppy, Ernest had somewhere to go.

Chapter 4: Ernest Joins a Cycling Club

Any lad who wants to enter a cycling race must join a club.
Ernest, his athletic capabilities, and his bicycle turned up on a Sunday morning at the designated meeting point for the East Lancashire International Cycling Club.
In his eagerness, he was fifteen minutes early. He looked at his pasty legs, his grey socks, his plimsolls.
Brian and Brenda Towers pushed their punctured tandem up the road. They were the treasurers, club secretary (and founding members) of the club. They had always loved
cycling, even on their wedding day, their
guests held up an arch of bicycle wheels for them, and not long after, their cycling club was born.

Named international, because the club needed ambition.

"Hello, lad, are you lost? You've not come to join our cycling club have you?" Brian asked.

Brenda took over all the talking.

"Eee look at him, Brian he's got one of our flyers!" She left her husband propping the tandem up and eyed Ernest's bike up and down.

"Is this what you'll be riding on? This sit up and beg? They don't usually have baskets on the front, but you'll do, you'll be robust enough for now" Brenda patted the seat of Ernest's bike. Brian Towers' eyes were wide, his mouth was open. Had this boy really turned up for a beginner's club run on a delivery bike? Was Brian Towers about to say so to his bossy wife? No, he shut his mouth and nodded at Ernest. Already, the carrier bicycle had proved an embarrassment, but Brenda's warm demeanour, her 'you'll do for now' had reassured Ernest it would be alright. Brian got his brown backed notebook and pencil out of his satchel and took down Ernest's details. Name? Name of parents? Just your mother?

Address? Ernest gave all the information. Brian took it all down. Brenda nodded and looked over the top of her spectacles when Ernest said that his mother 'Deserved a bloody medal' Ernest had a speech prepared for if they asked why he wanted to join their cycling club. He was going to tell them he wanted to win a race before the world blew up like his mother had said. Fortunately, Brian and Brenda didn't ask that question. Other cyclists arrived.

They all looked like they were taking it pretty seriously. Ernest looked at their racing cycles compared to the low gravity carrier bike. How fast could he go if he had one of those things? His mind was racing with ambition. Brian explained things to Ernest. There was much talk of "Club events. Ten mile Time Trials. Long hours on the bike" and that "Brenda always has a flask of sweet tea, in case riders get out of steam. Don't worry about the tour races for today" Brian finished.

Some of the other cyclists were nodding 'hello' at Ernest. He had only just joined!

"There's another lad, Christopher he's about your age, I don't think he's coming today, though, he... sometimes he can't make it" Brenda was nodding at Ernest, as though she had known him for years, he was 'one of them'.

Brian commenced his instructions through a piece of rolled up cardboard, required only to assert his authority in Brenda's company.

"You lead today, Sid. And look after the new lad, Ernest Bradshaw"

Ernest's heart sang at the sound of his own name, the new lad.

"Brian, are you mad? Have you seen what he's riding? He'd need a head start to flamin' well keep up!" Sid whispered to Brian out of the side of his mouth. Both men noticed that Brenda had clocked what was being said. Sid turned his cycle around, and Brian shut his mouth- again.

The riders pushed off, Ernest last, Brenda and Brian waiting for them on the other side of the road with their punctured tandem. Hearing the sound of his own name by a cycling club leader was enough to convince Ernest. If he didn't already imagine himself to be the winner of an international cycling race, he definitely did now.

The excitement of not knowing where he was cycling to. The challenge of keeping up with the man in front. Cycling up and down hills covered in straw and sunshine that looked like sand.

Ernest pushed the peddles up and down and round and round with all his strength. Life is meant to be a struggle. The wind rushing past his ears, his whole self wet with fine rain and sweat. His bicycle light, without groceries. His mind free of school and nuclear war, but full of freedom itself. The adrenaline rush, the rain stopping and the sun starting. The overuse of his heart muscle... because, at the other side of a downhill, is another uphill.

"Wait for me!" Ernest had wanted to shout. The winding road, losing sight of the cyclist in front of him, then catching him up again. Puny legs pushing peddles up and down. They were back on flat, it seemed

like an hour later. Ernest recognised the road, they were nearly back at the starting point.

Meanwhile, Brenda and Brian had forgotten about their puncture and had just had their daily argument. Brian, at the front of the tandem, had set off before Brenda was ready, therefore her shins had painfully collided with the back pedals. Funny for Brian, but not for Brenda.

Brian would be hearing about his mistake for the following week.

"There's Sid! Fetch the flasks, Brian, I'll put out

the plastic cups!"

Rows of sweet tea were set out on the church wall for the cycling club. One by one, they finished the ride and dismounted their cycles.

"I expect we'll have a bit of a wait on our hands for that new lad on his delivery bike!" Colin Sidebottom was a good natured soul.

"You absolutely should not turn up for a club run on an unsuitable bike, this is what happens, he'll show us up" Percy liked to take everything seriously, Sid was nodding at the side of him.

"Aww give the lad a break and drink your tea, Percy, besides, imagine the picnics he could fit in those pannier bags!"

"I think they've got a point, Brenda, do you think we should tell him the delivery bike is unsuitable for club runs?" Brian said.

"No! Don't be daft, he's got guts turning up here with his little legs and his... contraption. Rolling up a piece of cardboard because you
think it will make your voice louder is unsuitable, Brian. Anyway, here he comes
now!"

Ernest could see the riders, it sounded like they were cheering Ernest:

"Dig in! Dig in lad!"

He was sure he heard applause. He drank down his sweet tea, embarrassed as he was not sure if he should pay. Before he knew it, the cycle club run was over.

Ernest returned home on that sunny spring day, with his life mapped out in another leaflet from Mr and Mrs Towers :

"TIME TRIALLING FOR BEGINNERS"

Chapter 5: Allies

Ernest's teacher, Mr Cooley and his wife had twin babies and they were at the age of becoming vertical. This happens to most infants, although the Cooley children were in the minority, less than five percent of 1962's babies were twin babies. The other portion of infants in the UK in 1962 were in their cots,learning how to be vertical on their own. The two Cooley babies had learnt how to fill their nappies, how to cry, how to poke each other in the eye and most importantly, they had learned how to be together. The Cooley babies were allies. They had been growing and grabbing at the bars in the cot when Mrs Cooley had put them down for their afternoon nap. Egging each other on, gradually straightening their baby legs, wrinkled with baby fat until their padded bottoms no longer came crashing down on to the cot mattress.

Then came learning how to manoeuvre themselves over the cot side by swinging their legs over, one at a time. This took a lot of heave-ho and gusto, one twin could not have done it without the other. All whilst their mother was not watching of course. After a few attempts, the twins were successful. There had been a loud bang in the upstairs of the Cooley's new build house. Mrs Cooley jumped out of her skin and hit the deck. She had been mocking her husband for warning her of loud bangs followed by bright flashes of light which meant nuclear detonation. For a split second, she thought the bang was the sound of a bomb, but it

turned out to be something worse! The loud bang was followed by a pause, and then a loud crying noise. It was the sound of both the twins crying after jumping out of the cot. Mrs Cooley stood up and went to inspect the upstairs drama. That particular day in 1962, when the Cooley twins conspired together against claustrophobia was the day that there was another upheaval in the local
area, this time in the Dootson household.

Mr and Mrs Dootson were terrible at making decisions. It had taken them six months to decide on a new standard lamp for the dining room, and when they got it home, they did not
like it. So deciding to move house was not something they took lightly, but once the decision was made, they could not go back on it. Especially because they had told their daughter, Janet. Who could blame the Dootson family for not anticipating the global uncertainty that would be foisted on, not just the Dootson family but the entire human population? "It's not all about you, Janet" Her mother had chastised, but Janet told her parents, during the same argument, and in no uncertain terms, "She did not ask to be born!"
When the dust had settled, and the removal men had removed themselves, Janet found herself realising her own mortality at her young age. Climbing the adolescent ladder to maturity, whilst being confronted with the threat of nuclear war. No wonder she was a loner! No best friend to speak of, bicycles do not count as friends although Janet considered her bike a soul mate.

When she was not out cycling alone, investigating her new neighbourhood, Janet was hanging around with her parents. Mostly engaging in the silent reading of broadsheet newspapers. Her father was always on hand to discuss political matters, should she not understand them. Her mother was always on hand to flap and make light of the situation.

"Dad," Janet asked in the tone of voice that her father knew required an explanation.

"Are the Soviet's against America at the moment?"

"Well, err there's all this going on in Cuba, Janet. Hold on, which bit are you reading?"

"Weren't the Russians on the same side as Britain in the war?"

"Kind of, it was complicated," Mr Dootson shook out his newspaper, pushed his
reading glasses further up his nose and
 ran his forefinger over his moustache. This was a cue that he did not want to talk about it, probably because he did not have an accurate answer. Janet did not pick up on these signs.

"Well, America was on the same side as Britain, but now Russia is allied with Cuba" Janet wondered if she would need reading glasses one day "Dad, what's an ally? I mean, why are Russia such big pals with Cuba at the moment?"

More newspaper shaking from Janet's father. Janet's mother started to take an interest.

"Oh! I know this one! It's all to do with communism. Or is it capitalism? One of those, things, you know" Janet's mother flapped her
 hand and started clicking her fingers at Janet's

father.

"Americans are capitalists, just like us Brits, we live in a democracy" Dad stepped in with half an explanation.

"Russians are communists and so are Cubans I think, and America is worried that there are communists secretly living in America. 'Reds under the bed' they are called." Janet said.

"Janet! Have you been reading the Manchester Guardian again?!" Janet's father sometimes wondered why his daughter did not want to go out listening to popular rock and roll music, like a normal teenager. Janet's mother stood behind Janet's father, and swept her silk scarf around the other side of her neck "Maybe you should ask your History teacher, at your new school? Hmm? About allies, you know darling"

Her mother was only trying to help, but this annoyed Janet. She ran upstairs and slammed her bedroom door- a slightly over-exaggerated response to newspaper time with her parents. She flung herself on her bed and reached down onto the floor. Pulling out a copy of last week's *'Bunty'* magazine, it was either that or - how about a book of poetry? Janet loved poetry and hated it when people misquoted 'If' by Rudyard Kipling. It had been Marjory Smyth's older brother prancing around at the integrated school Christmas dance with incorrect orations: *'When all the world around you is...'*. Very annoying to Janet, she thought him most self-righteous. Everyone knows the poem 'If' reads: *'If you can keep your head when all about you; Are losing theirs and blaming it on you,'* ... Janet did not even think the word 'world' appeared in that poem! Or did it?

"Janet! Janet! It's time for bed! Turn your bedroom light off!" Janet's mother shouted up the stairs. This was even more irritating to Janet than Marjory Smyth's older brother, on this evening in 1962. She crept under the pink eiderdown, shining her redundant Girl Guide's torch at last week's local newspaper. Trying to keep her head, she read on... If Janet was honest, she did not fully understand the crisis. The newspapers were confusing, no one knew what and when or if and how. She could not imagine dying. If she was dead, then she would not know about it, would she? She could, however, imagine the desolation and destruction of towns, cities and countryside. These images, images of war were regularly flashed on the TV screen in black and white. Janet had no best friend, no ally, there under the covers to discuss this with. She looked at the local news, to find out if anyone in the town of Bury cared. There was absolutely no reference to what was going on in Cuba. There was a story about a woman who did not know her husband was a murderer. There was a story about how two men were in court after they stole an umbrella from a pub for a joke. There was a story about how a TV crew had been to visit a high school near Janet's house. They wanted to interview school children about the most important issue that week. "Is there going to be enough employment for teenagers when they leave school?" Janet's eyes were bulging, she was very irritated. That is not the most important issue!

1962

Employment figures will not matter when we have all been annihilated! She threw the newspaper to the side. Her eyes were drawn to a story on the open page:

"SCHOOL TEACHER MEETS PRESIDENT

 KENNEDY" Her eyes scanned the story, she read it again. Her forehead crinkled. She held the newspaper up to the light. Maybe she did need reading glasses? The story went on to say that the teacher, from Bury, had spent an entire year in America. She had taught at a kindergarten in Philadelphia. Then she spent some time in Minnesota and Seattle. She must have travelled around quite a bit. There was absolutely no mention of how she met the president, or what she had said to him. But the headline clearly said that she had: "SCHOOL TEACHER MEETS PRESIDENT KENNEDY". Maybe there is a conspiracy and the school teacher had asked him about nuclear bombs. Maybe the American secret service had infiltrated the British local press in Bury and instructed them not to print the conversation between the school teacher from Lancashire, 'Eng-land' and the President of the United States of America, the most powerful man in the world. Janet knew exactly what she would say to President Kennedy if she met him. She would say... She would say... Err she would say... She had no idea what she would say actually. If only she had someone she could discuss it with?

Meanwhile, on summer days when Ernest Bradshaw had been practising being a courageous, ambitious cyclist, Mark Crosby was practising his wolf whistle. They were not friends as such, nor were they enemies but shared a common goal. Mark Crosby viewed himself as 'top dog' at school, and Ernest did not mind this, as long as he, himself did not become 'bottom dog'. Ernest had not really been much of a target up to now, Mark Crosby saw Ernest as a kind of friend he could tease. And anyway, there were four other bits of information that balanced things out.

1) Ernest was really good at athletics, this was a desirable attribute in 1962.
2) Ernest was fast at sprinting, Mark Crosby was not.
3) There was another boy, who needed to be bullied more, his name was Harold.

That is three bits of information, but Mark Crosby was not very good at counting, another reason he endeared himself to Ernest without Ernest's consent. Ernest now had a passion for cycling, and Mark Crosby did not. He had a passion for, anything involving misbehaviour. Mark Crosby was not the cut of Ernest's jib, so to speak, but up until now, he was the closest thing that Ernest had to a friend.
Apart from his Uncle Billy, but he could not speak and anyway, he was family. That was until Mr and Mrs Towers introduced him to Christopher Cunliffe, an ally for Ernest. He lived on the other side of the Irwell to Ernest Bradshaw. Brenda Towers had been keen for the two juveniles to meet. She had ambition and arthritis.

1962

There had been a recent lack of junior competitors in the north of England.

Being a school teacher, she knew that putting two youths up against each other (in friendly competition) was a powerful thing.

Ernest was having a relatively uneventful week at school. Apart from Mr Cooley's ongoing nervous breakdown about nuclear bombs, and Mark Crosby wetting himself in assembly. He had done his provisions deliveries as usual. Mrs Smith had been in a state of undress again. He had been paid his wages and added them to his 'cycling fund' money box and set off for the club run.

"Christopher, this is Ernest, he's our newest member. You're a similar age. Just today I'll ask you to company ride, that way you can get to know each other" Brenda said.

The two boys weighed each other up.

Ernest was wearing his plimsolls and grey woolly socks. Christopher had all the proper gear, cycling shoes, brightly coloured tight fitting jersey. He even wore a helmet! ... A helmet with a hat underneath! Ernest was initially cautious, but Christopher seemed to like him straight away. He didn't seem to care that he didn't have the right gear. Ernest explained the origins of the bicycle he was riding, and that he was working and saving to buy a different one and all the paraphernalia that was required. Ernest wanted to know about his helmet and hat, but as he spent his school life avoiding questions about his mother and deaf uncle, Ernest decided it would be noble not to ask.

Christopher asked Ernest about the cycle club, had he read the leaflet on 'Time Trialling for Beginners'? Was he going to turn up and do training regularly? Where did Ernest live? Maybe they could meet up and train together? Christopher thought of telling Ernest he should buy a different bicycle sooner rather than later but thought it noble not to make his new friend feel like a fool.

Ernest told Christopher about his mother, who 'deserved a bloody medal', and that he was only available on certain days on account of school and his job.

"Oh yeah, school... I forgot about that. Sometimes I can't get out on the bike, I get these headaches, see" Christopher said, pointing at his forehead. Ernest looked at the helmet, he thought about the other cyclists in the club. No one had mentioned anything...   If Ernest was honest with himself, no one had *called* Christopher anything, apart from Christopher, his name. There was loads of information there! Christopher wore a helmet, he forgets about school, and he gets headaches! Ernest thought about all the nicknames he could for Christopher involving 'heads' 'rubber helmets' 'school avoider'. That's how it worked, after all, Ernest had the information, and Christopher needed a nickname.

"ERNEST..... ERNEST" Christopher prodded Ernest in his forearm... "Are you daydreaming? Oh, I do that sometimes" Christopher was pointing at his forehead again... it was all too much for Ernest, who hopped on his Hercules carrier bike to make a quick exit.

"Tell you what, I'll see you on Monday after school..." Ernest used all his new found strength not to come up with a nickname for Christopher and vowed to himself that he would stop wasting his time with the Mark Crosby's of this world.

Ernest Bradshaw and Christopher Cunliffe became friends, allies and teammates. They would courageously embark on a journey together over the next few months. Not just the ups and downs of roads and adolescence to handle, but the ups and downs of victory and defeat that cycling brings.

Chapter 6: The Pre-War New Hudson

"I'm putting my foot down Brenda, I'm not parting with it!" Brian and Brenda Towers stood face to face in their lean-to shed. Not by choice, there was little room, especially for both of them to be in there, nose to nose, stomach to stomach.

"Brian!" Barked Brenda "That Pre-war contraption has not seen the light of day since... since... PRE-WAR!"

This was true, the New Hudson bicycle lay cluttering up the final few feet of Brian and Brenda's lean-to shed. Gathering dust and rust like aphids feeding off a rose bush. The tandem and their newer individual bicycles plus Brenda's gardening paraphernalia also created chaos and clutter.

Brenda did not like this, it made her feel as though her house was about to fall down. If only everything could be tidy, all at once, organised and compartmentalised like the rest of her life. Brian did not see it this way.

"What if it comes in handy one day?" Brian pleaded.

"It has! Today is its lucky day! Young Ernest Bradshaw is crying out for a bicycle to race on, you said so yourself, I heard you and Sid whispering behind his back don't forget!"

"I'm not a flaming charity, Brenda! That cycle cost me... it cost me... err"

"You can't remember, can you? It was that long ago... you miserly old buzzard Brian Towers!" But it was too late, Brian was clambering over spades and cycle wheels to get to his beloved pre-war New Hudson. His hands turned orange as he grabbed the rusty back wheel, and disappeared under a cloud of dust and moths. The fumes from the back of the shed soon reached Brenda, who of course had her mouth open to continue her tirade towards Brian. She usually did not give up until she got her own way, but today the dust went right to the back of her throat as she sucked in her own nagging voice. She was blinded too by now, coughing, spluttering her eyes started streaming. In the dark of the final few feet of the shed, Brian had his foot stuck in a plant pot.

"Oh! I'll give you hoarder Brenda! This plant pot will come in handy will it?! I thought you'd given up on hydrangeas!"

No answer.

1962

"Brenda?"

Still no answer. Brian struggled to get out of the shed, the door was now closed and ... what was that? Brian heard a tearing sound as his trousers caught on a pair of garden shears right on his behind.

"Flamin' Nora! She's locked me in!" Brian rattled the door, which was indeed locked from the outside. Brenda, on auto-pilot as usual, had absentmindedly snapped the padlock shut on her way back inside to rescue herself from her coughing fit.

"Oh that's better," Brenda said to herself after swallowing a cold glass of water "Oh that's better, let me take the weight off my feet, get my breath back"

Brenda sat down in the sitting room catching her breath and dabbing her eyes. She thought about putting the kettle on but decided on a read of the local newspaper.

"Mrs Marigold Schofield wins the top prize at the church fair for her Victoria sponge," Brenda said to herself "She looks familiar, I'm sure she was the woman who won last time... Ha! I hope it's not the same cake!"

Brenda glanced up from the newspaper "Brian! I said... oh never mind, probably sulking somewhere" Brenda was still talking to herself. She started the crossword. A whole ten minutes passed (which seemed like three-quarters of an hour at least to Brian, still locked in the shed). "Three down, four letters, ticket price sounds reasonable. Fare. No, it can't be, that's bad grammar, they can't put bad grammar in a crossword. Sounds reasonable... Brian! Brian!

Come and help me with this crossword... Brian! Ooh, what's this?"
Still talking to herself, Brenda's eyes were drawn to an article about her husband's nemesis, Garth Pratt. Their ex-friend, their ex-*cycling* friend, a stuck in the mud who refused
to veer away from time trial only races in the cycling club they were all in together in their youth. Brian and Brenda had big plans, and that's how they came to break away from the pack. That's how they formed their own club, the ambitiously (and ridiculously) named East Lancashire International Cycling Club. But now it seemed Garth Pratt has big plans
too. There it was, as plain as day, Garth Pratt boasting mentorship for his new cycling protégée, Kenneth McKenzie.
Young Ken and Garth were pictured with Ken's racing cycle, and the article boasted big plans for junior time trial wins. 'Must be a slow news week!' Brenda said to herself "Brian, have you seen this in the paper, Garth Pratt showing off, this young lad has promise, and just because Garth lives on the same street he thinks he's responsible for the lad's talent. I ask you! It's nowt to do with him" Brenda shook her head (still to herself) "Brian? Are you listening, Brian? ..." No answer "Oh perhaps it's just as well..."
Brenda took her feet down off the stool and wiped her glasses. Then it dawned on her,
where was Brian? She thought he was right behind her when they came in after the tiff about the New Hudson bike. He was not in the back yard. He was nowhere to be found inside the

house... What's that faint banging noise? Oh! 'I've locked him in the shed!' Brenda rushed outside, where she heard a torrent of abuse from Brian.
"I've been in here for hours, I can't see a thing, Brenda! ... Open the door then!"
"I don't have the key Brian, and anyway it's been minutes not hours!"
"Well how did you lock it then and why did you lock it? If this is your way of getting me to part with my New Hudson, well I think you're being very childish Mrs Towers"
Brian only called Brenda 'Mrs Towers' when she was in trouble, deep trouble usually.
"No, I, I snapped the padlock shut automatically, Brian, I was all flabbergasted because of the dust"
Meanwhile, Brian had been rummaging around in the dark in his pockets. His forefinger brushed against something that had not seemed to have been there last time he checked.
"Brenda! I've got the bloody key"
Brenda was back in charge now, with this revelation. "Well, what are you doing with the key!?"
"I opened the padlock, Brenda"
"You're going to have to crawl right to the back and open the door at the other end of the lean-to, it's only on a latch" Brenda had half an idea
 to tell Brian he might as well bring the New Hudson out with him at the other end, but thought better of it.
 "Well, I can't see anything Brenda, I've crawled backwards and forwards in this lean-to twice already, it's very dusty at the back there. You'll have to fetch me the torch from under the kitchen

sink and shine it through this little crack in the shed door"

"Right you are then, Brian" But when Brenda looked at their front door, it had

blown shut. She was locked out, and Brian was locked in. She only had herself to blame but decided to admit to nothing.

"Brian, the batteries are flat in this torch... you'll have to crawl to the back, and when you

get out, you'll have to climb over the back wall!" "No, I'll just come down the alley and then I'll be at the front door"

Brenda did not answer Brian, she would tell him later that she had let the door blow shut. After much grumbling, pushing and shoving, Brian made it to the back of the shed, in the dark and unlatched the rusty back door catch. The lean-to spanned the entire side of their cottage, Brian had put it up himself not long after they married. And he had to concede that the New Hudson had been stationed there ever since. The light flooded onto its frame and memories of youth flooded back to Brian. He had raced on this bike in his younger years, when he was Ernest Bradshaw's age or there about, quite a bit older if he was honest with himself, it was the pre-war years. Brian patted its saddle.

"Don't worry old girl, 'appen I'll get round to taking you for a spin one day soon" Brian's humanising of the New Hudson had decided it was female. The shape of the Lauterwasser handles seemed to offer him sorrowful pleading.

Brian gripped the brake lever and it did not spring back. "You just need a bit of oiling, just like me!" he whispered.

"BRIAN! Brian, have you made it out of the other side yet?"

Brenda. He had forgotten about Brenda, why was she not inside?

"Right well, jump over the wall, and I'll meet you at the front door"

I don't know why I can't just walk around the alleyway. Brian grumbled to himself as he tried to get purchase with his left foot on the back garden wall. After much heaving, and grabbing on to one of Brenda's hanging basket brackets, Brian was now at the top of the wall. On top of the wall, and now on all fours trying to catch his breath after the daredevil, knuckle scraping feat. He swung his legs over and sat down. It was still spring, night time ground frost had not yet disappeared, yet the sun was out and

birdsong was in the air. Up there he paused to take in the glory of spring flowers, the last of the tulips and blossom, the first of the poppies and peonies. Or at least that's what he thought he recognised of May, nodding in that just sharp enough breeze, giving away that the summer of 1962 had not fully arrived, it was on its way, but it had not fully arrived. Particularly as Brian's posterior felt damp and cold sat up there

on the wall. He had forgotten about the rip in the seat of his trousers, and now his underpants were becoming damp. Oh crikey! Brian got up on all fours again. Time to think of a plan of action, if he jumped straight off the wall, he was sure to break his ankle. Maybe he could swing on the hanging basket bracket? If only someone was underneath him to put a chair or something to break his fall- but then there would be no need for him to be up there. He heard Brenda shouting at him to hurry up, she needed to spend a penny. Looking up, he saw one of the spinster sisters from two doors up pegging out the washing.

"Hello!" Brian waved.

"Oh!" She dropped her peg-bag "You gave me a fright" then backed into her own house.

Brian got up on all fours again and edged his way along the back wall. Each hand meeting moss covered bricks. If he could get to the other side of this hanging basket, then he could jump down onto the bin. But another shrill voice, just as loud as his wife's shouted over the backs.

"Yoo-hoo! Mr Towers, I've a ladder here, Nellie and me, we think we can push it over your wall" But it was too late, the shrill voice was the other sister, Gladys. Brian, just at that moment slipped and fell, his remaining trouser seat catching the hanging basket bracket and tearing himself what felt like an entirely new hole.

"Oh me favourite slacks!"

Nellie, with assistance from Gladys, climbed to the top of their ladder, only to check if Brian had landed correctly.

"Oh, hello, Mrs, err Miss Nellie, I err" Brian looked at his ripped up folded up slacks, he was now stood in his back yard in full view in his damp underpants, socks and shoes. The hanging basket bracket had come loose from the wall and

the bin was a bit dented, as was Brian's pride. When he reached the front door, Brenda's face was squashed up into the little panel window. "What are you doing out there?!"
"The door blew shut whilst you were messing about in the shed. Here, read this about Garth Pratt while I nip to the toilet" Brenda ran upstairs, and it only took her visit to the bathroom for Brian to read the article that changed his mind about the destiny of the New Hudson bicycle. Ernest Bradshaw might not be able to keep up on it, but it was not as heavy as the Hercules carrier bike. Ernest Bradshaw needed to train for speed, and Brian Towers needed to beat Garth Pratt. Brenda was back downstairs now, Brian, still in his underpants and jumper made an announcement, right there at the bottom of the stairs.
"Ernest Bradshaw is going to be the new owner of my pre-war New Hudson cycle, that's it, Brenda, I'm putting my foot down!"

Chapter 7: The Queen's Speech

On this day in 1962, Her Majesty The Queen, Elizabeth II was preparing to read written words out loud in front of a moving camera. These words formed a speech, drafted by civil servants employed in the utmost, highest
positions of the British central government war defence headquarters. Words of an imagined text, envisaging the possibility of war. Her

Majesty The Queen, Elizabeth II executes a busy schedule. Each morning, afternoon and evening are filled by the Lord Great
Chamberlain with official engagements. Officiously organised by five departments of the royal household, and safely delivered by the Earl
Marshal. State ceremonies and so on, the 1962 calendar never emptied.

Recording a speech is an unusual request from the ministry of defence. Nevertheless, it had been pencilled in by the royal private secretary's office. Decisions had been made; what would Her Majesty The Queen, Elizabeth II wear?
Decisions had been made regarding the location of the filming. Decisions had been made about the safe keeping of the speech; would it be sent to 10 Downing Street? Or straight to The National Archive?

This was an unusual state of affairs because the *request* for Her Majesty's time had been processed, but the final *decision* about whether
to record the speech or not was *un*decided. This was most unusual. The decision lay with
two men, the Prime Minister and the Secretary Of State For Defence.

What was more unusual, this secret speech, not intended for immediate public broadcast was to be the subject of a secret decision. Even though there had been multiple quandaries about the speech and it's filming, the final decision was :
'the speech is to be axed!'

The request cancelled, and the Queen's time about to be wasted. There ensued a catastrophe of excitement at Buckingham Palace. No living person at the palace could recall any such disruption to the Queen's official diary. Another decision followed. Who was going to tell Her Majesty that her morning was about to be ruined? That the speech was redundant? That Her Majesty's time was about to be wasted?

Straws were drawn over bated breath... there was not a member of the royal household that did not idolise Her Majesty The Queen. They would rather kill themselves than spoil her day. To each and every person in the royal household, Her Majesty The Queen Elizabeth II was *their* Queen. Gazing through the window with mournful reminiscence, Queen Elizabeth II thought she could see two cyclists in the distance. Remembrances of her father, King George VI brightened by wonderings about the Olympics. Will they ever be hosted in London again? She sighed a secret sigh to herself, whilst turned away from the court.

Arnold Smyth age twenty, footman and trainee butler of Buckingham Palace had drawn the short straw. A decision had been made that he was the one to deliver the news, thus spoiling Her Majesty's day.

The note from the Prime Minister, Harold Macmillan had been placed by gloved fingers upon a silver tray. Arnold approached the Queen, and, still in training

knelt before her. Bemused at Arnold's formality, Queen Elizabeth II took the letter and her spectacles (only worn for reading) and skimmed the Prime
Minister's words. Arnold Smyth the trainee footman anticipated the royal look of disdain; instead, he saw beautiful red lipstick lips impulse a small smile. Placing the note back onto the silver tray, Queen Elizabeth II turned to Arnold the trainee footman :
"Thank you, young man, you have just made my day"

Chapter 8: Never Mind About The Rust

"Cheer up Ernest, it might never happen!"
It was one of 1962's Sundays again, and three people had already told Ernest to 'cheer up' this week. First, it was Mrs Towers. Ernest saw her standing on her street and peeping through her own cottage window when he was on his rounds the other day. She had said something about locking herself out, and that Ernest should keep it a secret from Mr Towers.
"What's to do Ernest? Has someone stolen the jam out of your butty?"
Ernest did not answer Mrs Towers.
"Never mind, Ernest, see you at the next club run"
Then, it was Uncle Billy, who, after studying Ernest for a few days, gently put his hand on Ernest's forearm, and then signalled him with double thumbs up.

1962

Then, it was Mr Cooley, who did not exactly tell Ernest to cheer up with his "Pay attention Bradshaw! Five hundred words on why one should pay attention in class by tomorrow morning please"

Ernest, of course, had no choice but to answer Mr Cooley. Ernest had been daydreaming, he had a lot on his mind, and now Uncle Norman was telling him to cheer up. Ernest had not even bothered to pray for a new racing bicycle at church that morning, he knew it would be futile. He thought that all his problems had ended when he got the delivery boy job at Potts' Greens. He thought he had cracked it, improving his speed and strength on his rounds. But compared to the other riders of the East Lancashire International Cycling Club, Ernest was a slow coach.

"Oh, I'm just thinking about something Uncle Norman"

"Well don't think too hard, you might hurt yourself!" Uncle Norman nudged Ernest "Hmm!" Ernest had no choice, but to answer Uncle Norman with a shrug. Auntie Marigold and Ernest's mother, Rose looked and nodded at each other "Hormones?"

"I think he's worried about nuclear bombs, I told your Norman not to say anything" they whispered. But Ernest was thinking nothing of the sort. He had spent the last few weeks turning up at club runs and then turning up last at the finish. This was to be expected, of course. A new rider with no training and an unsuitable cycle could not possibly expect a fast result but this disappointment did not match with Ernest's imagined crowd cheering and trophy carrying.

Ernest had tried so hard to train and improve his strength on his rounds. He had even started eating his greens, spinach and so on. He had even gone out in the wind and rain, and even in the dark when he should not have. The other riders he had met were not beginners at all, Ernest was the only beginner. They had been friendly enough, told him about tucking his trousers into his socks to prevent getting caught in the chain. But that was the night it was raining, and Ernest had started to notice Percy rolling his eyes because Ernest had made them all wait. And even on the night that his new friend Christopher felt a bit 'under the weather'; Ernest still came in last. All his hard work had come to nothing. Colin Sidebottom was only being friendly, but on the last club run, he had told Ernest something that had unsettled him.

"When you get your speed up, you'll have to start training with the chain gangs"

Ernest had thought that joining a cycling club would be enough, then he finds out, not only that he does not have the correct bike, but there are other ways to train. The chain gang rides, to Ernest, sounded like secret meetings. They were for the experienced, confident rider and their suitable racing cycle. They involved ploughing along the A6 between Manchester and Chorley for thirty miles at seven PM on a Wednesday evening.

"You'll have to get a racing bike, mind" Colin had gone on to explain.

Poor Ernest, just when he thought things were going his way, his hopes were dashed and dreams were slashed. More fool him for thinking he could become a cycling champion in such a short space of time. If a nuclear bomb goes off now, he would only be famous for coming last. Last on a delivery bicycle. Ernest had hardly touched Auntie Marigold's small sandwiches, and it was time for going home.

"You're many things, Ernest, but you're not one for giving up," Ernest's mother said to him on the bus "And you're not usually one for being moody either, so turn that frown upside down will you son, you'll turn the milk into cream if you're not careful!"

Great, now Mother was joining the merry band of well-wishers. No one understood Ernest's plight, he had cycled one mile forward but rolled ten miles back. Ernest thought about his life before cycling became involved. He could hardly picture himself without it, he was nothing without that dream. He would have been gallivanting about with Mark Crosby, leading the life of a ruffian. No, maybe not, Ernest would not suit a criminal hobby. What of that garden hoe Auntie Marigold gave him? He could give up cycling for gardening. No, maybe not, Ernest was fourteen, not forty. And besides, his mother does not have a garden, so it was back to the drawing board for Ernest's internal dialogue. If only he had thought of this earlier on Sunday when he was at church.

Rose Bradshaw thought of her son whilst they were all sat there on the bus. She had enough to worry about with the Americans and Russians in the news without Ernest's hormones. Who was she going to get to teach him to shave? It was not as though she could get Uncle Billy to take a fatherly interest in Ernest. She looked at Uncle Billy dozing on the bus, he still had bits of tissue paper all over his chin from this morning's shaving disaster.

Uncle Billy kept his eyes shut on the bus journey home, and thought about his niece,

Rose. He was grateful to her, of course for keeping a roof over his head but wished she would pick up a better quality razor for him so that his face would not look like he had had an argument in an empty bathroom every other day.

The bus driver thought of nothing, except stopping a little further along the road, especially for Rose, who he had taken quite a shine to. He wanted for nothing, except perhaps not drawing the short straw in the depot over the Sunday timetable shifts.

"See you next Sunday!" The bus driver winked. Rose shuddered and drew her protective coat around herself a little tighter. Soon it would no longer be coat weather in 1962.

"Yes, thank you! See you then!" said Rose, who was already considering wearing a respectable pinafore apron when the weather improved. Maybe if she put a paper bag over her head, then men would cease their uninvited advances towards her. Ernest dragged his feet off the bus. No one understood him. No one except Mr and Mrs Towers. Ahh, Mr and Mrs Towers and their shared love of

cycling. Mr and Mrs Towers who had spotted potential in Ernest. They could not imagine that any cyclist would be able to start getting their

speed up on a Hercules
low gravity carrier bike but Ernest had. He did not
realise this himself because he was focused on
his place in the race, but Ernest
was certainly starting to speed up. It was down to
his strength, now what he needed was
speed. Mr and Mrs Towers understood Ernest's
plight and were now waiting outside the Bradshaw
family's door like a miracle. They had three bikes
with them.
"Oh! There you are, Ernest! Hello! You must be
Mrs Bradshaw!" Said Brian.
"Oh, yes"
"This is Mr and Mrs Towers, Mother. Oh don't
worry about Uncle Billy, he can't talk" Ernest said,
in brighter tones than he had all week.
"You've changed your tune, Ernest, and stop
being cheeky about your Uncle!" Said Rose,
who appeared to have adopted Auntie Marigold's
'outside voice' "Well I'd invite you in, but err" Rose
eyed the cycles and shoes that threatened extra
traffic in her house. Brenda looked like the sort of
woman who would understand about mud on
carpets.
"Ah, we've just come round to give Ernest
something. Erm well, we don't want to embarrass
you, lad, but..." Brian had a whole speech
prepared about giving up
his pre-war New Hudson Cycle to Ernest. Unable
to help herself, Brenda interjected:
"We're giving you this bike Ernest if that's alright
with your Mother?"
Rose opened her mouth to speak, she always
liked time to consider things. Without waiting for
her to answer, Brenda Towers almost

snatched the handlebars out of her husband's hands and wheeled the precious New Hudson bike towards an ecstatic Ernest. Rose looked at his face. How could she refuse this generous gift? But where the *flaming hell* was she going to keep it? She awkwardly scrambled around in the bottom of her empty handbag.

"Let me give you something for it... Ernest? Ernest has been saving up, haven't you Ernest? Oh, I'm sorry this is a little erm, my other purse is inside." Rose called after her son, who was already astride the cycle, the saddle being adjusted by Brian. Rose was losing grip of her tightly ran ship but soon, she felt the slightly tight grip of Brenda's warm hand on her forearm.
"Not necessary love" Brenda had only just met Rose Bradshaw, and certainly did not know her well enough to call her 'love' "I'm thinking of it as an investment... an investment in your Ernest. You might not realise this love, but he's got potential; Racing potential!" Rose turned her face away from Brenda Towers and her lavender perfume, to take in the image of Ernest, full of joy for the first time in weeks. Brenda tightened her grip in a friendly way. "And besides, I'm not taking it back, you should have seen the palaver we had getting it out of the shed, then one hand cycling to get it down here. And don't tell Brian, but I want the space in the shed!"
Rose wanted the space too, space in her front room, which she knew was where this new addition would end up.
"He'll need his savings to patch it up and keep it maintained. And then eventually, he'll need to

upgrade anyhow to a newer racer" Said Brian, who was accidentally adding to Rose's pressure.
Then it was Ernest's turn.

"I thought this was a racer? I mean, you just said I would have to buy a newer one?"

"Well, this is really a fixer-upper. A bicycle to race on, rather than a racing bicycle... I mean this was one of my first cycles, before the war" Brian said, as his grip strangely clutched the frame of the New Hudson. "I was very proud of it Ernest, and, well you can start training for speed with this and then you'll be very proud of it too. I'll show you how to oil the chain and the bearings. A great invention, bearings are. Same with these Lauterwasser handles." Brian was enjoying himself educating young Ernest about his bike. Brenda was busy chewing Ernest's mother's ear off, meaning that Brian had a chance to speak, also meaning he could not stop talking. Poor Ernest could not get a word in. "The chap who invented them, Jack Lauterwasser, he was an Olympic cyclist, and when he was a lad, like you, he was a cycling delivery boy for a grocers, like you Ernest. So you see. It's fate! Fate that you should be using the handlebars that he invented!" Brian had a crazed look in his eye, Ernest was his protégé, he just didn't know it yet.

"Well, let go of them Mr Towers, please, then I can have a go," Ernest asked innocently. Brian was still clutching the bike, sometimes it's hard to let go.

"Oh! Alright... erm, off you go then lad! Oh! I forgot to say! Never mind about the rust!"

Chapter 9: If It's Not One Thing, It's Another

"Ahhhhhh! Ahhhhhh!" Rose sat up with a start in her bed "Ernest! Ernest! What's that noise?!"
To the inhabitants of a two up two down, the crashing sound of a bicycle wobbling,
and then colliding with the back room's flagged floor in glorious fashion is enough to wake the deepest of sleepers. The sound of *two* bicycles giving in to gravity is worse. Even Uncle Billy had been woken, and in Rose's light sleep, the crash was of course compared with how she imagined a nuclear bomb detonation would sound. It was enough to test the patience of any saint.
"I'm sorry Mother! Oh! It must have been the bikes falling over!" Said Ernest, running two at a time down the stairs in his pyjamas. "I don't know what shoved them over! Maybe it was this draughty back door!"
"D'you think, Ernest?" Rose was exasperated. If it wasn't one thing, it was another. She had enough on her plate without worrying about a wind tunnel blowing through her kitchen. Every house has some flaw, some left over maintenance job that needs attending to. However, with no man about the house, Rose could not help but take any
imperfections as an insult. And now she had two bicycles stationed indoors... As promised,

Mr Towers had shown Ernest the way about how to maintain the pre-war New Hudson. And as promised, Rose had found a way to adapt to having yet
another bike in the house. Newspapers and old bits of carpet had been arranged on the floor to collect any potential oil or mud donated by either the New Hudson (Ernest's temporary pride and joy) and the Hercules carrier (which really should find its way back to Potts' Greens).

The following morning was one of 1962's fine days. Ernest had the chance to take the New Hudson out on its much promised 'spin'.
"Mother?" Said Ernest, as he stood astride his new bike "Do I look more like a proper cyclist now?"
"Yes, yes you do," Rose said without looking up "Now think on, Ernest, you promised to help me turn the mattress, so don't be back too late" The days had lengthened in the summer, allowing for more merriment for ordinary folk, and more training for cyclists.
"Thanks, Mother! See you later" And with that, Ernest was off on his own, just himself and his pre-war New Hudson. As Mr Towers said, it was a bicycle to race on rather than a racing bicycle, but much more suitable than turning up to a club run on Mr Potts' delivery carrier. Now it was time for Ernest to see if he could improve his speed. He just needed to set off. Tip-toeing along the main road, the bike was better, it was lighter but it was bigger.

Mr Towers had checked the saddle was in the correct place for Ernest. He had promised it was just right. It did not feel quite right though. He just needed to set off. Was he ever going to get used to riding this new bike? He just needed to push off from the side, get going, and then everything would be alright. So why did he just not set off? Thank goodness Ernest had not
just turned up to a club run without trying the New Hudson out. He still had not set off. Do all cyclists feel this way on a new bicycle? That somehow, compared to their other one, it does not quite feel like their own cycle? Like they might not get along with it, but they will get used to it, like getting used to a new pair of shoes?
Ernest was thinking through his next move.
Maybe he could continue to use the Carrier bike anyway, and just give up on the new one? Except it was not new... Maybe Ernest should just carry on saving until he had enough to buy a newer racer? But what if a newer racer put him in the same position? Walking along the side of the road with a bicycle,
when he should have been riding it?
'Oh no! He's everywhere!' Ernest said to himself as he spotted Mark Crosby walking down the street. Ernest quickly pretended to be doing some important checks on the New Hudson, just like Mr Towers had shown him, checking the tyres (that did not really need checking).
"Bradders? That you, Bradders?"
"Oh! I didn't see you there!" Ernest looked up as though Mark Crosby had interrupted a major and important operation.

"What you doing?" Mark put his right elbow casually on the wall behind where Ernest was stood, unfortunately, this meant he wanted a conversation. "Ahh just checking tyre pressure and the chain, before I take her for a spin" Ernest tried to bring to mind and copy what Mr Towers had said to him, whilst patting the bicycle's saddle. Accuracy was not required however, Mark Crosby appeared suitably impressed with Ernest's manly attitude towards his vehicle.

"Hey, don't forget to take me with you next time you deliver to your girlfriend, Mrs Smith. I've heard she hangs around that house all day just in her underwear!"

Ernest thought about how dangerous this would be. How wrong it would be to suddenly start taking Mark Crosby with him on his rounds, how did Mark Crosby know about Mrs Smith and her negligee hobby anyway?

Ernest had been dealing with him by 'being courageous', he did not want to have to kill him with kindness too. He ignored the quip about Mrs Smith being his 'girlfriend' and took a risk by lying with his answer. "Ahh, I don't deliver to her anymore"

"Really, well me mum's had a bottle of Old Potts' illegal sherry that Mrs Smith ordered under the sink at home. Are you sure Bradders? I thought we were mates?" Mark Crosby's revelation about his own mother's thieving forced Ernest to think on his feet. Be courageous, Ernest, wherever you are going.

"She's just not having me deliver it," he said.
"Oh, well, see you at school Bradders. Nice bike
by the way" Mark Crosby believed Ernest! He
believed him! Time to set off on this bicycle!
Ernest pushed off from the side and without so
much as a wobble, he set off towards his chosen
solitary test run ride. Getting used to the
 New Hudson already. What had Mr Towers said?
Never mind about the rust? What had Ernest
been worrying about? He was off and away his
legs had gained power in the last few months, no
longer pale and puny. Ernest had
 always had his athletic capability, riding a
different bicycle soon became second nature!
 Pushing along, how fast could he go on this?
Ernest had wondered why Old Potts had started
 adding bottles to the deliveries, illegal sherry?
Crikey! Pushing along, freedom, a chance of
hope, Ernest's dreams came back to him, he was
going to do it. He had told everyone he was going
to do it, and now he was another step towards it.
Ernest was sure. He had told everyone. Round
and round. Ernest did not like lying. Up and down.
The fib he had told Mark Crosby was
unavoidable, but Ernest felt terrible about it. Dig
in! He could not let his ambition statement
become a lie, that would be two lies in one day
and Ernest only goes to church once a week. The
day he blurted out to his Aunt and Uncle that he
was going to become a cycling champion could
not become a lie. Keeping his pace up! It could
not be an untruth. Ernest was cycling like he had
 never cycled before, he was almost in Bury now.
Ease off... Ahh, his mother had told him not to be

too long, what was it she wanted him to help her with again? If it's not one thing, it's another with Ernest's mother. Then he saw her, not his mother of course, but a girl out cycling, doing what he was doing, cycling on her own. Probably not getting used to a new cycle. Her parents probably bought hers for her with no question of frittered funds or pity cycles.

"Hello," She said, as she passed him on the other side of the road. Ernest did not answer. He pushed to get his speed up just a little faster, full pelt, as he had heard the riders say. Ernest was on his way home on his New Hudson, as he reached halfway on his chosen route, the New Hudson was his. It was definitely his. All fears of giving up cycling were banished... what had Ernest been thinking?! This was faster than he had ever cycled before, he was sure of it. But wait, what was that noise? Voices, wheels behind him, and whoosh! As they flew by. A group of cyclists, the power of numbers, allowing them to go much faster than riding alone. Much faster than Ernest was cycling, even if it was faster than he had ever cycled before. That must be the chain gang training Colin Sidebottom had told him about. As the group of cyclists disappeared in the distance, Ernest was disappointed to realise he was not going that fast, he had a lot of work to do when training for speed. Just as he thought he had resolved his problems, another challenge made his ambitions further out of reach. Poor Ernest, if it's not one thing, it's another.

Chapter 10: Is it a Bird? Is it a Plane? No! It's a UFO!

On this day, in 1962, when warning leaflets of US military tests had been forgotten, Randy Maroon was, as usual trying his hand on the fabulous Las Vegas Nevada Casino Strip. He chewed on a salami sub sandwich, sipped his bourbon and flipped a five dollar casino chip over in
his hand.
"What the cock a-hoodie is this playing, darlin'?" He said to the female bartender.
"Why it's Edit Piaf, French ballads set the mood..."
'La Vie en Rose' could be heard
warbling out of the casino speakers.
"Well, it's an old song. All this love loss and
sorrow does not get Randy in the mood for playing!" Randy made a clicking sound with his tumbler on the glass topped surface which Dolly had just cleaned.
"It ain't that old Randy, and besides, the kind of playing your referring to, well! The Flamingo casino ain't no place for rock n roll!" Dolly moved away from Randy and his sub crumbs.
.
She had a point. Randy Maroon (not his real name) was a player. He would sit and wait patiently until he spotted his next victim. It could be the wife of a business man sat alone, or a lone fellow female gambler up on her winnings, soon to be down on her luck, after Randy Maroon had swept in and taken advantage. He had been making his living this way for generations. But now in 1962, he was considering

settling down. He just had to play one more time, spin the wheel, shake the hand of fate and show his lucky dice (Randy's secret nickname for his man parts).

Randy spotted Frances Contra (not her real name) perched on a bar stool on her own, wearing teardrop shaped spectacles, dripping in jewellery and sipping what appeared to be a vodka martini. He placed his Stetson on his head, tipped it forwards and put his thumbs in his belt loops. Dolly observed the forthcoming exchange, and at that moment, decided to polish that section of the bar. Frances looked up towards Randy.

"Ma'am," He said, tipping the corner of his hat. Frances Contra made a giggling sound and squeezed her right earring.

"A whiskey sour, and whatever the lady's having," Randy said to Dolly out of the corner of his mouth. Dolly's right eyebrow raised, she fixed the drinks slowly as she listened in to Randy and Frances' conversation, she just could not help herself. As she slid the glass tumblers over towards the two day time drinkers, two large men in black suits approached the scene. It all happened very quickly.

"Mr Randolph Clutterbuck?" The first man said, Frances Contra, meanwhile slipped off her barstool and disappeared. Randy said nothing but gestured that he was, indeed Mr Clutterbuck.

"I'm arresting you for fraud and, and what's the charge for con-man activities?" He turned to his colleague...

"Racketeering," The second man said, placing his

heavy hand on Randy's shoulder. Dolly dropped the bar keys on the floor in shock, this was better than working at Denny's for sure.

"It's a honey trap!" Randy shouted as he leapt to his feet. Just at that moment, the entire Las Vegas casino strip felt a rumbling not dissimilar to an earthquake. Nevada is just over five thousand miles away from Bolton, England where Ernest's mother, Rose was peacefully listening to Edith Piaf. This day in 1962, was the day that the US military had chosen to test its nuclear missile in Nevada's desert. Five thousand miles away from Ernest, but only one hundred miles away from Las Vegas,where Randy, Dolly, Frances and the two policemen observed mushroom shaped clouds billowing up into the sky. Warning leaflets had been issued of course, but in a place like Las Vegas, when daytime is easily confused with night, the warnings had been forgotten.

"What is that?" Frances Contra said to her police colleagues.

"It ain't a bird or a plane, I ain't never seen a shape like it in the Nevada sky," Dolly said.

"It's a ..." The first man said, swiftly taken over by his slightly superior colleague:

"It's classified!"

"It's a UFO Dolly!" Randy Maroon, or Clutterbuck, or whatever his name was shouted. This was his chance, he had been thinking about it, and now it seemed his dancing days were over. Here was his chance, before it was too late. He was already on his knees, because of the shock of the bomb test, he could not reach out because his hands were already in cuffs. "Dolly! Dolly, I love

you! Will you marry me?"
Dolly could not drop the bar keys in shock, she already had. Randy's unexpected flying overture did not get him out of being arrested,
of course, Frances and her two policemen colleagues dusted themselves down and escorted him out of the building. Dolly looked out of the window again, the mushroom cloud had dispersed, Denny's diner was still standing opposite the Flamingo casino. 'Nope' she said to herself, I'll get better tips here, as she flipped Randy's five dollar chip into her apron pocket and picked up her bar keys.

Chapter 11: Waylaid.

Now that Ernest is courageous and full of determination, his two-wheeled friend accompanied him everywhere. With his feet firmly under the table at the East Lancashire International Cycling Club, a regular rider of Wednesday and Sunday club runs, Ernest has become a passionate peddler, unexpectedly able to handle any terrain in the saddle.
On this day in 1962, Ernest was minding his own business cycling home. His new ally, Christopher Cunliffe - also from the cycling club was at home with one of his headaches.

Riding home alone this Sunday after high tea,

Ernest avoided the estate by cycling down the dip. This morning's church sermon had been about God's bounty, this lunch time's lecture had been about his forthcoming final school year, and Ernest's prayers were now mainly about cycling. Peddling until the town centre could be seen just that bit clearer, he could either keep to the road or take a short cut through the wasteland with shin scratching hawthorn branches and uneven, unsuitable undergrowth. Worried that he might run out of steam and fuelled only by Auntie Marigold's small sandwiches, Ernest's determined and courageous mind decided to take the shortcut. This wooded area full of cruel prickles hid the ruin of a derelict factory. Maybe it closed down and then started to dilapidate? Maybe it had been bombed twenty years earlier?

"Bradders! Oi! Bradders" the intrusion called out, accompanied by a flying broken brick. "Come and see what we're doin' "

Ernest's front tyre collided with scattered rubble. The attention seeking missile landed in the dirt next to his bicycle, gravel ricocheted off his back wheel spokes. He shut his eyes and squeezed his brakes. His back wheel

drew a semi-circle pattern in the dirt. Flying broken bricks are not part of any nature spot. Neither is Mark Crosby, the person on the end of the careless catapult, thrown, after one of the Benson twins had spotted Ernest slicing his way through the hedgerow; Ernest, cyclist and recently promoted within the school hierarchy.

"Oi! Bradders! Bradshaw! Ernest Bradshaw! Over 'ere" Mark Crosby was now waving a stick at Ernest. There was no avoiding him.

"Who? Me?"

"Ernest, come and look at what we're doing!"

A most unwelcome situation that Ernest found himself in. Mark Crosby now appearing to befriend him by nearly killing him with a lump of rubble, and crowning him the neutral nickname 'Bradders'. Ernest was faced with a dilemma; pretending he had not seen Crosby would risk retribution at school the following day, so, should he enter the building deemed as 'unsafe' with the three most dangerous boys he knew?

He could always just have a look and then make some excuse. Ernest debated for too long, persuasion from the three boys prompted him to turn his bike around and enter the den of inequity.

"Look Bradders, your mate Mr Cooley told us to make bomb shelters, didn't he?... Remember when he went nuts in assembly?" Mark Crosby was gesturing

towards the makeshift den constructed that afternoon. There had been no such instruction by Mr Cooley, and six or so of 1962's weeks had passed since the

mention of the war in assembly. Mr Cooley's rant had been reported back by the boys to their bigoted parents, who, in turn, had suggested the making of shelters with anecdotes starting with "*They reckon that*". The den did not look safe to Ernest, and nothing like the shelter in his mother's backyard. The second Benson twin crept out from under the flimsy tarpaulin.

Mark Crosby had a deck of playing cards in his hand.
"You can join us in a game of poker if you like, Bradders" Mark Crosby was not asking, he was telling "My mate Benson here will look after your bike, won't you?" The first Benson twin's fat sweaty hands were already on Ernest's handlebars. This situation was most unnerving. Ernest had no idea how to play poker, but with some idea about bullies, he had an inkling that a rule would be made up and he would be fleeced of the two bob Uncle Norman sneaked him for his cycling fund. Courage, determination, a decision was made.
"Aye, I don't see why not" Ernest lied, he bobbed his head under the cover. And then out again, to the sound of screeching of bicycle brakes.
"Don't worry about those two, neither of them knows how to ride a bike" Mark Crosby chuckled the crashing sound away. "We were in the Ballroom up Bury last night" He boasted.
"What for?" Ernest half disgusted, half curious.
"Women of course!" Mark flung both elbows over the back of the tree branch sofa "This week, we're gonna sneak in on Friday, 15 to 21-year-olds special hour... older women" knowingly winking at Ernest, Mark Crosby's knees were wide, his stature manly, lazy. The first fluff of a five o'clock shadow on his upper lip. Older women? Mrs Smith from the top cottage is an older woman, older than twenty-one, her lipstick was probably older than twenty-one.
"Most women want to marry a man who is older than them, not the other way round!" Ernest

1962

corrected Mark, the sound of bicycle brakes and high-jinks now distant from their conversation. Mark leant back even further,
then jolted forwards slapping Ernest on the shoulder "Ha! I don't want to *MARRY* them Bradders! Ha, you do make me laugh son!"
 Mark Crosby, actually two months younger than Ernest shuffled his pack of cards. The den already smelt of testosterone "Marry them! Ha!
 Tell you what, Bradders, come with us on Friday and I'll show you what I mean"
 Ernest would rather poke himself in the eye with a bicycle spoke than go out fighting and womanising with Crosby and his posse. Crosby, who was in the throes
of persuasion, painfully repeating and talking over
 Ernest "Bradders, come on Bradders" he looked
 over his shoulder as if to make sure that the twins were not watching. "Ere, look at these cards of me old man's" Mark's dirty hand flicked over a dirty playing card, "Asked me to look after them whilst he's away on business" Mark Crosby lied, his jailbird father had not employed his son to safe-keep his smutty pack. Ernest
looked down, Mark grinned and nodded. A girl, an older woman dressed only in black underwear, head tilted back, stiletto heel pointing to her protruding posterior. Smile as dead and awkward as Ernest's was now. "What about this one?" Mark's voice in lowered, sexualised, naughty tones as he flipped the ace of hearts over to reveal a black and white full length nude female form, feathers covering her nether. A strained sticky silence, the image

reflected in Ernest's spectacles. Mrs Smith popped into his head again, she wore similar underwear to the first playing card girl.

Uncomfortable feelings provided an excuse "I've got my round on Sat'dee mornin'. 'Appen I'll sleep in if I went gallivanting the night before" Ernest said, Mark looked unimpressed pawing the deck of cards, images, objectified women, where had he learnt this? A girl's face smiled up at Ernest... A girl's voice screaming... Two girl's voices screaming. Mark Crosby and Ernest rushed outside the den with their hands on their hips like two old men squinting at the sunlight. The sound they heard was two bikes colliding. The girl's voice was the first Benson twin, who, at the threat of seeing blood, screamed. He was unusually high-pitched for a boy of fourteen who weighed fourteen stones. The girl with mousey-coloured hair covered by a navy blue bobble hat pulled her bike out of the bushes, shook the wheel by its handlebars and cycled away. "Hey! Are you alright?" Recognising her from somewhere, Ernest shouted after her.

"No! " The first Benson twin complained whilst standing on one leg, holding out the other bleeding knee.

"I wasn't asking you!" Ernest spoke without thinking, and so had the first Benson twin, who was not usually permitted to speak out loud without permission. Mark Crosby admired Ernest, promotion deserved, as 'he spoke up for himself'. That is how it worked with Mark Crosby.

"Give us me bike" Ernest grabbed the handlebars back "I'd better go and see if she's

alright" Ernest made to cycle off away from the den. Now, this could have been a fatal error. Chasing after a female,
unknown and possibly injured could cost Ernest his recent unspoken place within Mark's hierarchy. He was saved, however
by the second Benson twin's eagle eye on the horizon.
"A Bobby!" He pointed and shouted at the distant image of a policeman on a bicycle, appearing to have stopped to talk to the girl with mousey hair and bobble hat. She had delayed the policeman long enough for the four boys to make their exit. Going back on himself, on the path, now a struggle because Mark Crosby had decided to hitch a ride.
Clinging to Ernest's torso, repeating and shouting to quicken the exit pace. Ernest got stuck in, imagining a gruelling hill climb race, pushing pedals up and down, pushing the two of them out of the fix. The Benson twins puffing, panting and peg-legging behind.
"Seeya tomorrow Bradders" Mark Crosby slapped Ernest on the back as he leapt off Ernest's bike before it was stationary, breaking rule one of 'Time Trialling For Beginners:

'A cyclist is responsible for his own safety'
"Don't forget about Friday!" Mark Crosby threatened delivery round excuse ignored, and once again, his grubby hands were everywhere in Ernest's pockets. 'If the Russians are about to bomb the world

anyway, please can it be before Friday, so I don't have to go up Bury with Crosby and his cronies'. Ernest banished these thoughts from
 his mind, praying to himself does not count, he has to be in church to speak to God, and his thoughts should really be on the following day. "Look at you!" his mother would say when he finally arrived home, her mind on Monday morning.

Chapter 12: Weather

Mondays, being the first day of school always had a sense of freshness about them. Four doors down from Auntie Marigold's house, a bobble hat hid mousey brown hair. A woman swathed in a stylish scarf surrounded her.
"Janet! It is summer! Take that... hat off" said Mrs
 Dootson, the recent resident of this bay fronted semi-detached house, and disappointed mother
"Come on, let me back-comb your hair and put it up in a do"
Janet squirmed sideways.
"This is your first day in a new school" her mother hesitated "Try and make some new friends, won't you?"
Janet Dootson, soon to be sixteen, schooled and suitable for secretarial work, was not looking forward to today. The Dootson's move
 was not far, but far enough for a change of school. Far enough for Janet to want to cycle back to her comfort zone, returning regularly to

the old house since the move. Any fool will tell you that teenage girls do not like change. Two wheels once a hobby, now a necessity. Janet cycled away from the house that her mother already called a home. Janet was considering today with timid optimism, that this school might be different. In her previous school, Janet had been the girl always picked last for hockey and had never been acknowledged by the girls in the popular crowd. Girls with big hair, and eyelashes as fake as their hollow personalities. They were as bold as brass, these girls, that was how it worked. Janet, last in the queue in her bobble hat felt no regret about not being in the popular crowd or looking exactly the same as her best mate. Because Janet was an individual who recognised the need to educate herself about the world. She had read every book in her parent's house, including a book about politics. Then she had started reading her father's broadsheet newspapers, headlines that shouted anxiety and widespread pandemonium, fear of nuclear war. Russians busy transporting missiles to Cuba, the place that is only ninety miles away from Florida - a place that sounded familiar and nearby to Janet. There was more to life than being as bold as brass, provided, that is, that the world does not blow up before life begins.

Four doors down from the bus stop, a stressed out single parent feared perceived failure. "Look at the state of this bike!" Rose shouted out as if its appearance was the worst thing she had ever seen. Ever, in her whole life. "What's this? A bloody hedge? MUD! Again?"

Ernest knew he was in trouble if his mother swore out loud. Deep trouble usually. "Where's your hat, glove and scarf set?" her eyes were blazing.

Ernest knew this was bad. She always went ballistic when something had been lost, stolen or misplaced. That was three things he had lost, four if you count the gloves individually. Ernest had wanted to win a cycle race before the world ended, but now it seemed his mother was going to kill him first.

"Ernest! I am not *bloody* made of money, you are going to have to empty your bicycle fund and replace them" her eyes watered over.

This was two blows for Ernest. First, his bicycle fund is now to be spent on woollens, then he made his mother cry. Ernest could not think of anything worse. Why could she not just hit him over the head with a tea towel like other boy's mothers?

Rose rubbed the heel of her left hand up her forehead. She sighed. A double blow of guilt infected her. First, she could not afford to buy her son a bicycle, now she was shouting at him, his shocked face chastised and baby-like once again, his little hands risking frostbite. There was no immediate remedy, it was Monday morning.

"Right!" She slapped her hand on the kitchen table "Don't be too long faffing about! I don't want you to be late! Do something about that woollen set! It's going to be cold today! Said so ont' wireless!"

The wireless radio, the one Ernest is not allowed to listen to because of the news, Ernest

thought without speaking. His mother's French was fluent today, he
knew when to keep quiet. Rose questioned her own parenting skills, with
 no one at home to bounce problems off, she looked at Uncle Billy and blew him a kiss.
"Right I'm off now love, think on, school first, proper job. Old Potts won't keep you on next year. He reckons there is going to be an economic crash after all this business.... oh.. never mind... I mean.. see you later"
Rose put on her hat, the hat she kept near the door to protect her from unwanted visitors and left for work. Ernest composed himself, watching the back window until she disappeared.
"I can't win! One minute I'm the best thing since sliced bread, next minute she's telling me to start thinking about responsibilities! Find your hat! Get a proper job! Don't have any ambition, so what you do!" Ernest tore the final piece of toast in half to share it with his uncle, who was wriggling about on the high-backed chair. Billy knew that Ernest had something important to say because he was mimicking his mother.
"I'll show them. Me Mother, Auntie Marigold, Uncle Norman. I'll even show Mark Crosby! I bet he couldn't compete int' Olympics... they don't have a pie eating contest!" Ernest laughed. Uncle Billy laughed because Ernest laughed.
"Uncle, I'm off now to get me training in before school... Thanks for listening" Complaining was futile. Even if Uncle Billy could hear Ernest, he would take Rose's side. Uncle Billy watched the back window until Ernest disappeared, and

put the coins he had discovered down the back
of the chair in a jar marked 'ERNEST'S CYCLING
FUND'.
The weather in the Northwest is perpetually rainy.
This morning in 1962 could have been any rainy
day in March, April, May or June. The calendar
does not matter to the weather. Rain conspired
puddles, Ernest sliced through them. A smog
blanket cuddled the sky, but Ernest was cold,
water had gushed through bicycle spokes. The
steel enamelled
mudguards had failed him, and his bare shins and
spectacles were splattered. Water will get
everywhere, life is not meant to be fair. If a job is
worth doing, it is worth doing well, this mammoth
task of becoming a cycling champion. Ernest took
a long way round to school. He reached the top of
the hill rain-blind, having cycled right into a cloud.
This cloud had burst below and was spitting at the
summit. He looked from side to side, traffic like
ants,
his mother's bus a centipede scurrying along the
silver road. He reached into his
side canvas pannier bag for the local newspaper,
the inclusion of cycling results
provided protection from the weather. One of the
competitions mentioned a 'Hill Climb Event'
encouraged and inspired, Ernest folded the paper
away.
"I'm racing back down this one then! Get me
training in!" Ernest shouted out to himself up on
that hill, because up on the hill, inside that
 cloud, Ernest's ambition could not be heard by
his worrisome mother, by his judgemental

auntie, by his deaf uncle, by the dangerous
boys at school. Not even the Russians or
Americans with nuclear bombs could get to him
up there. Braced for increased downhill speed,
Ernest provided his own sports commentary:
"And Ernest Bradshaw is out in front! We did NOT
expect the day to unfold like this! The young lad
from Bolton... He's still out in front, he is taking
over his club, the East Lancashire International
Cycling Club! He's beaten them all, Mr and Mrs
Towers, Paranoid Percy, Christopher Cunliffe,
and that girl with the bobble hat!" Ernest slammed
his brakes on. Girl with the
bobble hat? Ernest had seen her cycling around,
up Lever Brew... near Auntie Marigold's, she had
even made an appearance yesterday on the
wasteland,
but she was not in the club. Ernest did not know if
girls are even allowed in the cycling club, Mrs
Towers is a girl, well sort of, a lady. Never mind,
Ernest thought, the last leg now then off to school
I'd better not be late.
"The crowd are three deep! Blink and you'll miss
him as he takes the corner!" He raced
down the hill at speed, skillfully manoeuvring
around puddles and potholes. Reminded of old
Potts' warning to 'be careful of that smaller front
wheel'... as it bounced off a stray brick. Round
and round interrupted, his bike skidded along in
the mud, dragging him from his daydream, and
flinging him under a gate into some unexpected
water.
"Ahhhhhh! I'm done for now! Help! Help! I can't
bloody swim! I'm drowning! When did they put

a bloody river heeeere!" Ernest was drowning in
an angry deluge, sliding down, writhing around
 in this apparent river. Fearing that time was
getting away with him, imagining he was dropping
deeper and deeper into the water, gushing and
rushing around his body. The news report would
now include not only news of nuclear war, not
only local cycling results, but also a tribute to an
aspiring young cyclist from Bolton who sadly
drowned in an unexpected, flowing torrent.
Eyesight blurred, body disorientated, Ernest could
make out a pair of wellington boots, a saviour at
the side of him. The farmer silently scooped
Ernest up, hoisted him over the wall, pulled the
bicycle to an upright position for Ernest to easily
get back on the saddle. Aspiring young cyclist
gasped for breath, coughing, wiping his face,
looking for his spectacles. "Err thanks... thanks,
Mister!"
 Continuing not to speak, the farmer turned away
and made his way up the field. He had been
 waiting for a dry day to dig his ditch free
of silt, it was now swollen and stream like at the
side of the path, but not a river. Ernest pushed his
bicycle forward, wet through right to his
underpants, spectacles wiped on his sleeve, now
muddy, St Christopher sovereign thankfully not
lost. He turned the corner... it was Lever Brew!
The street he delivers to after school.
'Please don't let her open the door.. please don't
let her open the door...' Ernest gulped as the door
of the nearest cottage opened. She stepped out,
 this woman as if she had been watching, noticing
everything that passed her cottage. Hair in

curlers, figure hugging housecoat, pink slippers.
Not ready to accept a visitor, but welcoming all
the same.

"Is that you love?"

Ernest carried on pushing.

"Coo eee Ernest! Is that you?"

"Err... yes, err sorry Mrs, you didn't hear me
swear did you?"

Mrs Smith had not heard Ernest.

"You what love? You're early aren't you?"

"Phew" Ernest whistled in relief, he would be in
deep trouble if a lady had heard him swear.
Twice.

"Twit-twoo" Mrs Smith thought she heard Ernest
whistle. How old did this young man say he was?
As she stepped further out of her door.

"Sorry Mrs Smith, it's, later on, I'll be calling with
your delivery. I've just been getting me... err,
getting on me bike before school." Ernest said,
Mrs Smith had already turned to look in her hall
mirror, drawing on lipstick, then turned to look
Ernest up and down, shivering on the corner.

"But you're wet through love! Why don't you come
in? See if I can dig out one of my Alf's old shirts,
that's Alf, my husband, he's dead you know" said
Mrs Smith, Ernest knew alright.

"Oh I know... err everyone knows your 'usband's
dead, I mean... No thank you, I'll just cycle fast,
most probably dry off in the breeze like!" It was
still raining, though. Mrs Smith fastened her
housecoat belt tighter around her waist.

Ernest cycled away in the direction of his school,
stopping only to retrieve his blazer

rolled up and secured by a satchel type strap at the back of his saddle. He held it to his face relieved it was still dry, but his mother had been correct, the woollen set was missing. Then he remembered. Mark Crosby had insisted on trying them on. Now he would never get them back, even if his initials are stitched into the inside.
"I've no choice now but to stay wet though. I've a full day of school, plus deliveries after to get through! Hope I'm dry before me mother finds out. She goes absolutely crazy if I get one thing dirty, now I've spoilt five things; that's if you count socks and underpants separately, not to mention the hat and so on" Ernest pitied himself aloud, his mother's voice berating in his mind 'what have I told you, Ernest,!'.
At least Ernest could be sure his time was improving, Mrs Smith is usually fully dressed by the time he gets to her house. Hair still in rollers, curtains still closed means his time has improved!
 And with Mr Towers' donation of the New Hudson racer, Ernest could now start training for speed. But what had Mr Towers meant about him having to work hard to keep up? He had mentioned that Ernest would still have to buy a newer racer. So was the New Hudson up to scratch? Ernest needed to find out. Rule number two of the Time Trialling For Beginners handbook:

 'Bicycle must be up to scratch'

Chapter 13: The Chain Gang

"Chain gang training rides, they are," Brian said, "A good way of training for speed, the only way, really" Ernest had dismissed his disappointment and embraced his next challenge, by asking Brian how he could get into it.

"It's difficult to explain how they work really, but the thing is, you can ride faster in a group err a gang" "Well, we do ride in a gang, in the club!" "No, it's difficult to explain, you sort of take it in turns to lead, and you go through; and off" Brian was not doing a good job of embracing Ernest's next challenge, but he would have to face it, Chain gang training was the best way to train for speed. Was Ernest ready? Not really, the decades that had passed since the New Hudson bicycle was built had increased the speed and improved the style of racing bicycles. Brian looked at his beloved old New Hudson. He had held on to it for so long, not realising how dated it was getting. The bicycle was not how he remembered it.

Like still trying to fit into the same pair of trousers from thirty years ago, especially in Brenda's case, it would not work. But Brian had opted not to tell his wife that, just like he was about to lie to Ernest... he had surprised everyone on that heavy old Hercules Carrier bike, so he might just succeed on this old New Hudson.

"You'll be fine, lad, just go for it! Best way to train for speed. You've built up strength, now you need speed. You need to learn how to cycle with speed. Through and off" Brian's skills at explaining things were not as he remembered them, like still being as sharp as he was in his thirties when he last rode his New Hudson bike. Later that same week, when Brian had been berated by Brenda for setting Ernest up to fail; Ernest Bradshaw had plans to catch up with some chain gang training. Not before he had to deal with the day's mundane normality. School, Harold Goatshead and his broken ankle made his comeback; crutches and all. Mr Cooley jumping out of his skin and screaming like a girl when the sound of a chemistry experiment went wrong and exploded in the next door classroom. The spinster sisters trying to keep him talking when he was completing his delivery round. This day of 1962 appeared to be conspiring
against Ernest, the clock was still ticking
same as it always did, but as excitement built, the day was taking longer. And if that was not enough, Ernest started to feel something unsettling in his stomach, it was a feeling unfamiliar to him. He felt like he had done, or said something he should not have.
"Ernest, eat something before you go out again, won't you," Rose Bradshaw said to her son, whilst absent-mindedly folding the newspaper and turning the radio off.
"I'm not hungry Mother, I don't know, I just feel funny in my tummy!"

Rose nearly tripped over Uncle Billy when she lunged forward towards Ernest, her right hand landing on his forehead. "Well, you don't have a temperature, what's wrong? Is it those school dinners? Tapioca?"
"No, stop fussing, Mother!" Ernest was not one for snapping at his mother, but here it came, the combination of hormones, and anticipation of the unknown. Ernest slammed the door on his way out, half on purpose, half not. Courageous, wherever he was going.

During that same evening, when Mr Cooley had been sent out on an emergency errand to his mother-in-law's house, his yellow scooter was making it's petrol powered way along Pilsworth Road. He heard voices behind him, was he imagining it? An accent he did not recognise? Yes, he was imagining it, there was no way he could hear another person's voice when he was riding his scooter. Calm yourself, Mr Cooley, he said to himself. The Russians are not coming after you! What interest have they in you?
 On your yellow scooter? But you have been taking an interest in the prospect of nuclear war... the *prospect!* That word had just popped into his head! His own mind! Pilsworth Road is quite a long road, enough time for Mr Cooley to convince
 himself that he was going mad, and then talk

himself out of it again.

Whoosh! They flew past him with powerful speed, a gang of cyclists. They were taking over the road! Triggering, even more unsettling intrusions in Mr Cooley's mind. Flashbacks from the hit-and-run accident he was not entirely sure he had caused with a boy, tall enough to be a giant, but a boy all the same. Mr Cooley saw his face when he went over the handlebars. Mr Cooley had looked for his face when he returned to school the following day, there had been no reports of a boy in a cycling accident. Mr Cooley thought he had got away with it, that is until the boy's face started haunting him, that and the threat of nuclear war... In the here and now, Mr Cooley realised that he had stopped his scooter dead on the road when the cyclists flew past. His twins would have to do without their comforter blanket that Mrs Cooley had left at her mother's house. Mr Cooley would make something up, the scooter was running out of petrol or something, yes, the Twins would have to do without 'blanket'. Mr Cooley was willing to suffer the wrath of his wife, and the trauma of his twins, he was not, however willing to tackle the roads, not if there were cyclists flying all over the place. It was not, of course, Christopher, the boy who Mr Cooley had seen go over the handlebars, flying past him on a bicycle. It was Kenneth McKenzie leading a team of chain gang riders, with Ernest Bradshaw at the back. Determined as ever, Ernest battled to hang on to the group of riders. The front position is the hardest, breaking against nature, against the wind. Two lines of cyclists had started at different speeds, keeping close together to maintain the pace. Ernest picked up that this tight system, riders not allowing gaps to appear, was chain gang training. One line was moving forwards, the other moved slightly back. Ernest had not needed Brian Towers' instructions, he watched Colin Sidebottom a little, got his ear ready for instruction, and then got the hang of it. They were riding much faster than riding alone. Although, Ernest did run out of steam, and was riding alone, dropping back, creating that unwanted gap. This made it all the more difficult to catch up, he thought he was going to manage it on the slight descent. They had told him at the start that if he gets left behind, he would get left behind. Ernest gave the training his best effort, the butterflies subsided after the first half mile. Not the same anxious feeling he used to have when dealing with Mark Crosby, but a feeling of excitement. Now though, he was worried about not pulling his weight. Was it the rust on the wheels that Mr Towers had told him not to worry about? Ernest refused to believe it was himself that had failed, he had built himself up on that delivery bike, why could he not be as fast as the others on the old New Hudson? It was Colin Sidebottom who said something after the chain gang ended.

"Don't worry Ernest, lad, I reckon by the end of the month, you'll start showing potential, they could see you had a pre-war bike"

And that was that. Ernest was now training for speed.

Chapter 14: The Green Viking

The month of September clings to its daylight
hours; challenging folk to make the most of the
month. Grownups are usually preoccupied with
preparations for winter, because 'before you know
it, Christmas will be here'. However, Christopher
Cunliffe and Ernest Bradshaw were enjoying the
last few evenings that included daylight. Monday
had involved his mother being in an even worse
mood when she got home, Ernest had heard her
trying to sing Edith Piaf songs to Uncle Billy, this
usually happens when she needs to 'let off
steam'. It is a good job Uncle Billy cannot hear
her.
 The first school week had involved the usual
rigmarole, and Mr Cooley still going on about
nuclear bombs. The other day he was giving out
leaflets from the ministry of defence 'safeguarding
your home'. There had been whispers in the
teacher's staff room, but the children disregarded
him anyway. Now it was Thursday. Deliveries
complete, Ernest met Christopher at their
designated telephone box meeting place. This red
beacon could have been in the middle of
anywhere, but it was in the
middle of nowhere. Ernest cycled towards
Christopher, a grinning rubber helmet in the
distance, a few feet away, it appeared
that Christopher's head could have been turned
upside down. The lines of his big teeth, the
 lines of the rubber helmet. One year older than

Ernest, he was twice the size and stature of him. Ernest guessed him to be at least seven foot tall. The bigger he is the harder he must have fallen. The two boys paired together by Brenda Towers (Mrs Towers to the junior members). She knew that two teenagers competing alongside and against each other provided the powerful potential for her cycling club, because like her husband said, 'the club needs ambition'. The two cycled away from the smog, up and down country lanes with no traffic, roads pointing towards their ambition - Ernest's ambition. They could cycle for hours in silence, with no purpose or destination, because the purpose was *cycling.* They reached the point where the sky met the ground in their black and white life. On a clear day, it is said that Blackpool Tower can be seen from this point.

"I wonder if you'd be better off cycling up here if a bomb goes off, instead of hiding in a shelter," Ernest said.

Christopher's thick brows frowned, he reached into his saddle bag with giant hands, his mother had packed drinks and snacks for both of them, her way of encouraging the two lad's friendship.

"Why do you keep going on about bombs? You're obsessed!" Christopher shoved a carton drink in Ernest's hand "The world can't blow up! I've already died once! I'm lucky to be here... or so they keep telling me..."

In a few short months, Christopher and Ernest's friendship had climbed a steady incline, with the exhilaration of acceleration in common. "I don't remember anything about it, you know"

Christopher shrugged, Ernest need not say anything "Apart from opening my eyes. That's

when it started. I felt the same, but everyone was
different. The same, but different y'know"
Ernest nodded, he did not know, though.
"My mother couldn't stop crying, crying and
hugging me, said she thought she had lost me,
but I was just there, in the same place! In bed!
Just opening my eyes!" Christopher finished his
carton drink in one loud slurp "Then over the next
few days, they kept telling me to 'calm down',
whispering at the end of the bed that I was 'so
angry'. But it was my parents who were angry;
slamming doors and all that. Mother blamed
Father for me cycling, I wouldn't have had an
accident if it wasn't for him, y'know" Ernest still did
not know, Christopher was now getting the
sandwiches out. "I looked at myself and I was
different. Taller... with hair... Y'know, down there"
Christopher pointed at his crotch, Ernest, a late
starter still did not know (but had an idea)
"It turns out I was sort of asleep for months on
end, it was a head injury and now I have to wear
this helmet if I want to leave the house,
my parents say it's a compromise. And I get
headaches, and tired, but I'm not angry, I don't
remember shouting, to be honest, they just tell me
that I did, tip-toe around me like they're on
eggshells" He shouted "I was the same person
but looked different, and everyone around me
looked the same but was acting different" He had
never spoken to anyone about his accident.
Ernest had never spoken to anyone like this, it
was not like a chin-wag with Mark Crosby. There
was no encouraging Harold Goatshead to climb
the stairs of a ruined mill, and Ernest was not

being asked 'why are you punching yourself?'
because Christopher was Ernest's first proper
friend.

"Right come on, did you ever play lollipops with
your Granddad?" Christopher sprung onto his feet
like a bouncy ball.

"No? Well there's only me mother and Uncle Billy
really"

Ignoring Ernest, Christopher scooped up handfuls
of ice lolly sticks from his saddle bag in giant
hands, grinning with his extra big grin "We used to
do this when I was about five or six" Christopher
was slotting the wooden sticks in Ernest's bike
pedals, weaving until both bikes had sticks
protruding from both wheels "The noise they'll
make when we set off!" Christopher was laughing
"Sounds like machine guns from the war haha ha
ha!"

"Oh crumbs Christopher, I'm not sure about this,
Mr Towers gave me this bike"

Christopher stood with his hands in the arch of his
back like he had completed a science experiment.
"Oh, don't worry, they'll be no
trace of these lollipop sticks by the time we get
down this hill. Right, we are ready for the off?
Over that hill like we are gunning down the
enemy!" Christopher felt a sharp pain in his head
and stopped in his tracks.

"Are you ok?"

"Yeah, I'll be fine, I forgot to tell you, sometimes I
get this weird memory, what do they call it? Déjà
vu? Like a dream. It probably has
something to do with the accident, it just
happened then, right; a bloke on a bright yellow
scooter, you know those two-wheelers with

motors... a motorcycle! Right, and he is looking right at me and his face is all like this Aaaaah!" Christopher pulled a face, and then shrugged "Then I'm back to normal again, but I can't remember who he is or what happened"

"BLIMEY!" Ernest's eyes were wide "One of our teachers at school rides a yellow scooter. Mark Crosby calls it a chicken chaser. Mr Cooley, his name is!"

"Who?"

"Mr Cooley?"

"Mr Cooley?" Christopher repeated.

"Yeah, Mr Cooley, and, Christopher, he's obsessed with nuclear bombs too, it's not just me!"

"Wow! Come on Ernest let's get him! Mr Cooley!" It is true that Christopher now had a habit of hanging on to one word that he liked the sound of, 'Cooley' in this case. It is true that Ernest respected Mr Cooley, but as he is a school teacher, he was fair game in this instance. Christopher set off first, Ernest closely behind.

"Mister Cooooooooley!" shouted Christopher

"Thhhhhhhrrrrrrrrrrrrrrrrrrrrrrrrrrrrrrrrrrrrrrrrrrrrrrrr" sounded the boy's bicycle wheels, like a war film with sound effects courtesy of lollipop sticks. Ernest started to laugh. This was like being five or six again. Responsibilities,

Russians or reprobates could not spoil this bike ride.

"Thhhhhhhhhhhhhhhhrrrrrrrrrrrrrrrrrrrrrrrrrrrrrrrrrrrrrrrrr rrrr" sound from the sticks clacking against their bicycle spokes made a huge racket.

"Mr Cooooooooooooley" Christopher shouted,

whilst Ernest laughed at anything Christopher said. This lollipop game involved littering and making fun of the Second World War. Both naughty, but Christopher's naughtiness was *innocent,* not dangerous like Crosby & co. Ernest and Christopher laughed and freewheeled all the way down the hill. This was not about preparing for a career in cycle racing, this was two teenage lads enjoying life. Just enough sunlight and just outside the smog, another cyclist could be seen. A girl, a teenage girl with mousy brown hair and a bobble hat. Both boys saw her. It was Christopher who noticed her.

Parked up on that same hill, Mr Cooley was catching up on the weekend's newspapers. He had purchased the motorcycle on the pretence of frugality. Mr and Mrs Cooley had invested in a new build with a frosted glass front door. Before too long, this three bedroom box was full, his wife efficiently producing twins. That was eighteen months ago. The scooter, with its speed appeal, had become Mr Cooley's only form of escape. Meanwhile, Mrs Cooley was at home with twins' bath and bedtime, whilst her poor husband could not get a moment's peace and quiet to read the newspaper.

'Soviets refute Kennedy's allegations'

Ah! the headline he had been waiting for! This was what Mr Cooley was so desperate to read! He had found it! Desperate to know the details of bad news! To make sense of it, up on the hill with his ridiculous vehicle, hiding from his noisy family just so that he could read about the world ending. Then to make matters worse, in the distance he thought he could hear his name:

"Mr Coooooooley!". He folded his newspaper, and set off home, promising himself to get more sleep.

Janet Dootson knew better than to be out until this time. She was already having a bad week, new school, hockey, meeting Rita and Elaine in her new class (who were just like the Rita and Elaine from her previous school) And now this. She had told her parents she would only be out for three-quarters of an hour. That was ages ago (a teenage guess). She was starting to panic because the sky had started to go down.

She had only intended cycling solitude and a glance at her old house, but trying out new routes she had taken a wrong turn and started cycling uphill. The more experienced rider knows that every uphill has a downhill, this was Janet's weakness and the real reason she refused to join a club because sooner or later, she would be expected to cycle downhill. And anyway, she was not sure if girls are allowed to join cycling clubs. Lost, but there were two other bicycles in the distance, one rider at the side of his bicycle, his friend on the floor, knees arched, wearing a hat that looked like a cross between a toast rack and a tea cosy. She did not recognise him at first, but then she did not know him. The boy she had seen cycling around since she had moved house. He was everywhere, when everything in her life had changed, this cyclist

had been her new constant. She had seen him walking at first across the field with a red setter and a man, presumably his father. She had scolded herself for thinking 'I wonder if he likes cycling?' but then the next time she saw him, he was riding a bike! On a bicycle, but talking to some boys that even a grammar school girl could identify as trouble. She had asked a policeman for directions that day, dismayed that her cyclist frequented with ruffians. But then! Just before the first day of school, she had spotted him bobbing in and out of cottages on a hill (that she made the mistake of cycling up) He had not noticed her, and now he was almost unrecognisable, nearly bent over, eyes crinkled shut making a whooping sound; was he laughing or crying? The other boy, or man or whatever he was, also laughing.
"Ernest! Pull yourself together! She's seen us!"
"She's seen us? Oh... hello, I wondered if you could point me in the right direction of Turton road?" Bold as brass Janet copied Rita and Elaine. More noise ensued from her cyclist "Diiiiiiyoooooseeee?"
"He's trying to tell you it's that way!" Christopher stood, eclipsing Ernest, and pointing down a hill.
"Oh, err is there a way I could go that does not involve cycling downhill?"
"No, but you can follow us if you like" Christopher had noticed Janet in the same way that Janet had noticed Ernest. Just before Janet arrived on the scene, the two lads collided and ended up on the road. Asking each other- 'are you alright?' but not getting their words out for laughing. Especially Ernest, who laughs like he is crying. The three teenagers turned their bicycles around. "That's

an unusual bike," Janet said to Ernest, she was not going to enjoy cycling downhill, but what could she do? What could go wrong with these two? Rear cycle lamps guiding the way in the twilight and smog, even a row of traffic joined them. Christopher and Ernest pointed at the turning Janet should take, and she waved "Thank you!" Her bicycle and her terrible week turned a corner. "Do you think she was being sarcastic about this bike?"

"Yeah, probably, girls are like that. It was probably the rusty wheels Ernest, girls are funny like that" Christopher said with mature authority "Oh I forgot to tell you, Paranoid Percy is selling everything, he's planning on doing a flit. Anyway, he wants twenty-five quid for his best bike... It's a Viking racer, though, green coloured it is, so I think it's worth it"

"I've got me birthday coming up, I wonder if he'll hold on to it?"

"Well, you'll need it if you want to get your speed up. You'll be the youngest champion, Ernest, you'll be int' the records, never mind the world blowing up!"

Chapter 15: Rose Constance Bradshaw

Rose Bradshaw's week was not going well. On the way to work, Cynthia Crosby delivered her weight on the bus seat, budging Rose along without saying hello. She had a permeation of cigarettes and body odour about her. Cynthia

Crosby, mother of Mark Crosby, general dogsbody and largest, sweatiest woman employed at Potts' Greens. Cynthia Crosby, who appeared to be, no... definitely was wearing Ernest's grey woollen hat gloves and scarf set. "My boy gave me these, early birthday present" She patronised, not to be outdone by Rose and her tweed coat with a fake fur collar, now sinking deeper into the synthetic textile. The brazen cheek of it! How could Rose ask for them back? They had gone missing months ago, but they were definitely Ernest's. Clothes were important to Rose, she always made sure she bought a new coat every two years, afforded because she did not smoke twenty-a-day. And with the likes of Cynthia Crosby about at work, Rose was wise enough to know she needed the armour.

"Is it true your Ernest is delivering giggle juice for Old Potts?"
"Pardon!" Maternal instincts heightened.
"You know, bottles of sherry? That Mrs Smith up on top, she's his best customer!"
"I don't think so it's me that bundles the deliveries up for him"
"Oh! It's you is it?" Cynthia's arms folded into a knowing knot.
"Yes, potatoes and so on" Rose faked a smile at Cynthia, who took her smirk, returned it, and put the grimace in her pocket for another time.
"You mark my words it's, giggle juice!" Cynthia said.
"Don't be ridiculous" Rose returned.

"Uppity cow" Cynthia Crosby silently mouthed at Rose whilst she put on her tabard.

"Common as muck" Rose Bradshaw silently prayed as she overall-ed herself into the shop side of the distribution centre. What on earth did she mean? This is a greengrocer, not an off-licence... Someone's eyes were on her.

"Oh, Rose! Hello, Rose!" Mr Potts' morning had just improved.

Rose provided an awkward smile... That man does not know the meaning of personal space. Cynthia Crosby stood in the corner, smugly sponging in the exchange.

Rule three of 'Time Trialling For Beginners' :
'Any suspicion of cheating must be reported to Time Trialling Association officials immediately'.

"You've dropped something, Mr Potts," said Cynthia. Her job, cleaning is a self-regulating industry; if Cynthia Crosby was to swipe her mop around too quickly, Potts would have no need for a full-time dogsbody.

"I'll take that thank you" Cecil Potts rummaged around his pockets for papers from his customers.

Cynthia read the paper and folded it knowingly. "Thank you, Mrs Crosby!" said Cecil, snatching it out of Cynthia's hand.

Rose was momentarily startled by their exchange, Cecil Potts immediately became worried about being short with Cynthia Crosby, but only because of Rose. To Rose Bradshaw, Cecil Potts must portray a permanence of

pleasantness, ahh Rose. Still on her own.
"Do you want me to put Mrs Smith's order
together for you Mr Potts?" Cynthia said, crafty as
a cat, glancing at her
counterpart..."Oh! I'm sorry Rose, I didn't mean to
tread on your toes"
 "No, don't mind me!" Not to be maligned, Rose
was not about to get into it with Cynthia, although
it was her job to bundle the packages.
 "No... err.. leave it with me, your Ernest is doing
an extra round for me tonight isn't he?...
 Rose make sure, I mean let me know as soon
 as you have finished those orders, no rush!
And Mrs Crosby, I thought you were employed
to..." Cecil Potts stopped, not about to get into
 it with Cynthia, who was now smirking and
rocking backwards and forwards on her mop.
"Employed to what, Mr Potts?" she asked,
innocently.
"Never mind" Cecil Potts was now patting his
sleeves up and down, he patted his upper chest,
his jacket pockets and his lower trousers.
 "Have you seen my lighter?"
 Cecil Potts and Cynthia Crosby shuffled into the
back yard for a smoke, with all that pocket patting
 and rearranging, the note had now miraculously
 unfolded and appeared in front of Rose for her to
see and read whilst the smoking of cigarettes
happened outside. Cynthia Crosby liked to take
her time, time enough for Rose to digest the facts
 written on the paper. She's a crafty one is that
Cynthia Crosby. Out in the backyard at 'Potts
Greens' Greengrocers', Mr Potts' mind was on the
 missing order, the missing letter. He knew the

woman who wrote it adopts a colourful way about her and he did not want anyone to get the wrong end of the stick. Particularly the member of staff left on the shop floor; Rose. Funny that. Cynthia Crosby sidled up next to him, selecting a cigarette from her packet, she offered Mr Potts one. He went to accept the cigarette from the dirty packet.
"Don't take me lucky fag, Mr Potts!"
"Lucky fag?"
"Yes, I always leave one upside down in the packet, just in case"
"Just in case?"
"Yeah, just in case" Cynthia Crosby sucked in on her cigarette, her cracked lips making a sound when she prized it from her mouth. Mr Potts went inside but came straight out again.
"Did you see where I put that piece of paper you found?"
Cynthia Crosby almost choked on her own smoky breath. Her years of training as a gossip taught her this, not to flinch when there was an opportunity to manipulate and use new information.
"What's that you say, Mr Potts? Sorry, I didn't hear you on account of this cough I've picked up. Nasty it is"
"Err ... never mind"
Never mind! He says, that missing order is none of my business, he said so himself! Cynthia Crosby chuckled. Mr Potts returned through the same door.
"Mr Potts! You'll wear that door out!"
"I was asking you about that note, that order from Mrs Sm... Never mind.."

Cynthia Crosby looked around herself.

"Well, I don't know what you mean, exactly, to be truthful, but I know it's not out here" Cynthia puffed on her cigarette, trying unsuccessfully to blow a smoke ring.

"I know, that's why I'm asking you!"

"Well, I was doing me mopping, you know doing my work. When I noticed Rose crying in the corner of the shop. she was reading something. I asked her what the matter was, but she said it was nothing. Her face looked funny"

"Funny?"

"Yes, funny, like this" Cynthia tried to do an impression of Rose "She looked like she was trying not to cry"

"Oh, I don't think she would've looked like that, what was she reading?"

"Oh I don't know, but after she left, I gave the till area a quick tidy up and there was a piece of paper on the till" Cynthia lied "That's when I said to you, have you dropped something, Mr Potts"

"I thought you picked that up off the floor? A piece of paper?" Mr Potts was anxious for Cynthia to get to the punchline.

"It was an order"

"Mrs Crosby! Just tell me!"

"It was Mrs Smith's booze order"

"What! I don't know what ...That's a secret!"

"Oh, we all know about it Mr Potts, and that's what made Rose cry!"

Mr Potts eyed Cynthia Crosby's cigarette packet. She held on to it tightly and popped it in her tabard pocket.

"Scuse me, Mr Potts, can I get past you? I've
scrubbing to do"
Both Mr Potts and Cynthia Crosby went inside.

Rose looked at Mrs Smith's order, at her tight
neat handwriting like painted flowers on the
scented note paper. This woman, Mrs Smith
had even added a motive to this order.
 "The need is there since my Alf passed" What
 kind of woman is she! Mr and Mrs Towers don't
add a commentary to their orders 'We need the
 carrots for our tea, the need is there, as we
cannot see in the dark!' their order is the same
each week. Mrs Smith is ridiculous "Same treat as
you gave me last week" what is all that
about? Kisses at the bottom? I don't want to
know; I've got enough on my plate. Rose
 Bradshaw, jumped in her seat, a figure, a man
was peeping at her from behind the green screen,
the partition in the warehouse to the shop side of
the business.
"Rose, have you.."
"Oh! Mr Potts! You gave me a fright!" Rose put
her hand on her chest, she wanted to slap him;
fancy giving her a start like that? "I'm not used to
men creeping up on me". Of course, Cynthia
Crosby was right behind him, infernal mop in
hand continuing her thankless cleaning, eyebrows
 lifted.
"I was going to say have you finished with the
orders for your Ernest's bike? "

1962

"Yes, I'm, yes they're over there, in that box, you know I leave it at the back door 'butcher drops his parcels in, labels them after his morning rush" Rose giving too much information in her rush. Cynthia noted Rose's blush.
"Right, right, I know err, I'll come back, don't let Ernest go until I've added to them"
Mr Potts swung the door behind him.
"What a strange man he can be at times," Rose said to Cynthia.
"I told you. You know what he's adding to the orders don't you?"
"No? What d'you mean? It's nowt to do with me"
"Well it is, it's your lad delivering. Wouldn't you like to know?" Cynthia propped her chin up at the top of the mop "Don't you want what's best for your boy?"
 "It was Mrs Smith's order!" Rose said, "You just flamin' well passed it me!"
"Yes, Mrs Smith's order" In hushed tones, Cynthia looked over her shoulder, Father Dunn was the only customer in the shop, browsing for peas and carrots so it was fine to talk "You know she's a ... erm"
"A widow? Yes we all know that she loves talking about her dead husband"
"No! Yes, that as well, but she's a.. y'know!" Cynthia was getting too close for comfort, Rose was now breathing in body odour and carbolic soap. She threw her head back and gestured draining an imaginary bottle. "She's a merry widow! A drinker!" Cynthia dropped the mop, put her hands in the prayer pose and bobbed up and down when Father Dunn arrived at the till.
"Afternoon Reverend"

"Afternoon, Mrs Crosby, long time since we've seen the Crosby family on a Sunday. How's Mr Crosby?"

"He's fine" Cynthia dismissed Father Dunn, he was getting in the way of gossiping this new and important information about Mrs Smith. He was feeling rather awkward with his peas and carrots, not knowing if Mrs Crosby's husband was in prison or not. Never knowing how to speak to Rose.

"Mrs Bradshaw" Father Dunn nodded. If only Rose knew, she would have plenty to say to God this Sunday, plenty of challenges ahead of her in the next twenty-four hours.

"Thanks, Vicar, would you mind shutting the door on your way out?" Rose said, her welcome shut out by the shop front doors until Sunday, her sister's outside voice to blame. She was not sure why but was keen to know Cynthia's bit of gossip. Wary about keeping her this close because aside from her odour, new information may come at a cost.

"Yes, it's Potts. Since your Ernest has been doing the deliveries up Lever Brew" Cynthia made a 'snob' face by pushing her nose up with her finger "Mrs Smith has been putting extra orders in, you know, booze!" Cynthia said in a whisper "Your Ernest is far too young to be carting those type of goods about"

Rose huffed, hark at Cynthia Crosby taking heed of the law! Rose's huff was duly noted by Cynthia, who could not help herself putting a cherry on top of the story.

"Yes, Old Potts is helping out the merry widow, if you know what I mean!" Cynthia winked.

"Gets her all greased up like int' day, then he pops and visits her after work! I betcha!" Cynthia was pleased with her little story.

"Don't be silly Cynthia, that note, wherever it has gone clearly asked for 'something fruity!' I read it myself! Although she .. never mind! It's nowt to do with you, or me for that matter. He'll thank us for keeping our noses out"

Rose stood up to Cynthia, who did not like it. That is how it worked with Cynthia Crosby.

"No! Thank *you*, Rose Bradshaw, don't get all pally with me on the bus, then when we get to work, start pulling rank!" Cynthia defended her place. Rose had to change the subject, especially if she was ever going to retrieve the stolen woollen set.

"It's our Ernest's birthday next week, he's been saving up for a racing bicycle, he wants to go in for a race"

"Oh, lad-id-a. My lad's going up Bury tonight, there is some teenage do on at the Ballroom, he's friendly with your Ernest, I'm sure they'll be going together"

Not my Ernest, Rose thought. I'm sure he said his mind was on the race, there was no answer to this, it was at times like these that Rose Constance Bradshaw wished for a loud French singing voice. Edith Piaf would not stand for any of this nonsense. "What do you think about the nuclear bombs in the news, Cynthia?"

"They reckon that we all need to build a shelter, but I don't know why it's only to do with the Russians and the Americans..."

Soon Cynthia was back on the subject Rose was trying to avoid "That reminds me, My Mark was out with his friends playing the other week, building a shelter, and then your Ernest gave him a ride home on the back of his bike"
This was the final straw for Rose, she would be warning Ernest not to hang around with the likes of Cynthia Crosby's lad when she got home.
The two women had not noticed Mr Potts stealth like movements in the corner of the shop, carefully adding to Mrs Smith's parcel two bottles of under-the-counter sherry.
'Something fruity!' he thought, these two minxes are conspiring against me.
The two most important women at Potts' Greens greengrocer wholesalers and distribution centre, Rose Bradshaw and Cynthia Crosby, were not what you might call friends. Being a respectable lady, a quiet person during the outside hours of the working day, Rose Bradshaw would not have said outright that Cynthia Crosby was an enemy either. Cynthia Crosby was a woman, a master manipulator, people were pawns to her in the great game of survival. You were either in or out. That is how it worked. She did not see Rose Bradshaw as a friend, but she would be stupid to keep her as an outright enemy. Rose Bradshaw was simply a commodity. Cynthia was the lowest of the low at Potts' Greens, the cleaner, the scrubber of floors. There was no big time crime going on, but Cynthia would often slip the odd potato in her

tabard pocket or a random carrot up her sleeve.
She was only keeping things ticking over. Mouths
to feed at home. Her husband's criminality
brought uncertainty, so no one would *blame* her,
stealing vegetables was a perk of the job, surely?
Rose Bradshaw had turned a blind eye, she had
other things on her mind. The news of a potential
war, her son, his life ahead of him, Rose had not
finished worrying about his future. She was
nowhere near ready to let go. If she could just
keep a tight rein on things at home, run a tight
ship so to speak, deal with the Cynthia Crosby's
of this world. Because Rose could not control the
news, no one could. Later that same Friday, when
dangerous boys and ballrooms had been so far
avoided, Ernest had a couple of extra deliveries to
deal with, accepted gratefully from Old Potts.
Ernest nearly had enough to buy Paranoid
Percy's Viking racer.
"Bradders! "
Oh God... he is everywhere.
"My mum tells me, said Old Potts is getting you to
deliver booze for him now!"
This is it, Ernest thought. The Russians have not
yet finished setting up camp in Cuba, but it's all
going to end here for me, right at the bottom of
Lever Brew... Mark
Crosby is going to kill me for one of Mrs Smith's
bottles of sherry. There was something slightly
different about him, though, the smell of cologne,
his hair greased back. A suit, not his school
uniform, but not his either. And he was alone.
 "Let's have a swig then!"
 "No! What are you talking about! I've got to

deliver it!"

"Oh, so there is something then?" Mark Crosby
asked and confirmed "Come on, my mam's
always getting free stuff from Old Potts, he won't
notice if the odd bottle of sherry goes missing"
What a position to be in! Mark Crosby always
seems to be involved in these dilemmas.

" 'Appen he won't miss it today, but Mrs Smith
will. She runs out of these bottles really quickly,
must make a lot of trifles or summat"

"Trifles!" Mark Crosby launched into
condescending Ernest, who had learnt this much,
the most stupid people have the most amount of
superior and patronising attitude. 'Know it all's' his
mother calls them. True, Old Potts would not get
to hear about a missing bottle of sherry today, but
he would eventually. Mrs Smith was out there in
her dressing gown on Monday morning,
desperate for her delivery of fortified wine. She
would tell Old Potts eventually, maybe even
tomorrow, if she can change out of her slippers
and housecoat, and walk down to the high street.
Then what would Ernest do?

"She is not making trifles Ernest! Ha! You do
make me laugh son"

Oh crikey, here it comes.

"She is getting tanked up! She won't notice, trust
me, and she won't mind borrowing to some to a
nice young man like you! Ernest Bradshaw, the
golden boy!"

"She will notice, she notices everything, she
noticed me wet through cycling past one day,
tried to get me into her house to strip off!"

"Wet yourself did you Bradders?"

"No I fell off me bike.. and it's lending not
borrowing... hey whatcha doin!"
"Trust me, she won't notice, anyway Bradders, we
need the 'Dutch Courage' you and me before
tonight" Mark Crosby had removed one of the
sherry bottles and efficiently opened it. Swigging it
down, coughing the tart ethanol away from his
throat.
"Try some! See, she lent it!"
The bottle was already open, the damage was
done, alcohol vapours filled the air before the
evening traffic took over. Old Potts would find out
about this tomorrow at the earliest; The President
of America may have had to push the button by
then, so why not live a little! What is all the fuss
about anyway? It is only liquid fermented fruit
bottled up... why the desperation Mrs Smith?
There was no money for drinking at home, they
did not have the glassware. There was an old
metal tankard but that is used for keeping spare
buttons and safety pins in. Ernest had no
experience of alcohol, but just like that, he
climbed another rung on the adolescent ladder.
He did not even bother wiping the bottleneck.
"Eww, that's awful!"
"Don't hog it Bradders!" Crosby snatched the
bottle back off him, he had done this before,
although fortified wine has a certain special
property to it; sherry is the strong stuff. Even Mark
Crosby had no tolerance for it, how does Mrs
Smith do it? Soon the two boys were straddling
the Farmer's stone wall, the effects had gone
straight to their heads.
"See this ditch here? See it?" Ernest pointed at
the edge of the field. "There was a river here the

other day.. s'gone now" He shook his head."Wow! I know why she goes through so much of it! Hey, she's always dressed in her underwear when she comes to the door you know"

"Who?" Mark Crosby's randy ears picked up "Mrs Smith?... In her underwear? I thought that was just a rumour. How old is she?" Mark greedily sucked the bottle. Ernest now had red lips, he shook his head.

"She's a widow, so... you know... shh" Ernest put his finger on his nose instead of his lips.

"Let's go and see her, is the rest of this for her?" Mark Crosby had eyed up the contents of Ernest's side pannier bags, carefully packaged by his mother, and added to by Potts.

"Oh crikey, yes"

"Come on then, let's go and see her"

Ernest hopped on the delivery bicycle, and pushed off, not expecting Mark Crosby to hop on behind him. Now, this was a challenge.

Underage drunk cycling, with increased cargo. Ernest stopped halfway up the hill. Dizzy, confused, exhausted. Mark Crosby smoothed his hair back and sniffed his underarms.

"This isn't Mrs Smith's house, I've just got to drop this parcel off to the spinster sisters" Ernest knocked at the door.

"Well, look at the state of you!" The first belligerent woman said "Nelly! Come and look at Ernest, come and look at him!" She shouted inwards "I hope to goodness this delivery is alright, I'm sick of getting them wet through, the brown paper makes awful smoke int' fire when..."

But Ernest Bradshaw and Mark Crosby were
gone. The final incline, the push, push, front
wheel wobbling.

"They're not sisters, Ernest they're dykes" Mark
Crosby had the crudest and most insulting way of
explaining everything.

"I think I'm going to throw up!" Ernest gave in, and
decided to walk the rest of the way, unloading his
cargo "Grab hold of this will you" Ernest
inadvertently made Mark Crosby responsible for
the short order... Only one bottle.

Ernest swung Mrs Smith's rusty gate.

"I thought it was you!"

"See I told you, she notices everything"

"What you say, love? Who's your friend?"

Mark Crosby, plus Dutch Courage plus brown
paper bag minus one bottle of sherry equals
uncharacteristic silence.

"Hello Mrs Smith, err you're dressed!" Ernest said,
trying not to sound drunk. Amused, Mrs Smith
wrapped her cardigan tighter around herself.

"Well, of course, I'm dressed, Ernest! What do
you take me for! My husband, you know he's
dead don't you?" She nodded at Mark Crosby,
who's mouth was wide open "My Alf used to say I
had the best pair of pins this side of the Pennines"
Ernest is trying to ignore Mrs Smith's teasing, he
handed the grocery parcel to her. She
dropped it accidentally on purpose. Ernest
picked it up, Mrs Smith
leant down to pick it up at the same time. When
Ernest stood up, he was met face to
face with her frontage. Mark Crosby grabbed him
by the arm, the two boys ran
off back to the delivery bicycle, Mark Crosby

 leaving the remaining bottle of sherry at the gate.
"Don't rush off, Ernest! Come in if you like!"
Mrs Smith has been one of Ernest's biggest fans,
she was the first to tell him that he should try out
for the Olympic team. Any cyclist knows he has to
endear himself to his crowd, but now he has
stolen a bottle of sherry from her, blushing and
smiling for a whole new reason. Inside her
cottage, Mrs Smith was singing and dancing
around her kitchen, she coaxed a glass out of a
cupboard, closing the door with her hip. She
poured herself a drink and says 'cheers' to a
single bottle of sweet sherry.
"One bottle!" She realised "One bottle! I'm not
being rationed! I'm a widow! I'm not being
rationed! Not by Rose Constance Bradshaw!"

Chapter 16: Sherry Power.

"Right Rose, love, the back door's all locked"
Cynthia Crosby marked the end of the working
week, although it was not quite over, a clip-clop
sound turning the
corner marked the start of an argument.
"What! Excuse me! You! Rose Constance
Bradshaw! My order was short!" A woman
appeared on the high street, full makeup, fully
clothed, full view.

Rose's heart was in her mouth, this apparition, this Mrs Smith on the high street, right there in front of Potts' Greens. Rose was having a bad enough time as it was, a bad enough week. Mrs Smith, not one for leaving the house, ill prepared in stiletto heels and smudged lipstick, had marched all the way down Lever Brew. Drunk, determined. Why? It was her business how many bottles of sherry she got through each week, that was between her and Mr Potts. She had a good thing going. The sherry had moved her, given her the power, the energy to seek out more. There had been rumours about Alf, rumours that fuelled Mrs Smith's isolation. The perfect marriage, the perfect cottage, the perfect wife, the perfect husband. Hidden away, hidden. But here she was, exposed on the high street, gesticulating at Rose, and fuelling those rumours herself. This was worth missing the bus, for Cynthia Crosby, a bit of fun on a Friday. There was a lot of panting and pointing. Rose was taken by surprise and fastened up her armour, the tweed coat. Maybe it was time for a new one, twice this week it has let her down, she felt unsafe at the talon end of Mrs Smith's finger. "Who do you think you are anyway?!" The delivery of her complaint was somewhat skewed. One bottle of under-the-counter, slightly illegal sherry. One glass of Sherry power had stopped her from getting to the point. "I beg your pardon?" "After all that's been said, who are you to cut my order short?" Cynthia Crosby perched on the bench opposite the front of Potts' Greens.

"What's all that about?" Cecil Potts could see Rose trying to shove her hat on, pinned against the front window. Mrs Smith, wearing unsuitable heels which she had toppled over on a few times on the way down there. Hair pulled and puffed from rollers.

"She looks like she's been drinking!"

"She has you daft bat!" Cynthia jumped at the chance of stirring things up for Cecil Potts. Out there on the street, he was not her boss. "She's shouting about her dead 'usband"

"Nowt new then"

"Dragging up old rumours. Don't tell me you don't know about those rumours?" Cynthia Crosby revelled in the chance to condescend, Cecil Potts, out there on the high street, he was not in charge, she was "Where were you fifteen years ago?" Fifteen years ago, Old Potts was not in charge of Potts' Greens. It was Even Older Potts, his father who was the boss in those days. Old Potts was only middle aged, but his bachelor loneliness made him appear older.

"Rumours about Rose?"

"Aye up! Your fancy woman's about to spill the beans about your..."

"Sherry!" Mrs Smith shouted.

Potts rushed forwards.

"Oh, Mr Potts!" Mrs Smith smoothed down her hair, changed her tone, and caught a glimpse of her own lipstick smudged face in the window. Rose removed herself.

"I'll deal with this Rose" Cecil Potts bundled Mrs Smith in through the front door, fumbling with his keys and hoping he had not run out of Sherry. "See, I told you!" Cynthia Crosby said, pleased with herself. Friday had been a good day for creative gossip. Rose Bradshaw's head full of Potts and Mrs Smith. Cecil Potts now wondering about Rose Bradshaw and Mr Smith (deceased). She's a crafty one that Cynthia Crosby. She waved goodbye to Rose. With her husband in prison and her son out gallivanting, there was no one at home demanding an evening meal. Cynthia Crosby put her feet on the empty table and poured herself a glass of Mr Potts' sweet sherry. "Oh, it's powerful stuff this," she said to herself.

Her son, Mark Crosby was indeed out gallivanting. His Dad's suit saved only for funerals and the pawn shop. Cologne, fortified wine, happy hour at the ballroom up Bury. Resulting in fifteen minutes of fame for Mark Crosby, making it into the local newspaper for all the wrong reasons:
'A bunch of hooligans, young people between the ages of 15 and 26, arrested and bound over for turning the town centre dance hall into a battlefield'

'Must've been the sherry' Mark Crosby muttered to himself in his cell.

It was not Mrs Smith's outburst, nor Cynthia Crosby's gossip that really got Ernest in trouble that Friday. Uncle Billy hopping up and down greeted Rose at the door, something was different. Ernest was asleep in the winged backed chair in the corner. No wonder Uncle Billy was jumping up and down.
"Ernest! ...Ernest!" Rose shook her son. Maybe he's tired? School... out cycling all the time, those deliveries look like they are getting heavy now that... what's that smell? Smells a bit like sherry! "Ernest! Have you been drinking?"
Ernest was in the middle of a drunken dream, his eyelids flickered ... *dig in, dig in lad!*
"Ernest!"
"Where am I?" Ernest's eyes rolled around the back room, seen from the different angle of Uncle Billy's chair "Oh, I'm going to be late for me rounds!" disorientated, Ernest thought Friday tea time was already Saturday morning.
"Ernest! You've been drinking! Where did you get it? Oh!" Rose gasped, do not tell me that Cynthia Crosby was right...
"You've stolen from Mr Potts? From Mrs Smith?" Rose's heart was in her mouth, still
shaken from the altercation on the high street.
No one to support her, to back her up. "Go to your room, Ernest. Go to your room and sleep it off. You can forget going out cycling after your deliveries, you can forget going in for that Time Trial race you've been going on about"
Ernest was sent upstairs for the night with an empty stomach, although that was not

part of Rose's plan, in her anger, she actually could not remember what punishments she had dealt out to Ernest, could not remember exactly what she had shouted. She had only meant to warn him off associating with Cynthia Crosby's lad, but in her vexed state, had rambled on, banning cycling. Had she forbidden him to go in for that race? She could not remember, and it was not as if she could ask Uncle Billy what he had heard. He was trying to help Ernest upstairs. Would Ernest remember what had been said? Ernest, who would soon be sleeping soundly, sleeping right through until Saturday. Rose made herself a cuppa, to take her mind off things. Being thoughtful is an attractive quality in a person. A thoughtful person, such as Rose, usually has a tendency to be over- sensitive, although this, in turn, is an unattractive quality. When Rose Constance Bradshaw has something on her mind, this usually upsets the entire equilibrium of her household. She, herself had fallen asleep on Uncle Billy's chair a few hours later, must have been all the upset over the sherry. She listened to Ernest shouting out in his sleep, "DIG IN, DIG IN" ... And then Billy got up in the night too, flinging the back door open. Being a creature of habit he was still using the outside toilet. The first night time chill of September intruded the back room. What had she shouted at Ernest? Sons need their mothers to be consistent, not contradictory. Constance was her middle name. What did she want to teach him? To stay away from Cynthia's lad?
Well, he would have to work that out for himself, she could not protect him forever. To punish him?

Take away the thing that he enjoyed the most?
Ban him from cycling? But which part? How far
was she to take it? Was Ernest banned from
cycling after work tomorrow? Or the race he
 wanted to go in for? And what had she said to
him? She was angry when she shouted, but if she
did not shout, then who would? It was now nearly
 midnight. She wasn't one for reading, but short
 stories in women's weekly magazines come in
handy late at night, too late to listen to Edith Piaf.
She heard Billy slam the back door shut. Bless,
he doesn't realise how much racket he makes, the
neighbours will be complaining again tomorrow,
she thought. Rose skim read the short story, it
was set in the 'olden days' a young scullery maid
had got herself pregnant, she was ever so pretty.
The lord of the manor was the father but denied
her. There were storylines of love, passion and
mild peril. Rose was losing interest. People read
at night to clear their mind, so they can get back
to sleep. Reading about pregnancies and secrets
sent Rose's mind off on a tangent. There was no
way she was getting back to sleep now. Ernest
started shouting out in his sleep again.
 "THIS YEAR'S JUNIOR TIME TRIAL WINNER!
ERNEST BRADSHAW! THE CROWD IS GOING
WILD!"
 She gave up, wondering if she could occupy
herself with quiet cleaning jobs and a cup of tea.
The newspaper she brought home from Marigold
 and Norman's house was at the top of a pile in
the kitchen. Left there for wet shoes. She
instinctively wanted to hide it from Ernest.
Fourteen, fifteen in twenty-four hours, the man of

the house, his life ahead of him.

It is easy for a person to take on the weight of the world, to listen to too many horror stories in the news. Turn the page over, make a cuppa and try and forget about it. A few months ago, a young actress had died in America, Rose was not that much older than her. What a life! Glitz and glamour and the movies. A life ended just like that. Rose couldn't even afford a proper fur collar for her coat. When it was nearly waking up time, she fell back to sleep on the kitchen chair, with the newspaper over her face. She dreamt of war. That she saved Ernest from death by pushing him to safety on his bicycle. "Save yourself, son, follow your dreams"

In the morning, Rose made a decision. Ernest's punishment would be to pay Mr Potts back for the missing sherry, he would have to own up to it. It would be easier for Ernest to broach the subject with Mrs Smith. But after the outburst about her dead husband, Rose Bradshaw was not about to suggest that.

Chapter 17. Uncle Billy Saves The Day

Rule 4 of Time Trialling For Beginners: '*Any indiscretion must be reported to the Time Trial association officials*'

"I'm sorry about the bottle of sherry Mr Potts"
"Shhhh! Ernest" Cecil Potts chuckled, and
glanced at his customer, shopping for groceries at
the only time she could, Saturday morning "We'll
discuss that in the back, excuse me, I won't be a
moment"
Ernest's eyes darted about the back of Potts'
Greens, he had eleven hours sleep last night and
his head felt thick. Old Potts, that is, Mr Potts to
Ernest was stalking up and down, patting his
pockets up and down, he pulled out a thin roll-up
cigarette.
"Well?"
Not a trick question, Ernest knew how to deal with
this.
"My mother told me to empty my savings out so
that I can pay you back for that bottle of sherry"
"Your mother? She didn't tell you to drink it
though did she?"
Not a trick question. "No, that was Mark Crosby,
he drank most of it to be truthful"
"Mark Crosby? Cynthia's lad? I didn't think you
were friends with him"
"Yes, I mean no, I know him from school. Only it's
my cycling fund, I've been saving up for a
new bike"
Cecil Potts should give Ernest the sack, his
father, *even* Older Potts would have, this was a
lot to think about. His illegal under the counter
sherry sideline... It would be difficult to find
another lad willing to cycle up Lever Brew on that
carrier bike... oh and he can't leave the shop for
too long... The pause made Ernest want to speak
, he knew that Old Potts could not keep him in the

back for too long, he had customers to serve.

"My mother didn't want me to mention it to Mrs
Smith, thinks something funny is going on"
"Something funny?"
A trick question?
"Does your mother think there's something funny
going on between Mrs Smith and myself?"
"Eh?" Ernest said, wondering why Old Potts was
talking 'proper'.
"Right, I've taken for the sherry, you can put these
small coins, oh and this button back in your
cycling fund... Err and don't let it happen again,
don't tell anyone about the sherry, tell
Mark Crosby my supply has dried up, yes that's
how you can pay me back, keep this sherry a
secret!" Cecil Potts, juggling the
sherry sideline, Mrs Smith and Rose
Bradshaw's bad books. Ahh Rose, still on her
own. This is why he did not want to say yes to her
when she asked for a job for Ernest.
"I'll take these when you're ready, Mr Potts. And
have you any cherries?" Mrs Cooley was nearly
at the end of her tether. This was the only free
time she had to get the groceries, and this fool
Potts had left the till unattended for an
unreasonable amount of time.
"What did you say? Sherry?" Mr Potts whispered.
"Sherry? No, cherries! They're not out of season
are they?"
Old Potts clumsily totted up what Mrs Cooley
owed. "I'll put this lot on your tab, Mrs Cooley?"
Ernest's ears pricked up, Mr Cooley's wife! Maybe

he's not as old as I thought he was! The door tinkled open. Mr Cooley popped his head in at the same time as Ernest came through to the shop, this could mean just one thing. Ernest had been kept in the back for long enough so that Mr Cooley started to fret about how long his wife was taking. This would be Old Potts and Ernest's secret, imagining his employment gave him a new kudos with Mr Cooley. Ernest had a few deliveries to do, this would be his only chance of cycling today, cycling fund nearly empty his heart nearly empty... he was meant to be going in for a cycle race.

The world was still turning. News flooded current affairs like a tidal wave. News that would affect us all. The news of American and Russian stand-off. Folk were going about their daily lives. It was Ernest's fifteenth birthday tomorrow, the second Sunday in September. Ernest's birthday is always on the second Sunday of September, every year. At age 15 in 1962, Ernest was old enough to leave school.
The correct and sensible procedure being when the school year finished. At Age 15, Ernest would not be old enough to smoke, drink or pass his driving test. He was, however, the man of the house in his mother's household.

Three cyclists had made their way to Ernest's house that Saturday morning, Ernest was still out on his rounds when they knocked at the door. His mother, not expecting anyone, popped her hat on, ready to say 'I was just about to go out'. She opened the door and was met by three smiling faces all clutching bicycles to their left sides. All wearing cycling clothes, matching jersey tops and matching smiles. It was Mr and Mrs Towers calling round again, and this time they had a lad with them wearing a rubber helmet. As always, Brenda Towers broke the silence.

"Oh hello love, where's the birthday boy?"

Brenda Towers shifted her body forward, grasping Rose Bradshaw's cold hand, she answered;

"I'd invite you in, but I don't know how you'd wheel your bikes through the house" Rose had not yet warmed to the Towers, especially as they had knocked on the *front* door, Rose had carpets to think of, her sister would be visiting tomorrow. Brenda looked at Rose, glancing down at her bicycle slacks, she realised her own error.

"This is Christopher, you've got quite friendly with Ernest, haven't you? Don't mention it, Mrs Bradshaw, we don't need to come in, we just wanted to see Ernest and give him his birthday present; from all of us"

"All of us at the East Lancashire International Cycling Club" Brian Towers interrupted. Ernest was now behind them, returning from today's round.

"Happy birthday" the three chorused. They started to sing, Ernest started to cringe. He tried to stop them a few times, but this was met with "Wait, shush Ernest, we haven't finished singing yet; happy birthday dear Ernest, happy birthday to you" from Brenda.

Christopher did not seem to be embarrassed by the singing, but then he was not the one forbidden from inviting guests in and having to conduct his birthday affairs on the front step.

Any cycling club worth its handlebars would have had colours. That is to say, a racing jersey with uniform colours for each member to wear. So that in the event of a big race, the club members could be identified.

Rule 5 of Time Trialling For Beginners '*Anyone entering a race must wear their identified club colours'*

Brenda Towers had decided on her club's colours. She had put her foot down and told the club members that now she had chosen the colours, they would not be changed. Never ever. Colin Sidebottom and Paranoid Percy had whispered and gossiped about rival club Bolton Clarion were 'changing their colours with remarkable frequency'. Brenda Towers would not be moved. And so serious was she about her cycling club, she had unnecessarily registered her club's colours with the British Cycling Federation. Who, upon receiving her typed and officiously written letter, did not dare reply to tell her that the club's name '*need not be emblazoned across the shoulders, nor be especially necessary for time trials and certainly not club runs'*. They were just too frightened to reply. And so, Brenda got her colours and corralled her riders into wearing them.

 The East Lancashire International Cycling
Club is an unusually long name. The first
tailor-ess Brenda approached refused, and so
Brenda took on the task herself. She quickly
shortened the embroidery marathon to the initials
E.L.I.C.C. And there it was, Ernest opened up the
birthday wrapping paper and pulled out his very
own racing jersey. He held it up to the light, and
yes Mr and Mrs Towers and Christopher were all
 in matching colours. Ernest really was one of
them now. Lime green and purple, with lettering
 stitched across the shoulders in pink thread.
Collar pristine and minus inevitable tide mark from
his neck. Pockets in the back for bicycle tackle
and small provisions. He shoved his head through
the neck hole and was now wearing the jersey
over his shirt, like a proper professional cyclist.
Rose was not best pleased.

Later that same day, when half the weekend had
been wasted away, Father Dunn shut his
 eyes, circled his finger in the air and dipped it into
the bible. "Look at that!" He said to the vicarage
cat "You know, I saw Mrs Crosby in the grocers'
shop the other day, I doubt she will come to
church, though, shame she will miss this one"
He closed the vestry door the following Sunday
morning, marking the start of his sermon.
"The book that Moses called Leviticus, '*You shall
not steal, neither deal falsely, neither lie to one
another*' how did I come to read this to
you today?..." His eyes darted about the church
pews. No Cynthia Crosby, it might be

too late to reach out to her anyway. He saw Rose Bradshaw, sitting lined up of course with Ernest and Uncle Billy.

You've got to be joking, God, it wasn't me dealing falsely. Is this why you're punishing me? Testing me, turning my son into a thief? Putting Mark Crosby in his way? I need all my strength for tomorrow, God. Ernest's birthday, not to mention the war. Rose's mind was elsewhere, no longer listening to the Vicar.

Ernest of course, was mainly concerned with wicked thoughts, how much money would Auntie Marigold and Uncle Norman put in his birthday card towards his bike? Only they could save him after the sherry incident.

' *For the love of money is a root of all kinds of evils. It is through this craving that some have wandered away from the faith and pierced themselves with many pangs*'Timothy 6:10. Uncle Billy's stomach rumbled, whilst Ernest hurriedly asked for forgiveness, deserved he felt on account of a hole free week for his socks.

Breaking with routine, Uncle Norman and Auntie Marigold had been invited to visit Ernest at his mother's house. Their own sons were fully grown and would not be joining the party. As Ernest understood it, fully grown adults do not really celebrate birthdays. Being the man of the house at fifteen, his next birthday would probably be in six years, his twenty-first.

Rose had thought of allowing and suggesting to Ernest that he invite a friend over, but decided against this after the sherry incident with Cynthia Crosby's son. Plus what if he had chosen his new friend, Christopher? She did not want to be shown up, there were not
 enough chairs for any more guests. Uncle Billy, who is not daft, had previously stumbled on and splintered the sixth dining room chair. Even though he could have fixed it, Billy put it outside for the rag and bone man to take away, because Billy understood that Rose did not like extra traffic on her carpets.

Ernest's need to purchase his very own racing bicycle had become imperative. He reckoned he needed between twenty-five and forty pounds to buy himself a good sports model
 bicycle with dropped handlebars and calliper brakes. The type of bicycle with gears that freewheeling was an impossibility. The type of bicycle for winning a race with. Christopher had told him that he could probably pick one up second had for fourteen pounds at least, but Ernest had his sights set on something more substantial. Legend had it that Harry Hill cycled all the way from London to Sheffield in 1936. So like Harry, Ernest would need a sturdy bike, especially if he was to make it to the Olympics. His mother had told him that good quality goods were more economical in the long run. Albeit more expensive. Buying a cheaper, poorer quality bicycle would be a waste of time, he would be back at square one riding a bicycle that was not much better than Mr Potts' second-hand heavy duty carrier or dare he think it? Mr Towers'

pre-war New Hudson.
"Happy birthday Ernest!" His mother knocked and
shouted through his bedroom door. Birthdays are
just another day, and in 1962 would generally be
celebrated on the same date as they had the year
before.

Later that same day, Auntie Marigold and Uncle
Norman had taken over the proceedings. Ernest's
birthday had become the 'Marigold and Norman
show' sitting in pride of place, all heads turned in
their direction. Uncle Billy, of course, could not
hear what was going on, but he sat appropriately
at the table, ate just the right amount of small
sandwiches and clapped at all the right moments
too. Of course, there was cake, and blowing out
of candles, Ernest had made everyone laugh with
his joke. "I'm fifteen, not fifty-one!" his mother did
not own fifty-one candles, but the joke was too
good to resist.

Joking aside, the wish Ernest made when
blowing out the birthday candles, of course, was
no secret, his ambition could be read like a
book. Then it was the turn of birthday cards
and presents. In 1962 presents for teenagers still
fell under the category of 'something useful' like a
pullover (cycling jersey excluded) or socks. Folk
had been starting to get more disposable income.
Especially the likes of Auntie Marigold and Uncle
Norman. This extra money trend had not yet
filtered into Ernest's life. Asking for money for his
birthday was met with derision. The skill of
buying a birthday present was something that

1962

Auntie Marigold was very proud of. With the autumn gardening schedule easing off, she had little else to think of in the past week. And after all, she had three sons herself, so she thought she knew exactly what to buy for Ernest. Amongst the small sandwiches and jelly Ernest's eyes had been drawn to a rectangular shape wrapped in birthday wrapping paper. This looked suspiciously like a book, rather than money. He had not yet counted the remains of his cycling fund since yesterday's sherry incident, no one wants to be disappointed on their birthday. Rose had given Ernest his card, containing what she could afford. Asking for money robbed her the pleasure of selecting a gift for him, she felt foolish making him pay back Old

 Potts and then replacing this herself in his birthday card.

The sight of the looming rectangular present was becoming a distraction to Ernest. What if Uncle Norman and Auntie Marigold had not given him any money at all? Now fifteen, fully grown and learning the lesson not to expect anything on one's birthday. No one likes a child who is constantly plotting what to spend their birthday money on. But Ernest was no longer a child, not in his eyes. The money would be an investment in his race winning future. He resigned himself to appear grateful for whatever was lurking behind that rectangular birthday wrapping paper. To return, or re-gift was not the done thing in 1962. There was actual anticipation in the room when Auntie Marigold made her way over to Ernest with the rectangle. It was true that She and Uncle Norman knew how to turn any occasion into the

'Norman and Marigold show'. Shoulders back, hair crowned her head, all eyes on her. There was almost an imaginary drum roll. She picked up the rectangular parcel, exactly making a right angle with each shoulder. She half closed her mascara-coated eyelashes and pushed the present into Ernest's hands.

"An Encyclopaedia! Wow, thanks, Auntie!" Ernest exhilarated with fake glee. Having educated her son on the notion of non-verbal communication, Rose Constance Bradshaw knew he would be prepared for Marigold throwing her shoulders back, with smugly pursed lips and wobbly head. No, he missed it, and Rose felt it necessary to kick her son under the table. This use of non-verbal communication to prompt him towards his auntie. Ernest being an obedient type of teenager got up to kiss Auntie Marigold by way of thanks for the gift.

"A British Encyclopaedia!" Uncle Norman confirmed the origins. Why would it be anything else? Ernest thought. He looked towards his mother, who had now ceased giving any nonverbal clues as to if he should thank his Uncle for the gift. Norman, grinning and perched on his wife's shoulder. Ernest, being an adult now did something he had never done before. He thrust his right hand out towards Uncle Norman. He was not about to kiss him, of course. Uncle Norman commenced his hearty laugh and his hearty handshake. Ernest sat down and started leafing through the encyclopaedia. Of course, the page had to fall open towards the end of the 'C' pages. 'C' for cycling, like a tongue finding a sore tooth.

Because it was only occasionally, that Ernest's mind would be distracted by other subjects. Although, this distraction usually and quickly led him back to thinking about cycling. And his lack of an adequate racer bicycle.

"May I be excused?" Ernest stood up as if to indicate he needed the bathroom.

"You may" Uncle Norman had taken over, mentioning the improved facilities "I see you're getting good use of the upstairs
bathroom" Uncle Norman flipped his tie out of his trousers.

"Well, of course, they are NORMAN!" Ernest picked up on Auntie Marigold's inside voice, just as he reached the top step. He did not need the bathroom but had just enough time to tot up his cycling fund...

Ohh just short of my optimum amount... If only Mark Crosby had not drunk it last night!

The shillings, pence and pounds added up to his estimated race winning amount. Enough to buy Paranoid Percy's green Viking that Christopher had told him about a few weeks ago. Ernest counted out to himself but was careful not to say it out loud. He flushed the toilet chain so as to make out he was not up there greedily reckoning his stash like an ungrateful teenager.

"He wants to go in for a cycle race next weekend" Rose admitted.

"Well, that's a good thing! That's a good thing isn't it Marigold?" Norman was really treading on thin ice now, Marigold batted him away, but he continued "I just think that lad needs an achievement, more than anyone, he

needs to be good at something" Norman looked
sheepishly at his wife "I don't know why I spoke
sorry
Marigold, why didn't Ernest mention it himself?"

Rose knew that if she revealed Ernest's
misgivings from last night that her older sister
would either give her advice that she had not
asked for or come out with a smug story about
her own sons. But it was Ernest's birthday, and he
would need his family, a crowd to endear himself
to. Rose had to admit that she was coming round
to the idea that her son longed to be a champion
cyclist. Ernest had become the character that
went everywhere on his bike, valued because of
his enthusiasm and drive. Demeaned because of
the sherry incident.
"He won't mention it, because of what
 happened last night"
"Oh?"
The pause was unbearable, and Rose nearly
 started her next sentence with 'never mind' but in
an attempt to be consistent;
"He stole a bottle of sherry from Old Potts"
"Oh!" There were gasps all around the table, even
from Uncle Billy.
"Right, when you say Old Potts, do you mean
Cecil, or his father, 'Even Older Potts'?" Norman
said, lunging forward, only to be batted back
again by his wife.
"Norman! What, Rose love, start from the
beginning, where did the sherry come from?"
"Well, I found out yesterday that Mr *Cecil Potts
junior*" Rose delivered his name without pleasure

"Has been running an under the counter illegal off licence. And to make matters worse, it was Cynthia Crosby who told me! That's how I found out"

"Eww" Marigold was without words, the grown-ups voices had become hushed on account of Ernest flushing the toilet upstairs.

"That woman was in my year at school, I haven't seen her since, well I wouldn't like to say... and there's a reason for that, let me tell you," Marigold said.

"Well, it was her son, I got it out of Ernest this morning. It was that woman, Cynthia Crosby's son who wanted to get tanked up before heading up town to the dance hall"

"At their age?"

Marigold took this in, she had her own story about her youngest son, Harry and some pints of cider that a landlord was stupid enough to serve him. She was not about to recall that tale out loud to Rose, her sister, the career woman of Potts' Greens. Because what did Marigold have in comparison to her little sister? Twelve rose bushes? even if Harry has turned out alright on the outside.

"That woman, Cynthia Crosby, her husband's in prison again, I read it int paper, stealing outside furniture from the Brown Cow, tried to pass it off as a joke to the judge! "

"Norman!" Marigold had had quite enough of her husband's anecdotes. She weighed things up, and passed her own judgement on the sherry incident;

"He's only a boy, he'll learn"

Rose was taken aback by her sister's lackadaisical attitude. Maybe she had been too harsh on Ernest. If she had banned him from entering the race in a fit of rage, she hoped more than ever that he had not heard her, and Rose had a full week to wait before talking to God again. Ernest was now looking glum and looking at his New Hudson bike, that even Rose knew was not up to scratch.

"That's why he won't have mentioned it, but I think he'll still be going in for it" Rose decided. She could decide for herself, after all, Edith Piaf did not have a sister, and she did alright for herself. It was Billy who had noticed Ernest's disappointment, his skill being non-verbal communication. He sat next to him. Ernest's initial disgust of a crusty handkerchief being shoved in his hand was soon replaced by the jangling of coins intended for Ernest's cycling fund. They dropped and rolled onto the table, like defeated riders clawing his way back to the finish line. Uncle Billy was clapping and making a muffled whooping noise.

"Oh, he's given you a present love!" Auntie Marigold always enjoyed providing a running commentary to the goings on.

Ernest himself started making a whooping noise. "Is he laughing or crying?" Auntie Marigold asked. He ran back upstairs. Yes! Uncle Billy who was not as daft as some folk would like to make out had given Ernest the remaining two shillings to make his cycling fund up to the twenty-five

pounds he had decided was the perfect amount it
should be.
Ernest would never find out if this had happened
by design, but Uncle Billy had saved the day! And
this day was Ernest's fifteenth birthday.

Chapter 18. Paranoid Percy

One more delivery. Mrs Smith at Lynchgate
cottage. Since the ditch incident when Ernest
nearly drowned, he had been delivering to Mrs
Smith last on his rounds.
 Then he could head home, having the option of
either cycling back down the hill or taking
 another turn at the top. It was as broad as it was
long, either way, would get him there.   Of
 course, after school deliveries are in the late
 afternoon. Mrs Smith was waiting, stood in her
cottage vestibule. Fully dressed, full face of
makeup. Full hair do. Full carrier bag anticipated.
Forgotten sherry incident. Funny that. He parked
the heavy duty carrier next to Mrs Smith's wall. He
hoisted the bag two glass bottles clinked inside
the paper. Two full red lips greeted him.

 "Ernest love, come in" Mrs Smith was all pink
and red. Pink clothes, red lipstick. Pink light
shining out of her pink front room because of the
red lampshades.
"Err, I'll just drop these off with you"
The delivery was not completely clinking glass
bottles, although there was one extra because

Ernest had to replace Friday's short order. It was a lot of sherry, though. Maybe Mrs Smith just enjoys Ernest's visits? Someone to talk to, getting through it, with no Mr Smith to share it. Must be lonely for her on her own, up on Lever Brew. No one to talk to except her tipsy reflection in the hallway mirror. Ernest's mother had no Mr Bradshaw, and in any case, he did not think his mother had the time for drinking. She had work to go to! Housework and Uncle Billy to look after! Plus Ernest's endless stream of holed socks to darn and lost items to worry about; not to mention the news... She deserved a medal. Uncle Billy was not much of a drinker it was not as if he could ever say... he had been retired for as long as Ernest could remember, a lot older than his mother. What if Uncle Billy dies like Granddad did? And what if Ernest does go off on tour with some (professional) cycling club, or join the Great British Olympic cycling team? It might be lonely for his mother in that two up two down... Ernest's first taste of alcohol had been hard to swallow, he had decided, that like Uncle Billy, he was not much of a drinker. Mark Crosby was now top dog again, even further up the school hierarchy after Friday night's brawl and appearance in the local press. All memories of Mark wetting himself in assembly, now forgotten. For Ernest, his punishment carried no secondary gain. Narrowly missing the total on his cycling fund, having to 'fess up' to Old Potts, and now he had to face Mrs Smith, pink and red house with all the fancy paraphernalia that went with afternoon drinking.

"One for the road" Ernest had heard grown-ups say from time to time.

"A little bird told me that you had your birthday this weekend!" Mrs Smith got hold of the bags, touching Ernest's hands as she did. What little bird? How could Mrs Smith possibly know when my birthday is?

"How old are you now? Sixteen?" Her mascara from the top lid was glued to the bottom set of eyelashes.

"No! Err, I mean No! I'm fifteen! Still at school Mrs Smith" Ernest was not sure why he was to protest his youth. It was his instinct. Mrs Smith stood up straight and buttoned her cardigan up. She had a wry smile, not that Ernest knew what a 'wry smile' was. "Oooh, shame! Old enough to know better, but young enough not to care!" Mrs Smith turned and sashayed into her cottage. Her kitten heeled slippers kicking the door shut behind her. Did she just forgive me? Surely not, Ernest thought. Ernest decided against cycling down Lever Brew. He took the turn at the top and would be home within no time. He could see the light on in his kitchen as he wheeled his bike down the back alley. He sprung the latch on the back gate. Uncle Billy could be seen through the window, wearing his flat cap inside, he probably had a cold head. Rose had just arrived home through the front door. She took off her green-grey tweed coat. "Hello love, feel any different at school today now you're fifteen?"

"No I hadn't thought of it, but the butchers have sent me home with these chops for you, someone

left them on the counter by mistake... I don't think
they gave them me because of my birthday,
though. I hope not anyway" his mother took the
chops in paper out of Ernest's hands. Ernest
wondered if he could have asked the butcher for
the 'money instead' for his cycle fund, there would
be entrance fees for races and so on.
"Mum, Christopher has found a newer racing bike
for me to buy, I've saved up the money now"
Rose did not say anything to her son's preamble
"So I said I would meet Christopher
 after tea" Still nothing "You know, at the
telephone box" Ernest was free to come and go
as he pleased. He was working and was nearly
 about to leave school. Once Christmas was out
 of the way, then it would be spring term in no
time. Well, that's if the Americans and Russians
 haven't blown everyone up. The delay in the
 conversation was down to Rose. The nineteen
sixties were becoming the dawn of a new era.
More freedom, more people and more danger.
They had even stopped chaining the swings up at
the park on a Sunday. Rose had no one to
bounce these daily mini-dramas around with.
Children and teenagers were free to come and go
as they pleased. Ernest was about to go round to
some strangers house with twenty-five pounds of
loose change and his friend who wore a crash
helmet. After dark. Well, he is fifteen, her sister
had reminded her. What would Marigold have
done in this situation? Probably sent her sons out
 in their gold-plated bicycles. If they lost any
money, their father would soon replace it. Holes in
 Socks for Marigold's boys? No problem: just buy

a new pair with Norman's money! Rose looked at her own hands. Cracked and dry. I look more like sixty-four than forty-four, she thought. What if Ernest gets knocked off that bike by the man who has been dashing about on the yellow scooter? "I'll set the table mum," Ernest said "Christopher's dad is going to drive us round to this chap's house, he's in the club. Christopher knows him quite well. If I like the bike, I can cycle it home "
"What's he called, this chap?"
"They call him 'Paranoid Percy' " said Ernest, his mother's eyes widened.

Paranoid Percy, age twenty-six from Bolton was amongst the people who had been paying attention to the news. A United States U-2 plane captured photographic proof of Soviet missile bases in Cuba. Paranoid Percy knew that the Russians were not the types to stand down, no meant no. This sweeping generalisation had stuck with him since school history lessons. If there was to be a war, a nuclear war, this would be a war that could not be won. The men-folk from Percy's generation had all been in the army. National service meant that Percy was on a reserves list, he would be the first to be called back if... when World War III started. The war that could not be won therefore Paranoid Percy was not being paranoid.
A cyclist since he was a teenager, he had thought about cycling away to escape. But worried that his bicycle would make him easy to recognise, he decided to sell it. Some folk had

said the news was sensationalising the threat, scaremongering.

Paranoid Percy had been advised to 'sit tight'. But as September was soon to become October, with its foreboding wind and rain, and the looming daylight saving, Percy had decided his 'sit tight' friends were wrong, it was time to sell his belongings. He would not need them where he might be going. The reasons, the story of Percy's green Viking being put on the market had gone right over Christopher's helmet. He was just focused on finding a better racing bike for sale for his best friend, Ernest. Christopher had promised himself that once he had helped Ernest, he could go about getting to know the girl with the bobble hat. He did not know her name, but it should be easy enough to find out, she was everywhere.

Christopher's Dad parked up at the address.

Ernest knew the street, it was near where Mark Crosby and his cronies lived.

"Is this where you meant, Christopher?"

"Yes, I've never been to his flat before"

Christopher's Dad was unsure if he liked the sound of this, but promised to wait in the car.

"You'll have to follow us home if you like the bike, Ernest. I'll tell Dad to drive slowly"

Christopher walked up to Percy's path. He often sounded amusing to Ernest, who was starting to learn that Christopher never meant to be funny.

Christopher rang the doorbell. There was no noise from the other side of the door, he pressed again. "Well he knows we're coming so I don't know what the hold-up is"

"Try rattling the letter box, that's what I do when I'm doing my deliveries," Ernest said as he stepped forward, and put his hand in the metal letterbox. The door opened, taking Ernest with it. Percy was stood firmly in the doorway, legs astride, muscles tensed. Shoulders back; ready, it appeared for an altercation. His demeanour caught Christopher's Dad's attention, watching Christopher and Ernest enter the flat, even Ernest was taller than Percy, so he decided it was alright to continue reading the newspaper whilst he waited.
"I didn't know what time you were coming, you have to be ready for anything when you answer the door these days" Percy suddenly appeared smaller than he had when he answered the door, and Ernest started to recognise him from the East Lancashire International Cycling Club "That was my mean guy stance, learnt it in the army"
"Crumbs," Ernest said "I've only come to look at this bike you've got for sale" he looked around Percy's flat. It was fairly sparse with a bit of paint peeling off the walls. Ernest wondered if this was what a bachelor pad looks like but quickly consoled himself that Percy had already sold his belongings. There was a huge pile of newspapers folded up at the side of an easy chair, with a solitary mug balanced on the top.
"Do you want a cup of tea? I've no coffee, I only drink tea" The almost empty flat echoed when Percy spoke.
"Oh no thanks, me Dad's waiting outside in the car," Christopher said.
"Good, I've only got the one cup. Let's have look

at this bike then" Percy got to the point, and Ernest was glad of it. He motioned for them to follow him into the kitchen then flipped the light switch on, a naked light bulb hung from an electric cord, without a shade, provided unnatural bright light. The tiny kitchenette had a back door with frosted glass. Ernest was about to remember everything from that moment. When he stepped forward out of the murky front half of the flat, he turned the corner and his eyes fell on something that was about to change his life. He felt a feeling he had never felt before. Ernest was falling in love.

The green Viking bicycle stood propped up and proud against the pale blue painted wall. As shiny as Ernest's ambition. A gleaming green promise of purpose, drive and desire. Even the tyres were clean. The saddle looked new. It had dropped handlebars like any proper racing cycle should. Ernest gripped one hand around the handlebar stem, and one hand on the seat. His heart was thumping, this bike was Ernest's bike alright, the green Viking had been built for him. It reflected in his spectacles, the image of Paranoid Percy standing behind him. Percy was talking about where he had originally bought it from, how much it cost, where he had ridden it. How he had spent a long time cleaning and polishing it up. About how the green Viking was the perfect bicycle really, he would be sorry to see it go. He asked if Ernest and Christopher had seen the news? Because this was the only reason he was selling it, there was no condition of sale, no wanting it back if the world *did not* blow up. Neither of them was listening to Paranoid Percy though. The extra bright ceiling light making Christopher's head hurt, maybe Percy had sold his lampshades as well. What a fool! Ernest was daydreaming about his new love, the green Viking. His mother usually took a long time on each decision she made. What would they be eating the following day? How often to have her hairdone? Which brand of cough medicine to buy? Decisions, decisions. But when it came to something big, such as buying a new coat, she had this ability to lose any indecisiveness, and choose the first one she saw. Or so it seemed to Ernest. He took a leaf from his mother's book and decided instantly that this was the bicycle for him. It was not Paranoid Percy's turn to talk, but someone had to. "I want twenty-five quid for it, no more no less" In the company of these two teenage boys, Paranoid Percy had adopted his tough guy stance again.

There was no room for haggling. This did not matter, as Ernest would have given Percy thirty pounds if he had it. He had no idea if this was a good deal or not. He could have bought a new one for that amount, but he trusted Christopher and the bike included sprints and tubs, special wheels made to take tubular tyres for racing, therefore, essential for Ernest's professional pursuits.

"Right - oh" Ernest unzipped the back pocket of his jersey and brought out a collection of coins, all adding up to twenty-five pounds. Paranoid Percy sneered at the small change but had to agree it was all legal tender.

"Don't you want to try it out first?"
Ernest already had, in his mind, the green Viking
was already his bike. Conscious that the other
two were watching him, he stood the
 bicycle upright. He held on to the handlebars and
swung his left leg over, almost scraping the
 pale blue painted wall with his Plimsoll. He
fastened his feet into the pedal clips. He just
 started to adjust the straps around his toes when
Christopher piped up.
"You don't need to go that far, just see if you like
the feel of it, you can adjust the saddle height you
know. Don't forget my Dad's waiting"
Nothing needed adjusting. Everything was just
right.
"It's just right, it's my bike"
Paranoid Percy, the bachelor had never felt so
lonely. He nodded at Christopher's Dad who was
giving instructions to Ernest that he would drive to
a point where Ernest would know where he was.
"Twenty-five quid! You could have had a new one
for that!" Ernest did not care, and could not stop
smiling.
Ernest pushed the silver crank-set down by its
pedal and started to cycle. Following the Cunliffe
family car part way home, on his professionally
engineered lightweight dream machine. Cycling
off into the night, taking Paranoid Percy's last
hope with him.
The next few club runs saw Ernest earn the
labours of experience on his new bicycle.

Rule number 10 of 'Time Trialling for Beginners' :
'Prepare to be impressed by lots of professional-looking cyclists, but do not be intimidated, they were beginners once'

Chapter 19: The Royal Palm

On this day, in 1962, the villagers of Villaneuva del Rosario awoke to find something different in their immediate surroundings. No one noticed it at first, farmers farmed, bakers baked, hummingbirds still hummed, something was not quite right but no one could put their finger (or feather) on it.

It was not until the Policia, the one law enforcement officer of the village picked up the telephone, purely to make an official call that it was really noted that something was different. The line was dead.

Now, this was not completely unusual; Crossed wires and deadlines happened occasionally to the people across Sierra del Rosario, such was its beautiful, green, mountainous terrain out in the sticks on the outskirts of society.

A place where secrets could be kept from the world, but not from the villagers. Alberto Gonzalez, the Palebra Para el Sargento of the village stepped out onto the dusty street, that's when he saw it. An

unusual event in the village of Villaneuva del Rosario. The main telephone mast lying there, on the side of the track like a
spent horse lying shiny on the roadside, dismissed of its duties.

"I saw them! I told you Sargento, I told you I had seen them during the night, working away,
 now they have chopped down our lines of communication!" shouted Sergio Lopez, the most superstitious man alive in the village.

 "No! You are wrong, the government has communicated to me, they are Russian agricultural scientists. We just have to let them go about their business" Alberto was used to Sergio's nonsense about conspiracy theories.

"Pah! Do you think the Cuban government would tell you, the surplus Policia out in the sticks about one of their many secrets?"

"There is no secret here, my friend, I have seen them myself, wearing chequered shirts, like farmers wear, they are agricultural scientists and no mistake!"

"Then tell me this, Sargento Gonzalez, why would the Russians spend good money to send good men to farm in our country? They have enough space of their own! And their space is cold space! If they succeeded at a farming experiment here in Cuba, it would not work in Russia. Their climate is totally different!"

"Callate tonto" Alberto slapped Sergio gently across the face "They are scientists! They know
 better than you! We have to leave them to it! I have official government instructions ... I mean business...

It's private business, only for the Policia!"
"Ahh I see, so you are part of the plan? I
should have known! I knew they would finally
track me down! Hiding out here in the sticks!"
Sergio started weeping and wailing, he
squatted down on the dirt track next to Alberto
Gonzalez, the tears ran down his dirty face,
pulling his hair out of his scalp with his bony
fingers.

"There, there, Sergio," Alberto patted the fool on
the back "No one cares where you are, do not
worry! No one cares about you, not even the
Russians!" "How do you know, Sargento? You
can't even make a telephone call" Sergio pointed
at the dead telephone mast and dissolved into a
puddle of distress.

Sargento Alberto Gonzalez stood in the middle of
the crossroads and scratched the top of his head.
This day in 1962 in the small Cuban village would
be a day of arguments, tears and secrets. Secrets
because what Sergio had said was true, their line
of communication had been destroyed overnight.
What could this
possibly have to do with agricultural science?
Alberto wondered. In 1962, it was difficult to keep
a secret from the population of the village.
Someone was listening in to Sergio and Alberto's
conversation... During the dead of night, an hour
or so before the sun came up, Marcia Martinez,
aged thirteen had seen everything. She lived with
her Abuela, in a house on the same side of the
road which the telephone mast had guarded the
corner of. But last night, in the dead of night,
before dawn even thought of rising, it was

 purposely cut down by the Russian soldiers. Marcia had heard them first,that's how she knew they were soldiers, even though they were wearing farmer's shirts. She peeped out of one curtain and saw one man commanding the rest of the troop. Even though they were pretending to be farmers, they marched and stood to attention at the telephone mast. Then they executed the instruction to cut it down, and roll it neatly to the side of the road, in a fashion only befitting of soldiers. What happened next gave away their secret. Marcia, like Sergio, had initially presumed that they were destroying communications to and from the village. But then she saw it, a huge vehicle, it looked to be nearly seventy feet long! A cylindrical shape covered in canvas. It had tried once, but could not make the angle of the corner without crashing into the Comisaria building. Marcia had stifled a giggle. What that would that have done to Sargento Gonzalez?! His precious police station bulldozed! Then she had watched the Russian missile-on-wheels smoothly manoeuvre around the corner, now that the telephone pole had been removed.

 She thought she saw it disappear into the deserted countryside. Maybe at first, she could not believe what she had seen. This over-sized vehicle looked alien and unfamiliar to anything she had seen before, so much that she wondered if she had been dreaming. Had she really seen it? Fear crept up on Marcia Martinez. Whatever this vehicle was, it could not be good. Was that the end of it? Would another, even larger thing come by tonight?

Marcia had borrowed her brother's bicycle and cycled over to Alberto and Sergio and listened to their earlier disagreement. They were now smoking and drinking coffee at the outside tables of the cafe. "I saw them, I saw them last night cutting down the telephone post so that they could drive their big... their big... thing through the village!" Marcia could not find the words to describe what she had seen, she did not want to say 'missile-on-wheels' for fear of being laughed at.

"See! See! I told you! The end of the world is coming!" Sergio slapped his hand on the table. Alberto was lost for words.

"The end of the world?" Marcia said, looking over at her grandmother's house and garden. "It will be the end of the world for them if they come back tonight and cut down Abuela's Roystonea Regia tree!"

That was the last time the Russians were spotted in the village during 1962. Marcia's grandmother got to keep her Royal Palm tree, which now permanently guarded that corner because the telephone pole was eventually relocated.

Chapter 20. The Glory is His!

It is funny how memories can jump about in a person's consciousness. Never in chronological order, one minute you are in your fifties, listening to the same daily argument from your wife. The next, you are sixteen again, then thirty-five, then a twenty-three-year-old college graduate, or a memory of a disappointed middle-aged man, suffering the realisation of a saddened wife 'we are never going to have children'... Today, the reality of tea and toast was a memory that Brian Towers' brain would never store because he had his mind on other things. Brian was thinking about his own halcyon days, just after the war, years of experience and athletic capabilities under his belt. A European cycling trip, the sun, roads and climate unknown. There was no breaking the rules with Garth Pratt because Garth Pratt had been Brian Towers' oldest friend. That was until he broke the *unwritten* rule.

George Fleming had been the first to complete a fifty-mile race in under two hours. In the cycling world, records become challenges. Brian and Garth rose to the challenge, aiming to be the next superstar. Brian won! Two seconds faster than George Fleming's time. But this was only recorded in a private race, in the North Lancashire Road Club, so therefore not recorded properly. That was when Garth Pratt broke the unwritten rule:

'Do not attack a record held by your own club mate'

Their last race together turned out to be the mother of all races, and Brian remembered it like it was yesterday. At Garth's suggestion, he drank an energy concoction of milk and eggs. Soured by the sun, Brian was violently ill, and the race became every man for himself. Garth Pratt was not going to let something like that deter him and he made his mark as the man who smashed George Fleming's superstar record. The upshot being that he also smashed his friendship with Brian.

And so newlyweds, Brian and Brenda broke away from the North Lancashire Road Club to form their own.

Garth meanwhile vowed to have nothing to do with road races ever again and was strictly a time trial man, experience earning him a position in the regional time trial association...

"Do you fancy a boiled egg, Brian?" Brenda's voice jolted Brian back to reality.

"Oh no... no thank you, Brenda, you know I don't eat eggs"

"Well you did when we first married Brian, they're good for you" Brenda took the egg refusal as a sign and whipped away the local paper.

"What's that! Hey, I've not read the local times yet" Brian took the newspaper back and found the cycling news.

"I see Garth Pratt's boy has done well in the time trial," Brenda said.

Brian put down the newspaper. He was not going to let something like that deter him.

"I think I'll try a boiled egg after all"

If Garth Pratt had Kenneth McKenzie to show off about, then Brian was going to have Ernest Bradshaw to bring home the glory, although Brian did not yet know the news about Ernest's new bicycle.

"Better be hard boiled though Brenda" Brian corrected.

"That's the spirit! That's my husband" Brenda had never enjoyed boiling an egg so much in all her married life.

Ernest's smile arrived before he did as he turned that corner riding his green Viking racer. Brenda Towers grabbed her husband by the elbow.
"He's done it, Brian! Look he's done it he's managed to get himself a new racing bike!"
"Is that Percy's bike?" Brian said to Sid, as one exchanged a wager to the other having taken bets as to whether Percy would really do his secret flit (that everyone knew about)
The juvenile club event, masterminded by Brenda would take the riders of the ELICC around a familiar circuit route in a park.
The ten-mile route had been measured using a revolution counter. A three shilling and sixpence fee from each rider would cover the cost. The prize was much sought after credit at the bike shop. Credit and achievement.
Achievement and notoriety if Brenda gets her way with the cycling report in the local newspaper.
"You know the way riders, the finish is opposite to the start."
The withering members of the ELICC looked like a coincidental group of people who just happened to be cycling in the same place at the same time.
    "It's a bit of a gamble sending Ernest and Christopher out on a road race isn't it Brian? Too tactical- you haven't given them any coaching!"
    "It'll just come naturally to them Brenda, you watch! And anyway, it's a circuit, not a road, not really"

"Don't tell the park ranger that. Thinks he knows everything that jobs-worth!" Said Brenda.

This was the life! Riding with ease alongside his friends, the green Viking felt lightweight, Ernest's mind was clear. Each revolution gave him new power, he was off with ease. The Hercules carrier had served him well in more ways than one, because Ernest was strong now, supercharged muscles, with double the power he had on that heavy bike. And the New Hudson had gifted him with speed. The route, he could manipulate without even looking. Ernest did not know he was doing it, but he had benefitted from Christopher being out in front, slicing his way through the roads until Ernest unknowingly, instinctively took his chance. This was tactical riding without the tactics.

He was on auto pilot, and soon he was off... his friends impressively left behind. Breaking away from the crowd, it was as if all the other bikes were clumped together. It was as if Ernest was in a mesmerising world of his own. The second half already, Ernest was not taking it too hard, with full confidence, no looking behind, Ernest was leading the group.

This is what they call being cheered on by the cycling world because in that ride Ernest was imagining all kinds of triumph. He was getting carried away! The route, the scenery all ignored because all Ernest could smell was his own success. The same length of time as one of Uncle Billy's afternoon naps, a circuit race is over and done with sooner than Ernest knew it. Time flies when you're having fun! And Ernest

flew on his new cycle, winning in style, the new
and improved Ernest.
There are Mr and Mrs Towers; the finish. I'm
winning! I'm winning!
"Come on lad! I knew you could do it! Blimey,
Brenda, he's a natural talent!"
Brian Towers had been right, road racing had
come naturally to Ernest, his muscles built up
steadily but swiftly during the spent weeks of
1962. He came careering towards that finish line
like it had cost him nothing.
"I've won?" Ernest asked in high pitched tones,
head darting about himself in disbelief "No one
else has come through here before me?"
"No, we were definitely all behind you, Ernest"
Christopher was at the side of him now, getting off
his bicycle.
"I've won!"
It all happened so fast ... The Glory was his!

The national rules and regulations surrounding
cycling time trials, road races and so on are
 lengthy and convoluted. However, the main aim
 of the game, the eyes on the prize do not include
any such rules or regulations surrounding the
actual *winning* of any such race. Funny that.
"You must be over the moon Ernest!" said
Brenda, the crowd of the club surrounding him.
"Erm err, yeah!"
"Well done Ernest!" Christopher, beaming
slapped him on the back. Everyone was a
winner tonight, now that Christopher had
helped out his best friend, he was free to

chase after Janet... Ernest had won tonight, and everyone was a winner. Even Brian and Sid once again passing that same two bob back and forth between themselves in wagers.
Garth Pratt might well be showing off about Kenneth McKenzie. But Brian had Ernest... Yes, Garth, the glory was Brian's.

Chapter 21: Time Trials and Tribulations.

Winter was just around the corner, meaning that netball was to be replaced by hockey. Up and down the country, hockey promoted comradeship and psychomotor learning. Hockey required team spirit; that grammar school girls were expected to own naturally. You had to be as bold as brass to be any good at hockey. That was how it worked. Janet was regularly chosen last in physical education. The practice of picking teams was an ancient tradition favoured by P.E. teachers, designed to teach pupils a valuable lesson about self-worth. Any girl who was good at hockey would know all about 'forming, storming and performing'. These girl's parents had paid handsomely for their daughter's French, arithmetic and physical education lessons. By the time they were sixteen years old, they would be schooled and suitable for secretarial work. That was how it worked.

Miss Little had engineered her entire P.E. lesson to incorporate the teaching of 'forming storming and performing' principles.

Even from word go in the changing rooms; teenage women would form groups, showing off with their bosoms displayed in an embarrassment of braziers. Camisoles, French knickers, grown up underwear, these teenage women pea cocked around the changing room in preparation for performing on the hockey pitch, and for storming into life itself. Out on the windy game's field came the next forming phase, the picking of teams. Miss Little would often mix it up, sometimes she would use the palm of her hand to gently strike each girl on the top of their head.

"You're a 1, you're a 2" or "You're an A, you're a B" she would storm. The girls would line up, then two bold as brass teenage women would be selected by Miss Little (usually the same two girls each week) to pick teams. This antiquated bullying was the highlight of Miss Little's week. Janet was sure of it. She was the new girl, and although she was physically fit (from cycling) she lacked the hand-eye coordination required for Hockey.

It was getting to the end of the line for the A's and B's. Bold as brass Rita and Elaine had nearly completed their teams. Standing there with their arms folded in the cold Rita was neither smiling or laughing. Her resting face predicted the sorry signs of ugly maturity.

"I suppose I'll have you. You can go in goal"
Rita's misplaced power destroying the self-
esteem of a girl that Janet did not yet know, with
one small sentence.

"Well I'll have you then" pointing at Janet, Elaine's
delivery was not much better.

"Don't you just want to punch her into shape?"
Rita sniggered behind her hand.

Janet heard her, but could not prove that she was
talking about her. This was the 'storming' phase,
and they had not even got on to the game yet.
The loneliness of being the last one picked met
Janet on that hockey pitch. She consoled herself
that the physical education lesson could not last
forever. She consoled herself that she would be
home soon, getting her dear two-wheeled friend
out of the garage. Winter was just around the
corner. She could tell by a number of leaves on
the hockey pitch, golden tears of hope for the
world that was about to crescendo into World War
III. And not only that, soon it would be too dark,
and Janet would only be able to cycle at
weekends. Stood there at school on the windy
games field, she thought of last weekend's
solitary cycle ride. The boy she had seen after he
fell off his bicycle. His laughter, his ancient,
 clumsy looking bicycle. He did not seem to worry
about looking a fool. Why had she been thinking
about him? His fair hair, his freckles, like speckles
of hope on his innocent face. His screeching
whistle sound....? Oh! Janet had been
daydreaming. The wind in the whistle belonged to
Miss Little's lungs and had distracted Janet from
her distraction. Miss Little, with her big voice, was
the next one to speak.

"Right nothing else for it girls, I'm joining the A team today. Janet move over there"
Miss Little shoved Janet towards the B team with her muddy cold hockey stick
"Let's start moving girls, I want two laps around the pitch before we start. Get some blood flowing through your corned beef thighs!"

No.

 "Why are we still playing bloody hockey when America is about to bomb us?!" All eyes were suddenly on the poorly coordinated new girl who had been picked last.
"I beg your pardon, young lady?" Miss Little brandished her hockey stick. Janet immediately realised her mistake, in the real situation of the windy hockey pitch, her protest about the threat of nuclear war did sound rather thin. Shame Mr Cooley was not one of her teachers. She had only ever sworn out loud under her breath before, and that was whilst cycling. Even Janet had to admit that her choice of timing was suspect for such a performance, it was obvious she hated P.E.
The two bold as brass team leaders Rita and
 Elaine sniggered behind their hockey sticks. Janet found herself frog marched, and forced to 'wash her mouth out with soap and water', a punishment she had only previously read about in Enid Blyton novels. Also, a note was sent home, with details of today's 'performance'.

1962
Dear Mr and Mrs Dootson
I am writing to inform you of your daughter's
performance in today's physical education lesson.
She has protested against the introduction of
hockey lessons, by using profanity. This is not
expected or acceptable for grammar school
girls.Yours sincerely,
Miss Little.

'Up yours' thought Janet. The end of the school
day had arrived as promised and she was at
home, steering her two-wheeled friend out of the
garage. No amount of chewing toffee could get
the taste of soap out of her mouth. The red acidic
soap with a distinctive smell. She wondered if she
would see the boy on the bicycle again. The
secondary modern school he probably went to.
Her mum met her at the front door, a shawl
around her shoulders.
"Are you ok, Janet?" Ruffling her hair, breathing in
the antibacterial smell of soap. Janet thought
about handing over Miss Little's note. "We had to
do hockey today at school" Janet pleaded.
 "Oh, how awful! Well, you will be expected to
perform, to learn about winning and so on"
 Not mother as well?
"Won't you have had enough exercise then?"
"I'm just going out for a bit, it will be too dark in a
 few weeks" Janet left, keeping the note to
herself.
Miss Little had been stupid enough to hand write
it and had not sent it through the post. Or maybe
she had done this on purpose? The 'forming'
phenomena, intending Janet to read the note and
be shamed into improving her performance.

Cycling along, she looked out at her surroundings. In the dusk, houses twinkled in the distance, homely lights of the cottages on Lever Brew, inviting pockets of warmth. Janet the teenager started to imagine herself living in a cottage just like these. She could hear the opening and shutting of doors down the hill. The muffled greeting of two voices, the giving and receiving of parcels. The boy with the carrier bicycle!

As Janet carefully tip toed her bicycle down through the pot holes of Lever Brew, her heart stopped. She could see Ernest now, weighed down by heavy bags on either side of his wheels. Janet carried on cycling. Her glance met his as their bicycles passed. How romantic! She thought.

Ernest, although the proud owner of his winning green Viking racer bicycle still used the Hercules Carrier for his delivery round. Oh! there is that girl with the bobble hat, Christopher reckoned she was being funny about my bike when we had to show her the way home... Maybe it's a female thing, no sense of direction.Come to think of it, I'm not sure if me mother is any good with directions, I remember one time ...

Ernest's imagination drifted off, on auto-pilot on his round. He had cycled right past Janet without noticing her! No sense of romance! Never mind, Ernest was at the next cottage now.

Maybe he did not want to say hello. Maybe he didn't recognise me? Maybe he doesn't speak

unless he's got his friend with him? Janet
continued cycling, Lever Brew was becoming her
favourite hill.

Brenda and Brian Towers had taken residence in
their conjugal cottage on Lever Brew and had
remained harmoniously in situ all their married
life. The winding and wet hill could only be passed
easily on two wheels, it was the shopkeeper's
nightmare, virtually impassable for a van. The
Towers' moving in day was a distant memory. The
movers, in their moving van, moved them in,
virtually scratching the side of their van up
and down Lever Brew, vowing never to move
anyone here ever again. Mr and Mrs Towers, the
newlyweds but with little to show for it. Brenda
had shut her eyes, held her breath, and told
herself the movers must have handled this kind of
road before, they know what they are doing.
That's what they are paid for. Moving day was
over. And from that day, Brenda and Brian had
vowed never to own a car. The pretty cottage
suited them, small, side door, hanging baskets
and a lean-to, to house their bicycles Perfect;
and who else could boast a 'guest bedroom' in
those days?
 Over the following years, carpet and furniture
specialists delivered to the cottage. Delivery vans
 struggled up and down that hill. Delivery drivers
that had been in this situation before, knew
exactly how to deliver, that was what they were
paid for. There had been an awful lot of pushing
 and shoving during those years. Finally, their
lovely home was born, Brenda delivered a
hospitable, welcoming cottage, and despite the

wind and rain battering the hill, anything that Brenda waved her hands over in the garden flourished.

Nowadays, Brenda and Brian, retired school teachers, still tended to their baby, the East Lancashire International Cycling Club. They had broken away from stuck in the mud Time Trial enthusiasts, Brian had the ambition to ride his club in the Isle Of Man Road Race. Brenda had her own ambition, to mentor the first female club rider in the area. Daily arguments with each other were only a show of matrimonial balance, Mr and Mrs Towers still had a lot to give.

Later that same evening, when twilight was creeping in, but sewing remained on the to-do-list, Brenda Towers looked up from her stitching. She had been completing the initials on the racing jerseys for the remainder of the club. Through her window, she caught a glimpse of a cyclist.
"Is that Ernest with the groceries?" Trying to finish her stitch she stood slowly and made towards the door, tangled up in the thread. Finger pricked and Colin Sidebottom's jersey on the floor. Brenda opened her door just as Ernest was about to knock on it, so the cyclist she had seen was not him. Was it that teenage girl she had seen cycling up and down? Brenda was desperate to speak to her.
Now; for no particular reason, the Towers' baby was only ever a daydream. Occasionally, Brenda would still think about her, the baby girl that she never carried.

She could not even remember what she had imagined... What kind of a mother cannot even remember her own imaginary baby's imaginary face? She would have been grown up by now, with imaginary children of her own, with Brenda's genes, continuing her dreams of female cycling victory.

"That flamin' Garth Pratt likes the sound of his own voice" Brian disturbed Brenda's imaginings by throwing the Manchester and District Time Trial association newsletter down on the kitchen table. "Who were you talking to at the front door anyway Bren?"
"Bren-da thank you, husband, It was Ernest with the groceries, but I just saw that girl again, the one with the bobble hat and bicycle" Always on the lookout for new talent, hoping for a new junior member of her club. She understood teenagers. They needed ambition, something to aim for. Competition and
comradeship were working well for Christopher and Ernest. And this decade was turning into a different age, with new opportunities for women. If Brenda could encourage that young girl to sign up, this would provide a new opportunity for Brenda to wipe the smile off Garth Pratt's face, her husband's nemesis who had just managed to get himself on the Association Authority Board.
"I see the nuclear bombs are int' news again" Brian plopped the folded newspaper on the pile of post.
"I don't know why people are so worried! It's between America and Russia!" Brenda Towers,

despite being an educated woman said to her husband. Temporary relief for Brian Towers, who did not have to fix anything today for his wife; although Brian Towers could not have fixed the news.

Janet Dootson had ten more minutes with which to conquer her fear of cycling downhill. Telling herself Lever Brew was her favourite because it was the only hill she could cycle down. The one she felt most comfortable with. Nothing to do with the sighting and spotting of the cyclist who helped her when she was lost. Today she had been too shy to speak. Janet reached the top of the hill, rain on her face, a droplet on the end of her nose. "Hello love, are you lost, love? Only, I've seen you going up and down here a few times tonight" Appearing to be lost on her bicycle was becoming a regular thing for Janet. This time, her hero was not the fair haired boyfriend potential that she had hoped for. This was a middle-aged woman, standing with her hands on her hips like any good school teacher should be.There was something about her demeanour, her 'hello love' that made things alright.
"I'm sure I've seen you cycling around here love, do I know your parents?" This, of course, was the sanctioned question from an adult to a teenager. Janet said nothing, and Brenda Towers suddenly remembered herself. Janet was a stranger, not a teenager in school that she could speak to whenever she wanted...

However, remembering that she was almost sixteen and grammar schooled, Janet decided to speak.

"I don't think so Mrs erm. We only moved around here this year. Their names are Mr and Mrs Dootson" Janet searched her brain for how this dowdy looking woman could possibly know her parents. "Erm, do you play bridge?"

Brenda Towers laughed out loud.

"Oh! No love. I was a teacher at the secondary modern. Which school do you go to?"

"Bury Grammar for girls" Janet embarrassed herself. Brenda Towers gave Janet a knowing nod. Oh, she's that type, is she? A grammar school girl. A grammar school education! You would think she could figure out how to get home!

"You know if you turn right at the bottom and keep going, the road will bring you out at the top" Brenda pointed, but regretted hinting that she had watched Janet cycle up and down her road before. Janet flushed also at the thought of being spotted on her solitary ventures. This was what made her say yes to what Brenda was about to ask her.

"Just hold on here love, let me get one of my leaflets" Brenda darted back into her own hallway. "Here you go love, any lad," Brenda looked at Janet over the top of her glasses " Or lass, who is wanting to race must join a cycling club"

"Oh, I'm not wanting to race, I just like riding around" Janet looked at the leaflet 'EAST LANCASHIRE INTERNATIONAL CYCLING CLUB'.

"Well have a think about it, love, we don't have any girls actually. Well, apart from me that is!" Brenda chuckled at her own joke "We do have two boys that are around your age, though, Christopher and Ernest. Anyway, there's a Time Trial race next Sunday, come along and see what we're about at our club run before then"
"Oh!" Janet's heart actually skipped a beat, Christopher and Ernest? She hoped that the fair haired boy was Ernest. That name sounds so *trustworthy!* How romantic. She felt as bold as brass, waving goodbye she cycled down the hill. Turning right as Brenda had advised. Brian, who had caught the end of the conversation from inside their cosy cottage beckoned his wife inside.
"You can't just apprehend teenagers in the street Brenda!"
"Ah well, I was recruiting for your cycling club if you must know. That girl has got some skill!
You know I saw her dodging puddles a few weeks back"
Brian did not make the connection.
"Brian! Our club could have the next flying housewife, just like Beryl Burton! That will give the Pratts summat to think about!" Brenda was getting carried away.
"Brenda, I think you're getting carried away. 'The flying housewife' was an athlete, not a cyclist" but it was too late. Brenda was doing excited star jumps in the kitchen. Janet had not said yes to joining the club, but Brenda was already imagining being interviewed by the BBC.

Typical. Thought Brian as he shut the front door. When something goes wrong, it's *my club,* but when something goes right, it's *our club!*

Chapter 22: Janet Joins a Cycling Club

"I'm surprised at you, Janet Dootson!" Miss Little was at it again, belittling Janet in front of the class. "I thought she was supposed to be good at cycling!" Rita whispered to Elaine, at it again, rolling their eyes with folded arm smugness
 "Just let her pass, just sign her off, Miss" PC Swift said.
"Excuse me, officer, the Cycling Proficiency certificate should not be given unless the pupil
 has passed all the stipulated safety tests" Miss Little berated the policeman "Rules of the road?"
 PC Swift did not answer, he simply shook out his newspaper, and waved Janet on, he pushed a pre-signed Cycling Proficiency Certificate across the foldaway plastic table towards Miss Little. Who in turn, despaired of the policeman. She often despaired of men who refused to take things seriously. And here she was at school, with Rita and Elaine, not taking the Cycling Proficiency test seriously. She was teaching in a grammar school for girls, with a male headmaster who was also not taking the Cycling Proficiency test seriously.
 It had been rolled out in schools since 1958, it was 1962 now, for goodness sake! These girls were past any interest in cycling, they would most

probably use public transport and never ride a bike anywhere after they have left school
 Apart from Janet Dootson, the new girl. Miss Little had seen her cycling to school, on quite a nice bike! Money must be no object at the Dootson house, these grammar school girls!
So when Janet Dootson failed to weave her way around the pattern of traffic cones, Miss
 Little despaired of her, she was obviously not taking things seriously. Just like Miss Little's ex-boyfriend... five years she had invested in Gordon Roberts. Five years of cancelled dates
 at the last minute, rectified by weekend adventures out of sight of anyone local. That was until Gordon Roberts announced he did not
 want 'anything too serious' with Miss Little.
 Turned out he was a bit too... *married to his wife* to be taking things seriously, with Miss Little, anyway. Now here was PC Swift, not taking things seriously... it was 1962 for goodness sake!
"Janet Dootson, you'll take this test again, but this time, you won't let Rita or Elaine put you off. Rita, you're up next" The wind inside Miss Little's whistle screamed suddenly, loud, and long.
PC Swift dropped his plastic cup of coffee and was forced to mop up the mishap with his newspaper. Rita wiggled her backside sideways onto the saddle of the test bike. She fluttered her eyelashes at PC Swift and wobbled forwards towards the traffic cones.
"You're supposed to weave around them, Rita!" Miss Little shouted. "WEAVE AROUND!"
"So, is it true you have to be tall to be a policeman?" Elaine was almost sat on the plastic

foldaway table. PC Swift stood up, really on account of the spilt coffee. "Oh you are tall, I love tall men"

"ELAINE!" Miss Little turned around sharply towards the flirtatious scene.

"This one passed Miss, next girl, erm lady" PC Swift struggled to find the right words. Elaine made a tutting sound at the tall policeman before she swapped places on the bicycle with her partner in crime. She performed the same half-hearted attempt at the rules of the road.

"You're dismissed now, girls" Miss Little shooed the bold as brass girls away, who trotted off to their smoking club, behind the bike sheds. Then it was Janet's second turn. She had no need to prove herself in front of Miss Little, Janet knew she was able to cycle safely, not once had she come off her bike, not once had she crashed into anyone or anything, despite her fear of hills. No one likes an audience though. Janet's bobble hat turned to observe Miss Little and the policeman deep in conversation.

"Are you married?" Miss Little asked "Intended" PC Swift answered waggling the fingers on his left hand.

"Ninety-five percent, Miss... erm"

"Dootson, Janet Dootson" Miss Little said. "Well, well Janet, seems you do alright when you don't have an audience"

"Ninety-five, well done Miss Dootson. There was a lad last week in Scunthorpe who got one hundred percent, can you believe it? You get to join the top ten club!"

"Well, he must have been taking it seriously" Said Miss Little.

"I think he was part of a cycling club, Miss, erm, Miss"

Later that same day, when Miss Little decided against taking life too seriously, and somewhere - out there, Gordon Roberts suffered a flat tyre; Janet Dootson reflected on today's events. "I got ninety-five percent in my Cycling Proficiency test today, mother"
"Never mind darling, your supper is underneath a plate, I'm going to make myself useful at bridge club" Janet's mother had not been listening. She rubbed Max Factor lipstick across both her lips and smacked them together for maximum coverage. "Well, where's Father then?"
Janet's mother looked quizzically at her daughter. "Hmm, do you know? I can't remember, he's probably gone to some debating club or other" Mrs Dootson waved her hand in the air and snapped shut her makeup compact. "No, no, I tell a lie, Janet, I remember.He received a telephone call from a box on the other side of town, Mr Roberts from next door has a puncture in his tyre and he called on your father to help him, it was the only number he could get the operator to find! Between you and I Janet, I think he's been playing away from home... got some woman who isn't his wife in the club!" Mrs Dootson continued talking to herself in the mirror before she sashayed off to her bridge club. Everyone around Janet seemed to be in some sort of club somewhere. Bridge club, smoking club, grown up club, 'in the club'. Janet had no desire to be in the smoking club with the likes of Rita and Elaine,

she would probably be picked last to have her cigarette lit there. No desire to join her mother in one of the many clubs and societies she had ingratiated her presence with since they moved house, like the trophy daughter Mrs Dootson wanted Janet to be. Her mother's whisper had made it clear 'in the club' meant pregnant, imagine being pregnant with some other woman's husband? No thank you. But what had that lady on Lever Brew said? *Anyone who wants to race must be part of a club?* Racing meant competition and competition meant the likes of Rita and Elaine. Competing about who has the biggest hair, who has the most fluttery eyelashes, the most grown up underwear. Oh, it was all too much for Janet. No one had ever asked her to be in a club for 'who has read the most books'. Her mother's book club held on the last Thursday of alternate months always sounded like some sort of reading club for the stupid. *Jane Eyre* had been confused with Jane Austen and Janet's mother was still trying to paper over the cracks that had splintered into the local gossip club because of this. But what had that policeman said about her Cycling Proficiency score? *'You get to be in the top ten club!'* So what of Mrs Towers? The fair-haired boy? On this day, in 1962, hormones got the better of Janet, she set off to join a cycling club.

The Miss Little's of this world can keep their mock surprises and Cycling Proficiency badges! Janet was cycling to her dream destination, cycling towards her future husband, the fair-haired cyclist! She did not know it when she got on her bike that evening, but the ride to the club run meeting point would be the last solitary bike ride that Janet would have in a long time.

Chapter 23: Hang on in There Christopher, Dreams Can Come True!

"Oh, Aha hahaha ohhh Brian! What did you say about me not accosting teenage cyclists to join our club?!" Brenda loved it when she was right, as she always thought she was, and she was thrilled to bits to see the silhouette of Janet cycling towards her. It was a beautiful scene, the rain had stopped, the sun was coming out, a rainbow framed Janet cycling towards the group. Brenda recognised Janet immediately, well who else would it be? Brenda had not given any of the club's leaflets to any other females, even if it was 1962...
"Good job I fetched my brown backed notebook and a copy of the 'Time Trialling For Beginners' " Brian said, licking the end of a pencil. He hated it when Brenda was right, as so often she was. The members of the cycling club present on that unsettled evening took in Janet's arrival.
"Nice bike" Colin Sidebottom nudged a begrudging Paranoid Percy. "Aye up, cupid's been firing arrows everywhere!" Colin nodded in the direction of Christopher and Ernest.
Janet pulled up next to the safety of Brenda

 Towers, as she had invited her to ride with her
club. Christopher's heart started racing, it was like
a dream come true. But Janet Ernest, trying to fix
her gaze on his. She turned away, waited a few
seconds, and then tilted her head over her
shoulder for the second time, in Ernest's direction.
However, Ernest had not noticed and was looking
up at the sky, then at the palms of his hands,
checking if the rain had really stopped.
Christopher had noticed though. Janet, of course
had her eyes on Ernest and knew exactly what to
do. She had seen Rita and Elaine at it during Miss
Little's class. She looked over her shoulder
towards Ernest. Christopher looked at Janet, and
then he looked at Ernest, and then at Janet again,
who had not noticed Christopher at all.

"Are you okay love? Something wrong with your
neck?" Brenda said.
"Oh, no, I've come about your club, like you said"
Janet clutched her brake levers anxiously back
and forth. Ernest was still paying her no attention.
Soon, Brenda and Brian were taking Janet
through the rigmarole of 'Time Trialling for
Beginners' and so on.
"First they let a lad on a jalopy join, now a
female!" Paranoid Percy whispered to Colin
Sidebottom. "Wind your neck in, Percy, it is 1962
for goodness sake!"
 "Hello, you can ride alongside me tonight, I
mean, if you like, I'm Christopher" He had decided
to go for it, and introduce himself. Janet could not
look more displeased. Brenda looked over the top
of her glasses at Christopher.
"Aye, that's a good idea, lad, you show young,

miss, err, miss" Brian was struggling.
"*Beryl...* I mean Janet, this is Janet" Brenda
interjected "Christopher will show you the way,
don't worry"
"Worry, err are there any hills?"
Janet's question led to a huge guffaw from
Paranoid Percy "Of course there are
bloody hills! Where do you think you are?
Lincolnshire?"
"Language, please, Percy, we have a female
amongst us now," Said Brian. Colin Sidebottom
burst out laughing, "Oh, you can say what you like
in front of Brenda, but not in front of this young
lady!" He winked at Janet, who made her cringe
obvious, so Colin ceased his teasing. Christopher
observed the exchange and felt like dying inside.
"Right! Come on then folks!" Brenda got on her
bike to start the club run. Janet rode alongside
Christopher obediently at first, she was part of a
club now, a cycling club. Just like that, she was
one of them, and she had only just met them! This
was almost like a competition, and soon her
whole attitude changed. Push, push, up and down
she went, forwards onwards against the wind,
this is how bike rides should be. That feeling of
freedom, forgetting that it is your own legs
pushing you on, cycling, like second nature. The
further she went, the further she disappeared into
her own private thoughts. She had no designs on
hearing her name read out by sporting
commentaries, she had no eyes on the trophy,
Janet was simply mesmerised by the feeling of
belonging, cycling with like-minded people. She
knew she was riding at an increased pace and

was starting to enjoy it now. As her energy grew, the cycling felt easier.

Twists and turns in the road, avoiding hazards in unison with her fellow cyclists, although there were few on that route, no traffic lights, and a few pot-holes. Janet could feel a slight downhill at the turn in the road. Christopher watched her legs pull back, then start cycling again on the flat. Did she not realise she must not stop pedalling on a 'fixie'? But Janet was moving away from him, and closer to Ernest. Had she forgotten she had agreed to cycle with him? To show her the way? Janet could see a hill ahead, she did not mind going uphill, she started breathing into it as she climbed, she knew she had a fight on her hands now. Christopher caught up with her. Experienced at this course, he knew that the uphill meant a downhill, and if Janet carried on the way she had been doing, there would be danger ahead. Girls can be dangerous, Christopher thought, but his romantic instincts took over. He pushed and panted to catch up with her. Ernest, of course, had gone over the hill already on his fast new green Viking. Christopher knew that Ernest would be in a world of his own, imagining he was cycling away from nuclear bombs and towards the finish line of some imagined race. Janet reached the summit, just as Christopher was at her side again. Her eyes were no longer fixed on the back of Ernest's head, she took in the sight of the steep decline and gasped.

"JANET!" Christopher shouted. "Don't stop pedalling, you'll go over the handlebars!" Janet gasped and took Christopher's advice, her legs stopped protesting on the downhill and for the first time, she started to enjoy it.

Christopher's heart was racing for the second time that day, Janet risked a crash, and only started moving her legs at the last second, he was sure. Girls are dangerous, he thought, and Janet is *irresistibly* dangerous...

Later that same evening, when the club run had ended, and emotions were high on tomorrow's promise, Colin Sidebottom made an observation.

"Lucky I saved you at the top of that hill, Janet" Christopher dangerously addressed the object of his affection.

"Oh, I knew! There was no need to save me!" Janet dismissed Christopher's protection, she had recently received ninety-five percent in her Cycling Proficiency test, of course. Her head craned forwards, the only person she wanted to speak to was Ernest.

"If you're looking for Ernest, he's already set off home," Colin Sidebottom said. His habit of laughing at the same time as speaking was already starting to annoy Janet.

"Oh, no, I'm looking for..." Janet headed towards Brenda Towers, who was anxious to know if Janet had enjoyed herself. Christopher, feeling invisible, breathed a sigh of unrequited love out of his nostrils. Still laughing his slightly condescending laugh, Colin Sidebottom put his heavy hand on Christopher's shoulder;

"Hang on in there, Christopher, dreams can come true!"

1962

Chapter 24: Going To The Pub was Ancillary To The Plot

Later that same month, when Janet had settled into being a permanent member of the East Lancashire International Cycling Club, Christopher still pined; and Rose Constance Bradshaw considered how she had not set foot inside a public house for as long as she could remember. Public houses were not places for ladies or women who saved up and bought a new coat every two years, no place for quiet women who could not afford such frivolities. In 1962, Rose Constance Bradshaw was no longer a young woman she was a full-time supervising fruit and vegetable charge-hand. She was a mother to Ernest, who, yes was nearly grown up but was still at home, eating her meals and partaking in her laundry. She was the niece of Uncle Billy, who also counted as a child in her home. The thought of the public house in the village had upset the careful equilibrium of Rose's world. She had mouths to feed! Housework to do! Socks to darn! She could not go, it had only been a suggestion, a hint, a silly remark.
Cecil Potts, Mr Potts junior regularly set foot inside the pub on the village high street, the Rose and Crown. Why shouldn't he? He had no children, no mouths to feed. No woman. If he had holes in his socks, no one would see them. He treated himself to a pint and a read of the paper at lunchtimes and tea times, usually on his own. The suggestion, the hint, the silly remark had been a mistake really, a slip of the tongue.

Earlier that morning, Rose Bradshaw was doing a stock take of green palettes. The palettes themselves were not green, just the contents. Cabbages, green beans and so on. Cecil Potts had often thought of
making a humorous suggestion to her. "He's off to the Rose and crown, why doesn't she
join him? Rose?" or, "You be the Rose, and I'll be the crown!"
Sentences played and replayed in Cecil Potts' mind. Rose Bradshaw had rejected him before. Well, that must have been over ten years ago. Time had stood still for Cecil Potts. No wife, no children, no Rose. Debating whether to ask Rose out again risked the upsetting the equilibrium of Cecil Potts' life. Son and heir to the small-time but modestly lucrative fruit and vegetable monopoly created by his father. But there she was in front of him, Rose. Hands red raw from handling fruit and veg for goodness knows how long. Her little frame hidden behind a greengrocer's overall. Her hair swept up in a hair net. Obviously
waiting to be asked to the pub? Surely waiting for someone like me to take care of her? Oh,
Rose, why did you forsake me all those years ago?

Cynthia Crosby crashed through the doors. Straight away, she noticed Mr Potts junior staring at Rose Bradshaw. 'The flamin' snitch!' She thought because observing the two statues had made her think the worst. That the two of them were *obviously* talking about her, Cynthia, and all the thieving she had been doing. Better brush this scene under the carpet, Cynthia Crosby style.

"Everyone alright then?" She said cheerily nudging Rose, and tapping her boss, Mr Potts on the shoulder "Did you miss me? Haha, I've only been gone a minute, cleaning the toilets" Cynthia was starting to babble now. "What are we talking about then?" As the two had appeared to fall silent when Cynthia entered the room, and still continued to stare without speaking, Cynthia became even more worried they were talking about her. It was Cecil Potts who thought it was his turn to talk.   "Oh! I was just about to ask Rose to come t'pub with me" he blushed.

Rose Bradshaw dropped the cabbage she was holding, and this nugget, this question, this new piece of information was the best bit of news that Cynthia Crosby had heard this week, no this month. She could not help but laugh.

"Ha! Rose Bradshaw going to the pub! You won't catch the likes of this one in a public house Mr Potts" Cynthia said, thumbing Rose's arm. And then she saw it. Mr Potts disappointed face. Not knowing what to do with his eyes, darting them at his feet. Just at that moment, he looked like a boy again. A glimpse of vulnerability, wonderfully power giving to Cynthia Crosby. He cleared his throat. He turned around. He left and went off to the pub alone to read the paper and sup a pint.

Rose Constance Bradshaw gently tapped Cynthia Crosby on the forearm and whispered "Thank you" in her ear as she scurried away in the opposite direction.

Cynthia Crosby leant on her mop one hand on top of the other, she put her chin on her top hand "Fancy that!" she said to herself, whilst slipping a couple of potatoes in her front tabard pocket.

Cecil Potts walked through the doors of the Rose and Crown public house as usual. He sat on his usual barstool and as usual, he passed pleasantries with the landlord, who was stood in his usual place. He glanced at the headlines of the newspaper, placed in its usual location on the bar as a reminder of life outside this one horse town. He could not concentrate, though, he supped his pint, his mind filled with Rose. She had rejected him once, and this was once too often for Cecil. This was the problem with newspapers. No one really read them, especially if said reader had other things on their mind. But the threat of nuclear war, the speech especially broadcast by President Kennedy from the Whitehouse about America's close surveillance. The details of a discovery of a military buildup on Cuba, the purpose of which can be none other than to provide a nuclear strike against the western hemisphere.... and so on... Yes! President Kennedy's speech was so important, it was reported in the British Press, in a newspaper which tomorrow would be soaked in salt and vinegar. Today's news would be tomorrow's fish and chip paper. That was the problem with the news, folk would not remember what was going on from one day to the next, from one week to the next. Do not ask a British person what was in the news last month, no! A newspaper is not like looking in a history book because no one knows how each story is going to unfold. In 1962, history was being written. Right there in today's newspaper. A newspaper hardly took notice of by Cecil Potts, a man regretting his bachelor existence whilst Rose Bradshaw was in his life, flaunting her single status every day in her smart coat, and defensive hat. History, he wished would repeat itself.

Friday saw Rose Bradshaw treating Ernest and Uncle Billy to a fish supper, wrapped up in yesterday's news. She had thought about running her mini-drama with Mr Potts' past her sister Marigold, but this would risk receiving unwanted advice from Norman. A man who liked nothing better than giving out unwanted advice. Rose put her Edith Piaf record onto the turntable and reached a decision. Rose would see her sister Marigold on Sunday because this Sunday was going to be a special day for Ernest. Yes, a decision made. This scene was swept away, Rose style with a trip to the chip shop.
Saturday brought Ernest to his weekend delivery round, the Ainsworth's, the Spinster's all on Lever Brew. And of course, Mrs Smith at her cottage. Ernest always called on her with caution these days, there was no need to race himself up and down Lever Brew. He was no longer timing himself against Mrs Smith's state of dress. Anyway, today, she was in a state of undress, although her face was fully covered in makeup and red lipstick.
"Cooee ! Ernest love!"
He could hear her before he had even propped

his delivery bicycle up against her wall.
"Why don't you come in Ernest!"
The blush on his cheeks was enough to make
Mrs Smith's week. She should get herself out, find
a man a new husband to take her out for fish
supper and a drink at the pub. An idea of playing
cupid between Mrs Smith and Mr Potts crossed
Ernest's mind... She fastened up her dressing
gown, blew Ernest a kiss and shut her porch door.
That does it! Ernest thought. All I want to do is win
a cycle race before the world gets blown up, but
Mrs Smith is going to kidnap me before I get the
chance!

Janet Dootson had also been invited to compete
in the junior time trial event. Brenda Towers'
protégée, Janet was scheduled to be the next
Beryl Burton in Brenda's eyes, whilst ignoring
Janet's fear of cycling downhill, because
unfortunately there were plenty of hills about.
Brenda Towers had also skimmed over the
entrance rules of the Manchester and District
Time Trial Association's time trial. The meeting
place would be at a pub further away from the
village, up in the hills, but central to the junior
competitors. Of course, Janet thought this early
attendance at a pub on a Sunday would give her
parents no choice but to forbid her from
participating. When Janet reported to her parents
the unreasonable arrangements for the Time
Trial, she found them less than supportive.
"That's wonderful sweetheart!" her mother said
 "Our daughter, specially invited to compete in a
cycle race! That's wonderful!" Her mother gushed

and displayed no sign of disapproval whatsoever. Meeting at a pub had become ancillary to the plot. "Yes, after that business with the hockey team at school, it's only right our daughter should join in with at least one sporting activity" Her father was equally unsupportive of Janet's fears of entering this time trial race.

"I can't wait to see their faces in the women's circle! You'll be like that woman, what was her name? The cycling housewife. Oh, Janet!" Mrs Dootson was obsessed with showing off at the women's circle and had been waiting for her solitary daughter to be invited to achieve something. Some of those women had news of their son's becoming teachers or worse! Doctors! That was the trouble with the news. Word was always getting round, and this news, this new information was quick to be acted on by mothers everywhere. It was nothing but a competition. Janet Dootson, however, was not competitive. Meeting up with a bunch of teenagers on a Sunday morning in a pub to compete in an event, riding her two-wheeled friend was too daunting for Janet. Even if this did include the fair-haired freckled Ernest, who was no nearer to noticing Janet. Maybe she could make an excuse, she could say that as it was a Sunday, she would be busy reading her father's newspaper, she needed to keep abreast of any developments regarding the prospect of nuclear war. Brenda Towers had seemed keen to dissuade her from such an interest.

"It's between Russia and America!" she had said to Janet. That was the trouble with Brenda Towers, she had spotted Janet's distraction;

Ernest. And with this new piece of information, she manipulated her protégée.
"Janet, you should definitely compete! There is nothing like bonding with your new friends when you compete together! I should know!" Brenda inferred to Janet, whilst glancing at her own husband. Brenda dreamed of interviews with the local newspaper, a photograph of herself and Janet. One of her on her own if she was lucky, they could go all the way to the Olympics!

Mr Cooley was continuing to keep a keen eye on the news. Especially on a Sunday when there was all day to ruminate and evaluate. His wife, of course, had enough on her plate; Twin babies in a twin buggy, Knee deep in terry nappies and sterilisation. Night time feeds cansettle a child but keep a parent awake, disrupted sleep patterns are impossible to reverse, Mr Cooley, the victim of long-term
insomnia found staying awake too tempting, even though the twins were sleeping soundly. He could get loads done, burning the filament in his bedside lamp, because every self-respecting graduate knows that a person should not believe *everything* they read in the news. Mrs Cooley, like any self-respecting wife and mother, knew that her husband should be saving his energy, because soon, those twin infants would be in junior beds, crawling, walking, opening cupboard doors and potty training in no time, it was every infant's plot. On the same Sunday of the Manchester and District Junior Time Trial event, Mrs Cooley glanced up from the floor where she

was sitting with one hand on each twin. Through the frosted glass in the hallway, she saw the image of her husband disappearing on two wheels, off to buy a Sunday newspaper. This was definitely not ancillary to the plot.

Brenda and Brian Towers, especially Brenda had been putting all her spare energy into training her junior cyclists for Sunday. This was going to be a special day, the junior Time Trial race where Brenda's club, sorry, Brenda and Brian's club had the chance to compete against junior teams from around the area. Heywood, Salford, even Todmorden. Brenda had been surreptitiously training her junior members, taking them out on twenty-five-mile club runs, taking Brian, herself and the tandem down the shortcut to meet them at the other end, no stopwatches, but a quick glance at Brian's wristwatch over his shoulder she knew that the three teenagers were ready. Even Janet appeared to be improving in her cycling confidence. Brenda being a woman who thought of everything, had been to the pub nearest to the meeting point for the junior time trial, and being a woman who knew everyone recognised the proprietors of said public house as the parents of one of her ex-school pupils. Brenda, being a woman who had been fair in her line of work was instantly recognised by the couple, and was welcomed into their pub. Everything was arranged for that particular Sunday. The East Lancashire International Cycling Club would have exclusive use of the pub's facilities. Even though they were junior members.

Ernest had not yet arrived at their meeting place,

the phone box in between the two boy's houses.
Christopher waited, he looked at the phone box,
he regretted not having Ernest's neighbour's
phone number about his person, then again the
sun had not yet come up and even Christopher
knew it was not an appropriate time to be
telephoning Mrs Basset, to ask her to nip next
door to wake up Ernest. The light attached to
Christopher's handlebars delivered him to
Ernest's house.
"Dig in lad! Come on Ernest! Dig in!" A shouted
somniloquy could be heard from Ernest's
bedroom. Uncle Billy was asleep in the wing-
backed chair in the back room. Christopher's
bicycle headlight shone through the window, right
on Uncle Billy's face. His mouth wide open, his
flat cap over his eyes. Christopher watched as the
flat cap slid further and further over his nose, he
wondered if Uncle Billy could hear his own
snoring inside his head. If he was unable to talk,
then why was he able to snore? Christopher
clutched his rubber helmet. His head was starting
to hurt. Uncle Billy's cap slid over his face and
tickled his nose. In his sleep, he dreamt of a
wasp's nest. The crashing sound of Uncle Billy
fighting for his life against a swarm of dreamt
flying insects broke Ernest's sleep.
"The time trial! What time is it?" Ernest ran down
stairs. "What time is it?" Ernest, like a baby
elephant, lit only by Christopher's bicycle
headlamp "Christopher! What time is it!?"
"Time we were gone, Mr and Mrs Towers wanted
us at the pub at the crack of dawn!"
"Give me five seconds!" Ernest bounded back up

the stairs, meeting his mother at the top.

"Ernest it's the middle of the night! What are you doing!?"

"The junior time trial, mother" Ernest shouted through toothpaste and tinkles. He struggled his racing jersey over his head and pulled his socks up. Downstairs, he had a swig of milk and pulled his cycling shoes on. Christopher was stood in the kitchen with Uncle Billy.

"Does Uncle Billy always sleep in his underpants and cap in the kitchen?"

"Err yeah sometimes" Ernest pulled his green Viking off the wall and wheeled it out into the yard. Uncle Billy muffled his goodbye.

It was not raining, but the ground sounded wet as the two boys sped off to the pub on the circuit course, the Welcome Inn. The weather had turned chilly with the foreboding of a terrible winter. Ernest, parched in his racing jersey looked amongst the bobbing heads for his team's colours. He dismounted his bike as he spotted Brenda and Brian in matching lime green and purple jerseys stood at the doorway of the pub. Ernest and Christopher wheeled their bikes towards them.

"Hello, lads!" Brian was blowing into his hands and Brenda was clapping both arms repeatedly around her middle to warm herself.

"We're just waiting for Janet now," Brenda said, she pursed her lips when she noticed Ernest rolling his eyes. Christopher's eyes darted amongst the crowd.

"She'll turn up, don't worry love" Brian dismissed his wife "Now then, which of you two lads is going to win?" Brian rubbed his hands together with

anticipation.
"Me!" Ernest blurted out, embarrassed by his own
confidence. They all laughed, Christopher's eye
line was still looking for Janet. In the dawn light,
he spotted a tiny bobble on a tiny hat turning the
corner and making her way through the crowd of
Junior time trial riders. In Christopher's mind, he
could already see her freckles glimmering on her
button nose like kisses of loveliness. Ernest had
not noticed Janet and was in deeply excited
conversation with Brian about 'keeping his pace
high' Brenda was nodding knowingly at Ernest.
Janet was freezing in her East Lancashire
International Cycling Club jersey. Her mousy
brown hair protruding from the bottom of her
bobble hat. She turned the corner and met the
peloton of junior riders. They were all boys and
Janet noticed what Ernest and Christopher had
not. Every boy it seemed had his back to Janet,
standing up and urinating against the dry stone
walls. Her nose filled with the smell, Janet
disgustingly tiptoed towards the unmistakable
club colours stood in the pub doorway.
Christopher's rubber helmet reflecting light at the
front of the little group. Brian and Brenda in lime
green and purple. And there was her Ernest, deep
in conversation, arms waving around his little
blond hair flick at the front bobbing up and down
in excitement. She did not notice that Christopher
was not listening, but was anticipating her
entrance to the race more than the actual race.
One of the boys from the Salford cycling club
noticed that the person under the bobble hat was
a girl, nudged his pissing colleague and turned to

face Janet.

"Wooo" he squealed "Aww what's up darlin', have I made you blush!" Janet shuddered and carried on towards the pub, trying not to notice the steam coming off the walls. She was out of earshot when it was asked: "What's she doing here?" The trickling sounds had stimulated her own bladder, she was so glad to see Brenda at the pub door who ushered her inside to the ladies toilet. Even inside it felt too cold to pee! She sat on the cold toilet seat, grateful as she would not have wanted to squat behind a bush in front of all those teenage boys. It turned out that meeting at the pub was ancillary to the plot.

Chapter 25: Going all out.

Before leaving his new build home, Mr Cooley had gazed admiringly at his wife. How does she do it? Not a care in the world... she does not even bother reading newspapers! How does she put her mind at ease? Mr Cooley then set off on his quest to buy every Sunday newspaper available .

Back at the Welcome Inn, the East Lancashire International Cycling junior members were itching towards the start point of the time trial.
"Now boys, and err" Brian Towers wound his

forefinger around as if he was trying to find the correct word for 'Janet' "And young lady: when she returns from the facilities... Remember the time trial rules. If you are caught, you must let them go and not ride alongside them or get behind them for the wind breaking advantage" Brian looked over his shoulders as if he was about to say some secret winning code to the boys. Ernest and Christopher stifled a giggle at Brian's 'wind breaking' comment. It was true, however, that failure to observe the rules would mean instant disqualification.

"Here, have a barley sugar each, oh and Janet welcome back. Suck on one of those sweets, save you from running out of steam" Brian handed out the sweets in a clandestine manoeuvre, his wife, Brenda already sucking on hers squinted her eyes nodding at the three youngsters.

"Go all out!" she whispered through sucks as if this was a secret code to ensure success.

The riders would be starting the race at one-minute intervals, according to the order that they signed on. And all of those riders would have signed up to a start sheet with Garth Pratt, Brian's nemesis.

Brian stopped listening until his own club's name was called out. Ernest's chin was extended towards the crowd to give him a better hearing angle. Brian muttered under his breath about Pratt being a 'stuck in the mud'. "Shhh," Brenda loudly whispered at her husband. The junior riders lined up in turn. Each competitor starting the customary one

minute apart. The riders would ride today to
secure a place at the future Manchester and
District Time Trial Association Autumn race.
Twenty-five-mile course. Ernest was fixated
that he would complete this in less than an hour,
he knew that this was physically possible because
Harry Hill had achieved this before him. But Harry
Hill was an Olympian, a grown man with years of
training and experience under his belt. Ernest was
a teenage delivery boy, his rounds and chain
gang rides on the pre-war New Hudson being his
only training. His mother's work ethic made him
believe that with grim determination, anything is
possible. He was worried about the stopwatch
business, though. He had never been officially
timed before. Janet wheeled her bicycle next to
Ernest's and was wondering what she should say
to him. She could not remember if she had
already complimented him on his new Viking
racer bike. Tension and anticipation were
mounting. She looked at Ernest weighing up the
other riders. Strangers on bicycles, some wearing
caps, peaks upturned with their club names
emblazoned on them. The other riders looked at
Ernest. He knew how to deal with other
teenagers. They might be from Salford,
but they cannot be any tougher than Mark Crosby
and the Benson twins. Ernest had seen that
crowd off and would apply the same tactic today.
No one can hit a moving target.
The three junior 'East lanc-ers' lined up with their
bicycles. Janet was desperate to speak to Ernest.
And Christopher was desperate to speak to Janet.
"Hey! I should go next to Ernest, not you Janet!
You should be right next to me! You just slipped

into the middle of us without me noticing!"
having not been to secondary school recently,
Christopher knew very little about the opposite
sex and how to talk to them. The last time he had
tried to get a girl's attention was Sally Muldoon,
and pulling her pigtails had not gone down very
well. Brenda Towers was, of course, listening
nearby. "What's this? Your starting order has
already been sorted out. It's on the start sheet!"
Always the teacher, she thumbed the official
paper and shuffled her team around. "That's it! My
junior winning team!" She winked at Janet, who
would have the hidden advantage of being last,
Brenda imagined Janet catching up to
Christopher on his wheel. Ernest was oblivious to
Janet's attention and unaware of Christopher's
green eyes. He was soaking up the advice from
Brian, even though his words were mainly cycling
jargon, which Ernest did not yet understand.
"Now Ernest, it's a false flat course, so keep your
pace high. If you are caught you must let them go
and not ride alongside them or get behind them
for the wind breaking advantage. You get
disqualified for that, see" Brian's voice had
lowered, he saw Garth Pratt approaching and
slapped Ernest gently on the back "Go all out
son!" making sure he could be heard.
"I didn't know you had children, Towers?" Garth
Pratt knew very well that Brenda and Brian
Towers had no children of their own. He had a
crumpled race sheet in his hand "The East
Lancashire International Cycling Club, just need
to check your permission slips"
Brian pulled his brown notebook out of the pocket

in the back of his racing jersey. Bound with elastic bands, he had letters with signatures from the junior members' parents. Brian was convinced that Garth Pratt had not scrutinised the other team's documents as carefully as this. Entrance forms and fees had been paid by postal order and sent to Garth before the race. Everything was in order, except Ernest was convinced he saw the man double check his form, and he was right.

"There's only one signature on this form, Bradshaw"

"That's right Pratt, it's the boy's mother, she's on her own, see" Brian Tower's stared Garth Pratt out with steely unblinking pride. Brian Towers could not speak to Garth Pratt without bitter suspicion. Ernest, in addition, puffed out his chest. It took him all his might to refrain from giving his little speech about his mother who deserves a medal.

"And this entry form, 'J Dootson' There is only an initial. Who is J Dootson?"

"Me!" Janet stepped forward "Me, err Sir err Mr" Janet struggled to find the right word for 'Pratt'. Brenda Towers swiftly stepped further forward than Janet had.

"Hello, Garth! How are you! How's Jean?" Brenda Towers, a woman with pockets full of charm was able to work anyone, so she thought, as she took over the conversation.

Janet was now completely hidden, disappearing behind Christopher's wide back and Brenda's chatter. She was virtually stood on her own, rather than stood next to the real reason she was there, Ernest; he was deep in conversation with Brian. Even Brenda had

abandoned her to talk to the official, 'Mr Pratt'. And if Christopher, the giant was not stood in her way, she could have easily joined in Ernest's conversation with all her new found knowledge of cycling talk. Deflated, Janet turned around with her hands on her hips. she huffed and pulled her bobble hat off her head, revealing her mousey bob to the cyclists behind her.
"Hey! She's a girl! This is a Time Trial!"
Brenda's equivalent of the Trans-Pennine cycling club stepped forward, with a whistle around her neck.
"What's that Fred? I thought I told you to line up first and do not shout!"
"She's a girl! My mum's gonna kill me if girls are allowed, my sister is sulking at home!" Fred said.
"Are you riding today love? Have you filled in the application form?"
"Yes," Janet hated being patronised. Of course, she had filled in the form, did she look stupid? Although when Janet thought about it, Brenda had filled the top part in for her, she had just got permission from her (unhelpful) parents and along with a postal order for the fee, had sent the form off. Janet was not lying because she had popped it in the letterbox herself. The woman from the Pennines with the whistle was staring at her with blazing eyes. She bossed her way past Christopher and got Garth Pratt's attention. The woman from Trans Pennines took time trial regulations very seriously. She had bossed her way to the position of general club secretary and was not pleased to discover a sudden change to the rules.

1962

"When since are girls allowed to ride in a junior time trial? Hmm? There is, clearly marked out in the rules a separate event for girls" This woman did not stop for breath "There is 'time trials' and there is 'girl's time trials' we don't want girls chasing after boys do we?"

Even Ernest was staring at Janet. Bloody women getting in the way again, come on! Let's just race! Before we all get blown up! Why had Brenda invited her anyway? She is frightened of going downhill, probably little hills too! Thankfully, he decided against saying this out loud.

Janet, conscious of her hat hair put her bobble hat back on. Brenda gave a little 'don't worry' shake of her head.

"Too late for that, love," The Pennine woman said to Janet.

Garth Pratt had weaselled his way onto the official's committee of the Manchester and District time trial association; but before he got the chance to speak, Brenda spoke for everyone. "Actually, it does say 'Junior time trial' on the application form... But, nowhere does it stipulate 'boy's only', so yes, here is our junior member, Janet Dootson" Brenda knew full well that she was manipulating the rules when she filled in the form for Janet with 'J Dootson'. And Janet felt as though she was back in Miss Little's physical education class line up.

"There wouldn't be a separate 'girl's event' if the time trial was open to females!" The Trans-Pennine woman exasperated, she hated being patronised. Does this woman from the East Lancs club thing she is stupid? Fortunately, Brenda was just a little bit taller than her.

"Well it's about time girls are allowed to compete. Look at Beryl Burton! The times she is getting! We must not be seen to discriminate against female talented juniors! Must we, love? It's 1962 for goodness sake!" Brenda was convinced of her argument. There was much chatting and debating breaking out amongst the cycling folk. Janet was mortified: 'young talented female'? I can't even cycle downhill, and Ernest is even less pleased that I'm here, she glanced over at him, he was now jumping up and down now in anticipation. Garth Pratt weighed up the situation. On the one hand, he could send this bobble hat wearing female rider home. On the other hand, it was getting close to the start time, each eager rider was raring to go. "Alright, alright!" There was no need, but Garth raised his voice

"You, J Dootson will ride last. You, J Dootson won't officially be part of today's Time Trial, but you will get a time so that you can compete in future events, should it be a good time, that is" Garth trotted off down to the back of the queue. "Oh, this is just delaying things! I just want to get riding!" Ernest's muscles had warmed up on the cycle to the meeting point, and now this momentum would be lost.

When he was out of earshot, Brian turned to Ernest, mimicking Garth.

"Did you hear him? There's only one signature on here! There's only one initial on here! Likes the sound of his own voice, always been that way. We'll show 'em, lad. You're going to win this race, just like you said" Brian Towers' leant in so closely, that Ernest could tell he had kippers for breakfast. But that did not matter. Brian had just told Ernest he was going to win. And that was all that Ernest needed. That was called belief in your junior team member, even though the junior female division of Brian's club now had to do the walk of shame to the end of the line because of his wife's ambition.

It was one of 1962's early mornings and daylight had finally reached the time trial riders. Today's race was starting to unfold. Arranged at this time on a Sunday as there was little traffic on the roads, to maintain safety and obscurity. On the outskirts of the course, not far from a newsagent's shop, was a man perched stationary on his yellow Vespa. Arms long enough to stretch out the broadsheet newspaper. Printer's ink highlighted in the rising sun. Mr Cooley read and reread the round-up of the week's news. President Kennedy's speech, the Soviet government making false statements about nuclear weapons. This speech listed the weapons that could be confirmed, and how far they would be able to bomb. It did not list Britain, but the newspaper reported there could be other weapons, yet to be discovered.
Mr Cooley inhaled and exhaled slowly, that was the problem with the news, what it *doesn't* tell you, keeping people in a state of perpetual fear. His arms were aching holding the newspaper out in front of him. Still, it was peaceful slightly outside of the suburb. Except what was that sound? The sound of tubular racing wheels flew past Mr Cooley. He just made out the letters on the back of the racing jersey 'HEYWOOD

FLYERS'. He folded up his newspaper, and then another cyclist passed him wearing the same top. Surely not the same lad? Then another flew past, then another, then another. He felt trapped in that corner like a cat up a tree. Ever mindful to avoid accidents, he did not want to go through that trauma again, he had no choice but to wait until all sixty-three junior riders had sailed past him. Every time he tried to set off, another would appear on that bend. Junior riders competing early on a Sunday morning, because there was not much traffic about... Just one lonely yellow Vespa. Was that Ernest Bradshaw on a green racing bike? Mr Cooley hid his face behind the newspaper. As the time trial set off one minute apart, even though they were all only going round once, Mr Cooley had quite a wait on his hands, the cyclists reminding him of when he first started riding his scooter; Rushing home to his pregnant wife eighteen months ago, he had a strange feeling she was going into labour. That day, the twins were born, but had he heard the screech of bicycle brakes in his haste to get to her? Or had he imagined it? He did not want that to happen again, he was still haunted by it, and so he waited until the coast was clear.
"5-4-3-2-1- GO!" Ernest's back wheel was finally pushed off after what felt like hours of waiting, the excitement of every rider setting off in front of him, at one-minute intervals. Ernest had imagined sixty-three stopwatches for sixty-three riders. Ernest's time would be the hour, plus whichever minute he passed the finish line. The timekeeper had a special way of knowing which minute he

was measuring and then waited exactly for the second hand to sweep round. That is how time trials worked, using one sophisticated stopwatch. And sometimes these times would appear in the local newspaper. Ernest's dream was to finish in less than an hour, his time being marked as whichever minute he managed *before* the hour, not past it. He had reckoned that if he could cycle fast on the unsuitable, heavy delivery bicycle, he would be able to cycle even faster on his green Viking. The race route was guided by marshals, all wearing yellow waterproof ponchos navigating the way to the riders like giant tropical birds. Ernest was going full pelt! His life depended on it! There was no time to waste, no tactics about saving his energy for the final push. He had nothing to lose. Ernest was not entirely sure if he had cycled this twenty-five-mile route before, was some of it was in the countryside? He could have stumbled upon a tricky turn or a perilous puddle. It was not worth slowing down just in case, and anyway, the farmer's ditch down the side of Lever brew had not been too much of a challenge for him, (forgetting that a farmer had to pull him out). Ernest remembered his Saint Christopher sovereign, and his confidence grew. Without hills or dips, the miles were no problem. It was all working out in Ernest's favour. As he managed a sharp corner, he spotted a man parked up in a rest area, sitting on a yellow coloured scooter. Hey, that looks just like Mr Cooley! The man's face disappeared behind the newspaper. Had Mr Cooley positioned himself there to cheer the riders on, in this low profile time trial? Mr Cooley on his scooter had had to rely on

petrol! And I've got here under my own steam! I've got here by pure pedal power! This alone made Ernest feel stronger, and he actually cycled just that bit faster, as he left Mr Cooley behind. Blink and you would have missed him, or so he thought. But Mr Cooley recognised him alright, he had pondered the ambition of youth. Here were these youngsters flying past, Sunday morning, taking in the fresh air. Training themselves up, for what? To be called up to a war that could not be won? What is the point in anything? He started up the chugging motor of his scooter. Legs like Giraffe's concertinaed on each side. He turned back on the road, keen to get home, having decided to make nuclear proof helmets for his wife and the twins. Then, sometime after the others riders, yet another cyclist cycled towards him. Pushing with effort, pedals up and down. Is that Janet Dootson? I know her father!
Janet was pushing down on those pedals with the punishing mite required to keep up with the rest. She was the last rider, so was she to appear last on the start sheet? It was 1962 though, why should she not ride her bicycle? She forced those pedals up and down. Hair itching under her bobble hat. The morning sun, low in the sky, blinding her. This really was unpleasant. What had started as a hobby, a solitary escape on her two-wheeled friend had become an all too serious matter.

She had only wanted to take her mind off things when she was too frightened to sleep because of nightmares about nuclear bombs. And then she had met Ernest. The first boy she had really noticed, and now she was up against him today, that one-minute interval had kept them apart, two minutes if you count Christopher's interference. She turned the corner, passing a middle aged man riding on a young person's scooter. She thought she recognised him as one of her Father's friends. She realised she had slackened her pace but was starting to enjoy the feeling of freedom. Taking in Sunday morning, on her legs and her two-wheeled friend. In the distance, she could make out coloured dots. Lime green, bright yellow, red, blue. Yes, I'm still in this race, she started to move again. She flicked her elbow, set her mind to it, and soon her pace was high again. Guided by the yellow cycle caped tropical birds, with all those miles under her belt, the marshal pointed her in the right direction :"Keep going that way, watch out for a dip! We've had a few come off today!" His voice trailed off, fortunately, because if Janet had known she was about to cycle downhill, this would have ruined her momentum. She kept going, but then there it was! The undulating enemy. She should have known that if she felt the uphill punishment, this would be followed by a downhill. What goes up must come down after all. Fear can make you see things differently. Today's course was mainly flat, with a slight gradient, but when the road opened up, all Janet could see was down. The wind took on a different feel, rushing right into the very holes of her bobble hat. She struggled to catch her breath. Palms sweaty involuntarily clutching for the brakes on her handlebars. No! I must not apply the brakes! What would Mrs Towers say?

Oh! That woman is relentless! Janet started to breathe, she was going downhill! Slipping, whooshing sensation. Her eyes could not catch up with the speed. When other riders thought nothing of hills, Janet saw them as her enemy. She had to overcome this. She could not have her mother reporting to the women's circle that she had fallen off her bicycle! Janet shut her eyes, to complete the distance of the (very slight) downhill. She could not bear it, she opened her eyes and met her own reflection in the stream, the puddle at the bottom. How deep was it! She had not seen any other cyclist ride through, but too late! She was in the water, or at least her wheels were... And then out again. She had done it, and she was still cycling! On! Forward! Tears welled up in Janet's eyes she had done it! Janet could get off her two-wheeled friend right now. She had done what she had never done before! She had cycled downhill! Not something her mother could boast about at the women's circle, but something that Janet could be proud of.

Christopher was not having a good day. First Ernest had forgotten to arrive on time at the telephone box, and Christopher noticed that after this, he had a headache. He was not sure if he had always been like this, but every morning, he would wake up, check what day it was, and then think about what was going to happen. The time he ate his breakfast got dressed, the time he went out on his bike. What time and how long he would spend cycling, the time he spent on school at home. He could rely on his parents, particularly his mother to do things at the time she said she was going to. But today, Ernest was not there at the time he said he would be. And then he had seen Ernest's Uncle half dressed in the kitchen. Then, Janet was goggle-eyed for Ernest instead of him. And then! If that was not enough, some bloke came along and said that Janet should not even be there. And now he had ended up wet through in a puddle. Christopher fell off his bicycle at the bottom of the (very slight) hill. There was not a soul around, no one saw him. He stood up, put his bike back on its side. He felt fine but wet. Knowing this would affect his time, all he could do was cycle on, fast and in the wind. It might help him dry off before he had to be home, for dinner at a certain time.

Ernest could see and hear the crowd in front of him "Dig in! Dig in lad!" he thought of a crowd, but he actually meant the timekeeper and Brenda and Brian Towers. Ernest, however at the end of the race with the buzz of adrenalin, glory was back in his imaginings. In his mind, the crowd was ten deep and the words he could hear were from a BBC commentator. Ernest passed the finish and shouted out his number.

Brian and Brenda were the 'crowd' at Ernest's finish line, and Brian's mind was in a similar place to Ernest's. Brian was thinking that Ernest, the natural athlete could take his club to the annual milk race. Brian's mind could not help wandering into ambition. Ernest could go for the Belgium Fast Criterion! Now that is international

"Come on Ernest!" Brian shouted.

"That means Janet won't be long behind" Brenda nudged Brian "And Christopher of course, Christopher"

"Sixty-one, time of one hour and eight minutes"
The timekeeper shouted to his sidekick who
entered the time, in black biro on the time sheet.
"Well done lad!" Brian ruffled Ernest's hair when
he got off his bike.
"I'm eight minutes over!"
"What are you talking about? One hour eight is a
great time! You're a natural athlete!"
"It was great Mr Towers, when will I find out how
the other's did? "
"It'll be in the paper" The official shouted over. A
few minutes later, Christopher arrived.
"Sixty-two, time of one hour, twelve minutes and
ten seconds"
"I fell off my bike, don't tell my parents, please"
Christopher was keen to put his cagoule on and
get warm again. Brenda went to give him a
motherly embrace but spotted Janet in the
distance.
"Sixty-three, time of one hour, fifteen minutes and
forty seconds"
"Are you alright love?" Brenda rushed to her
favourite's bike.
"I'm great. Mrs Towers, I cycled downhill! I started
to enjoy it!"
"Oh Janet I am pleased," Brenda said, trying to
calculate and remember her own time trial results
"Now you didn't forget you were competing in a
race did you?"
"Well I do remember taking in the view when the
road widened out, but then I thought I had better
get on, so I did! And here I am, Mrs Towers, I'm
not bothered about the time, the best bit was
getting over the hill!"

1962

"Well done Janet," Brenda said, dragging a smile out from somewhere as she turned to her husband "They're not going to put that in the paper, are they! She got over the bloody hill!" Brenda whispered to Brian "I'm 'over the hill' myself! That's why I'm training her up!"

The East Lancashire International Cycling Club returned to the Welcome Inn for a celebratory lemonade, supplied by club funds. Janet spent time in the ladies trying to rearrange her 'hat hair'. Christopher was silent, keeping one eye on the door waiting for her to come out. Ernest, full of the buzz of cycling was exuberant, reliving the time trial in speech, trying to throw in some cycling jargon. He could not stop talking! They all had plenty of time left that Sunday to tell the good news to their families about competing in the junior time trial. It was not over yet, however. Garth Pratt appeared at the doorway, he looked deflated, like the last balloon at a children's party. "Well, you got your way, but in future, there are separate junior girls events"
Brenda sucked her mouth in like she had tasted the sourest lemon sherbet.
"Alright Garth, but in future, you need to be a bit more specific like on your race applications!"
Garth lifted his right arm, thus letting it be known that he was trying to silence Brenda. Brian Towers stood up and squared up.
"Oh wind your neck in, Pratt, she's done the race, she's got her time, and she paid up fair and square"
Garth's voice suddenly became high pitched.
"Rules are rules! You should know that! Teachers

and all! You cross your T's and dot your I's don't you?"

Ernest's exhilaration had left his body, his very first cycle race, eight minutes over what he expected and bedevilled by a girl! The Janet's of this world had not appeared in his imaginings, he was too busy weighing himself down with imaginary silver trophies 'fastest hill climb' 'fastest time trial' 'Road Race winner'...

Janet was not sure how she would report back to her mother, for the women's circle news, she had competed in a race that she was not supposed to be in, and only had a time to show for it. How was her mother to convey the sense of achievement that Janet felt? She had cycled down a hill! A hill! And she had really quite enjoyed it. But to the women's circle with their medical student sons, 'Janet cycled down a hill: a little one' would be the same as saying 'The sun came up today'.

Amongst a tray of baked goods that never looked the same out of Janet's mother's oven, as they do on the recipe card. She might as well have said 'I'm exaggerating, amongst all you women to make myself feel better'. Janet dreaded the thought of her mother making a silk purse out of her sow's ear news, nevertheless, she would tell her mother straight, and probably in front of her father.

And true to form, Mrs Dootson glowed and floated about Janet with skills that could rival a peacock "Oh my wonderful darling! Fighting for women's rights! Competing against all those boys in a cycle race! Some of it was a downhill struggle you know!" she would report at the next meeting. Christopher, of course, had ridden many a cycle race. He had only fallen off his bicycle once before, and that is when everything changed.

He had fallen asleep, that's what it felt like, and when he woke up, everything was different. So today, as if things were not going badly enough with Janet fawning over Ernest when Christopher fell off his bike, it all came tumbling back to him and he decided not to say anything.

Chapter 26: Ernest's Fan Club

Of course, Rose was the founding member of Ernest's fan club, his mother, she was Ernest's biggest fan, secretly talking to God, praying that he would succeed, and join the Great British Olympic cycling team, but it would be madness to let him know that. Rose did not want it to go to Ernest's head.

Mrs Smith, one of Ernest's customers, was also one of Ernest's fans; and she had no problem letting him know! She was one of the first people to note Ernest's talent, she encouraged him, told him he was going 'like the clappers', during the spring when he started his rounds, not Mr Ainsworth from one of the cottages, no! It was Mrs Smith. She knows how to spot a talented young man when she sees one.

And Ernest, on that heavy carrier bicycle,
had become her special messenger to Mr Potts,
and her secret under the counter alcohol
supply. Did she mention that she is a widow?
Yes. Mrs Smith is one of Ernest's biggest fans. A
proper little go-between is he. Would Mrs Smith,
her lipstick and tales of her dead husband be so
keen on Ernest's cycling abilities if she knew that
Mr Potts was keen on Ernest's mother? It is a
sure thing that she would continue to use Ernest's
delivery service. Bottles of sherry can be heavy,
after all.

Uncle Billy had always been a big fan of Ernest's.
Fifteen years ago, the screaming of a hungry
baby in the night. Followed by the giggling and
cooing of an infant, and the chattering of a
toddler, could not, of course, be heard by Uncle
Billy. When Ernest was learning to speak, when
he had his first day at school, and when he was
asserting his ambitions, Uncle Billy was unable to
say anything to encourage Ernest, but
communicate he did. He had always been one of
Ernest's biggest fans. Because Ernest was Uncle
Billy's best friend.

Janet Dootson, soon to be sixteen, a cyclist and
loner until hormones had taken over and she had
fallen in love with Ernest. They had so much in
common. They both loved cycling, he had
relatives on the same road... they both loved
cycling, yes Janet did not really know Ernest, but
then there was little more to know. Janet's
adoration was unrequited because she had two
legs, not two wheels. But she had even named
their children, both wearing glasses and bobble

hats. Both on bicycles. Ernest was very distracting to Janet, who was also in his fan club. Then there was Mr and Mrs Towers, Brian Towers in particular. When Ernest arrived on the scene with his athletic capabilities, Brian could not help but imagine success for his cycling club. Ernest was already delivering the wins, showing promise, learning the tactics. The glory was bound to be his, and Brian Towers... could he? Should he take the credit?

Christopher Cunliffe had previously idolised Ernest, they became friends very quickly, almost like a whirlwind romance, Christopher was a fully paid up member of Ernest's fan club. It is funny how you can go off a person, though. Christopher's mother could not believe her luck when Ernest and Christopher became friends in the summer months. She too had joined the fan club. Christopher had been at risk of becoming something of a loner after his accident. His previous friends had all dropped off. Boys are not the best at keeping in touch, especially as they all have their own growing and schooling to occupy them. But here was Ernest, someone he could go on cycle rides with, become part of his routine, never letting him down at the meeting point telephone box. But then Janet appeared on the scene with her button nose, her bobble hat and her points of views. Christopher loved her, but it was as clear as day that she loved Ernest. She was always asking about him. 'Would Ernest be going to the next club run?' 'Do you think Ernest likes my bike?' She never asked after Christopher. And to think, Christopher had already imagined Janet and himself on a tandem, a bicycle made for two riding off together into the sunset, he was finding Janet very distracting. And then there was the green Viking. If it was not for Christopher's efforts, Ernest would never have found that bicycle. Alright; so Ernest had to earn the money to pay for it, but that was not Christopher's fault. First chance Ernest got, he was away, breaking away from the crowd and breaking away from Christopher. The jealousy that Christopher was feeling was a new feeling, that he did not know what to do with. And so, Christopher, with a broken heart, had dropped out of Ernest Bradshaw's fan club. He was even considering reporting him to the officials at the junior time trial national committee. Remembering the leaflet that Brian Towers had given them both a 'Junior Time Trial Rules and Regulations'. One of the rules, number four :

'Any injury no matter how insignificant is required to be reported to the event secretary, as soon as possible.'

Ernest had broken Christopher's heart and Christopher had been injured.

Chapter 27: The Fallout Cows

In 1962, Prime Minister Harold MacMillan had regular telephone conversations with President Kennedy of the USA. The young president, aged 45 (but did not look middle aged) had the most fantastic set of teeth. Harold MacMillan had the most wonderful plummy British accent, resonating with the Queen's English and acquired at public school. The two leaders, unbeknown to the British public (who had been told half a tale, of course) had regular telephone contact during that time. One telling the other that he would not do 'anything drastic, without telling the other' but of course, even the most powerful are told what to say sometimes. They were neither friends or enemies, they were allies.

Now, any such emergencies known to man should be planned and budgeted for by any local government worth its salt. The social changes that had followed two wars of population decrease and
expansion had led councillors up and down the country to search for an idealised system of local government.
 In 1962, the central government gave local councils the power to decide how to spend public money, so long as their national view
 was cascaded down to the community of people. The threat of nuclear war was a unique situation.

Those up high in authority had to think on their feet, find the right words and some of what they knew (from the Prime Minister) could not be cascaded down to the people. Harold MacMillan asked his ministers to speak with their ministers to speak with Mayors to speak with councillors, to provide some form or preparation (just in case anything drastic happened) for the good people, the harmonious communities of Bolton, for example. So it was no surprise that the good people did not get the full story.
Any new policy or procedure would be scrutinised by a committee before being put out for consultation. Not having the full story, the councillors in Bolton tasked with nuclear survival strategy had no choice, but to arrange a meeting about a meeting and possibly re-word and re-tell former policy and procedure designed for protecting the good people of the community.
They did not have much time. Speeches had been prepared. Hideouts had been dug out. Television and radio announcements had secretly been recorded. Local councillors up and down the country had been thinking long and hard about contingency plans, in the event of a nuclear strike. Time had been stolen from their days of meetings about meetings regarding traffic liaison, planning applications and of course, the minutes of the last meeting to discuss the new agenda: Nuclear Fallout.
Councillor Lesley Philpots and Councillor Hilary Green (Mr) did not quite know where to start the agenda and minutes of the 'Nuclear Fallout' planning department meeting at Bolton Council.

1962

"Morning councillor, Morning!" Lesley Philpots said.

"Afternoon, councillor, afternoon, let us put something together" Hilary Green bluffed his way through, but at least he knew what time of day it was... The brief to local government from the houses of parliament was to 'follow any such pandemic plan'. Typhus, influenza (of varying degrees) and Tuberculosis, to name but a few disease endemics currently feared in 1962. And without knowing the facts, figures and details of up and coming vaccination schemes, these pandemics were thought to be killers.

Just like the nuclear problem. The two councillors both scratched their heads.

Neither knew where to start writing a fancy policy or procedure to protect the townsfolk of Bolton community. They had to write something.

Afternoon cigarettes were puffed away at. Minds started wandering. Hilary Green was wondering what Mrs Green was putting on for dinner that evening. Lesley Philpots was starting to regret having black pudding for his breakfast when there was a tapping sound at the council chamber door.

"Hmm hmm," Lesley Philpots cleared his throat "Enter"

One side of the mahogany double doors opened to the room that permanently smelt of varnish, and often smelt of cigarettes. The tea trolley tinkled into the room, followed by Maxine McPherson. Stubby fingers worked the tin lid which promised exotic Christmas type treats but delivered plain and crumbled snacks.

"Custard creams? Shortbread?" Maxine jangled the tin and then poured out two cups of tea.

She turned to exit. Wiping her nose on the back of her hand, dolled up in hair net and tabard, she would be back to retrieve the tea trolley in half an hour. She reminded both councillors of something. The basic need for food would be everyone's basic need in the event of a nuclear fallout. And if any such survivors should survive, they would need the comfort and safety of school dinners, provided by a generous local authority. Who better to deliver this than an army of dinner ladies?

So it was settled then, cobbled together, and presented on Council lecterns in the 'Full Council Meeting' on a Thursday (the meeting that the Mayor attends) would be the policy proposal that school dinner ladies across the town would be trained in the art of providing staple survival food for any survivors of nuclear bombs. If enough training was cascaded amongst the dinner ladies over the next few weeks, then this would overcome the problem that some of the dinner ladies themselves may not, unfortunately, survive and recover any such blast. In order to protect the good people of the harmonious constituency, Lesley Philpots councillor and the right honourable Hilary Green finished their tea break, dusted away their crumbs and set to work writing the draft of said policy proposal. They would like to have reported that they looked into it, but there was not much time. Not having the full story had created a sense of hysterical anxiety in the town hall... So they made it up.

And on Thursday, in the Full Council Meeting, although not having the full story, the Mayor of

1962

Bolton signed off the policy proposal, thus having been scrutinised, the document became an official policy and was duly cascaded amongst dinner ladies across the town.

The following Monday, even though Ernest's school was on the outskirts of the harmonious community, eleven dinner ladies had been offered overtime, to come in early and learn all about food preparation for survivors of nuclear war. Mr Cooley, of course, was at the forefront of the meeting. He had put himself in charge of lecturing the information to the dinner ladies, which of course he would be unable to do, had one of the council typists, Sylvia Smith not agreed to overtime the previous Friday. Time was of the essence, and she was the most valuable and speediest words per minute audio typist in the entire Town Hall.
Now, being a teacher, Mr Cooley was aware that the word 'cascade' meant to successfully pass on information or knowledge, that he himself had received from a higher authority. Today, however, he was slightly out of his comfort zone.
The school kitchen was by no means ideal for a lesson, a lecture actually about safe and staple diets. There was no blackboard, and no desk fit for slamming a ruler on, to create a loud warning that the children should listen. And he was not entirely sure about stepping into the realms of adult education. The dinner ladies, only eleven in number sat around in a semi-circle, white caps, hair nets and tabards,
"Shhh! Girls" Elsie Seddon motioned, thus creating a loud warning that the dinner ladies

should listen. They had all helped themselves to a cup of tea, and one of them was even smoking!

"Just a moment please, err" Mr Cooley frowned, his hands out in front of him, both fingers poised to negotiate a thought, he was unable to think of a word at which was appropriate to address the dinner ladies. Girls? No, Ladies? Perhaps. He turned to exit the school kitchen, hoping to defer the lecture to Mrs Ogle the music teacher. She was almost 100 years old, after all. Mr Cooley caught a glimpse of himself reflected in the window of the school kitchen. He appeared middle-aged when he was actually thirty-six. He looked back at the gossiping dinner ladies. Most of which had taken the job whilst their own children were in school, some of whom were young enough to have been taught by Mr Cooley when he first qualified. Edwina Stone was, like her counterparts only there for the extra cash. Her mind was wandering to the sheets and her husband's shirts that she could have pegged out on the washing line that morning if she had not of been required to turn up to work two hours early. She was looking out of the window, and only half listening to Mr Cooley's flow of abundant words.

"So this, girls, err ladies is a diagram of how deeply into the meat, the cow's hide you will have to cut into to avoid radiation poisoning"

"Oh, I could listen to you all day, Mr Cooley!" Elsie Seddon teased "I'd make a deep indentation in his hide" She whispered to her neighbouring dinner lady.

"So this, as you see is a list of safe and staple foods that you will be required to prepare in the event of nuclear fallout. And it won't be just school children you'll have to feed. No, most likely schools, obviously the buildings are owned by the local government will be most likely used as shelters for the public, should there be a war" Having heard only half a tale, Edwina, sat up. "So right, cut into the cow a bit deeper so's not to radiate folk. But what if we get blown up, Mr Cooley eh? "

"What?"

"Well, if all us lot get blown up, then they'll be no one to turn to will there? And what if the farmers get.. What if all the cows get blown up? Eh? They'll be no one here to dish out meat cuts then!" The room was filled with 'Ooos' and giggles. Mr Cooley looked at the school kitchen clock, desperate for the bell to ring as was his trademark rescue from the pinnacle of any altercation with a pupil, always letting them think they were in hot water, but timed it right for the bell ringing, so he did not have to dish out any punishment. The stupid pupils, those most likely to be in hot water had never managed to figure this out. But now that Mr Cooley was in hot water himself, the bell was not for chiming.

"Well, 'appen we won't all get blown up if it comes to it," Elsie Seddon said, matter-of-factly. She folded her arms, slightly superior to Edwina, the folding of arms indicated a serious tone in her conversation. The other nine dinner ladies nodded. Cups of tea were now drained and the lecture should surely be over.

"That's right err Mrs err" Mr Cooley did not know

any of the dinner ladies names.
"Elsie, your honour" Elsie curtseyed at Mr Cooley.
"As Elsie has pointed out, in the event of a nuclear bomb, any survivors... Err, those who have not been blown up will have to pull together to help each other survive. Find shelter and water. We all need to be prepared for what is and is not safe to be consumed" Mr Cooley was getting exasperated and looking for a way out.
"Yeah, what he said!" Elsie Seddon still had her arms folded but was now swinging on the back of her chair, the same swinging manoeuvre strictly forbidden in other parts of the school.
"In that case, it might be better if you all take away one copy of these council briefings, read it, digest it, and don't bloody well forget it and if you really want to make use of yourself, cascade the information to your families and neighbours" Mr Cooley had enough of adult education for one day. Much giggling and gossiping followed Mr Cooley's swear words. Until the most important question was asked :
"Err Sir... Are we still getting overtime up until lunch time?" A dinner lady enquired.
"Erm yes, I suppose you will be, use the time to read it, though!"
Edwina Stone could not believe her luck, she had enough time to nip home and put
her husband's shirts on the washing line in time for her return to the lunchtime shift at Ernest's school. For this fallout cow, at least life continued on as normal despite the Cuban missile crisis.

Chapter 28: Olympic Teams Have to Meet the Queen.

The next Olympics will be in less than two years.
Any cyclist who wants to become a champion
must think about joining a professional team.
This is where the intrigue lies for most young
cyclists. It might have been the widespread
hysteria about nuclear war that had infected
Ernest. It might have been his age, but Ernest
saw the Olympics, two years away as a distant
dream.
Now, cycling time trials are a solitary, tactical
sport. Lone riders swinging out into the
countryside against the clock. In a club event,
 the likes of Ernest had endeared himself and
benefitted from the encouragement of the crowd.
This only need be one lone cheer: "Dig in! Dig into
your reserves!"
But should this lone cheer be absent, it could set
a rider off his game.
On this particular club event, another time
trial on a Wednesday night, the entire East
Lancashire International Cycling Club. Not just the
juniors. The entire club. That is all except for two
of the junior members. Janet, being Wednesday
she would be exhausted from Hockey or whatever
punishing activity had been chosen by Miss Little,
Rita and Elaine. And another junior member was
also absent, Christopher.
"Don't worry Ernest, love, Christopher is not riding
tonight, but his mother said he might come over

and cheer you on"
"Oh, thanks, I feel a bit put out competing against all the experienced riders" Ernest could hear titters from the grown up riders.
"Just go for it, lad," Colin Sidebottom said. Brenda Towers ran alongside Ernest as he set off, Brian Towers gave the 'off' signal.
"Go all out, Ernest!" Brenda shouted. She was one of Ernest's biggest fans after all. Ernest set off on the familiar route. The wind cutting into his pale legs the rain. The rain whipping his face. The grey clouds greying further and turning into the dark night sky. Still, Ernest had his eyes on the prize. This was all part of training. He had his mind set on improving his time. One minute apart, the solitary riders. Even on the flat of Pilsworth road, Ernest could not catch a glimpse of the rider in front of him. Pedals up and down, wheels round and round. Inhale, exhale, just keep going until you have got there. Ernest passed the phone box. His and Christopher's meeting point, the lonely red box stood still as a solitary beacon, Christopher is not here to cheer you on Ernest. Your friend has abandoned you on this punishing time trial. Pedals up and down, wheels round and round. Inhale, exhale. Ernest shut his eyes against the raindrops corrugating his spectacles. Is that a figure I see stepping out of the phone box? Ernest imagined to himself. No. He had imagined Christopher stood there.
"Come on, pal! Dig in! Dig in Ernest! You stole Janet!"
"What?" Ernest kept going, nearer to the phone box, avoiding potholes and puddles, the wind

burning at him. "What?" but there was no one there, no sign of Christopher. No single cheering on of his friend. His friend and teammate Christopher. Ok, so he had fallen off his bike at the last time trial, and the weather was rather gruesome on that club run.

Yes, Ernest had decided to forgive his friend. But did he imagine he said something about Janet? Ernest kept going, safe in the knowledge that he was the only dedicated member of the junior section of the East Lancashire International Cycling Club. Neither Christopher or Janet were as dedicated as him. Push the pedals up and down. wheels round and round. Inhale Exhale, don't they know the Russians are going to blow us to kingdom come! Cycle while you have the chance! Win! Get your name in the Bury Times! The Radcliffe Times! The Bolton Evening News! Pedals up and down! Wheels round and round! Inhale exhale! I'm going national, I'm going global! I wish Christopher was here, I don't fancy meeting royalty on my own...

Mark Crosby and the Benson twins were sitting on a wall when they saw Ernest fly past on the Green Viking.

"Bradders! Woohoo! Hahaha!" They chorused. Crosby and his cronies would shout at anything, their hollering was not as good as Christopher's, he pushed on forward. Wheels round and round pedals up and down.

"One minute three Ernest!" Brian Towers shouted. Ernest did not get off his bicycle, inhale exhale. He swigged the sweet tea foisted on him by Brenda Towers in the plastic cup. There was a tall man stood with the grown up riders that

Ernest did not recognise, he was wearing a waterproof cape.

"Right, I'm off," Ernest said, seeing no sense in hanging around.

"But you've shaved three minutes off your time, lad, why are you making a dash for it?" Brian Towers nearly spat out his tea.

"Aye, I'm going home to tell me mum" Ernest took his achievement for granted. He was disappointed with his own feelings. He thought the news he was getting quicker would thrillhim, but it meant nothing without his teammates. Any rider who did not value his club earned the reputation of arrogance. Before he knew it, Ernest was back home. It was dark, might as well have been midnight. His mother had lost enthusiasm for having several bicycles propped up in the corner of her kitchen, that's for sure.

"One hour three, mother," Ernest said. Rose could not tell from his demeanour whether that was a good thing or not. So she said nothing but nodded. Ernest trudged upstairs to bed. Uncle Billy peeped out from under the covers on his side of the bedroom, being one of Ernest's biggest fans, he wondered what was up.

"Hoooo," he said, in sympathy to Ernest, who fell asleep almost immediately, knowing that Uncle Billy was still on his team.

In the news, the Russians, it seemed were moving missiles across the sea to Cuba. Discovered by an American spy, it seemed listening to gossip in a bar in Havana. Not the type of enemies to keep close.

The Manchester and District Time Trial Association Autumn Race loomed. Ernest had made the grade. Christopher had not, and of course, Janet only competed in the last time trial on a technicality. They were not competing, but Ernest really needed his friends behind him. After his deliveries one Thursday, Ernest rode over to the phone box, the symbol of their friendship. He got off his bike, opened the door. Lifted the receiver and put it down again. He had not memorised Christopher's telephone number. He thought about hanging around for a bit, surely Christopher would still be riding his bike? Ernest started to worry that Christopher had another problem with his head, had another tumble, and asked everyone to not mention it to his parents... What if he had one of his headaches? A funny turn? Collapsed in his bed, and his mother none the wiser? Ernest had chemistry homework to attend to at home, but the value of team and friendship won over the table of elements.

"Mrs Cunliffe!" Ernest rattled the front door knocker. He was not a regular visitor at The Cunliffe's house. They had a driveway and a front garden! Mrs Cunliffe was pleased to see Ernest, there was formality, though, at their house, no 'come in love!' Ernest was asked to wait at the front door, whilst she went to fetch Christopher. Mrs Cunliffe had seemed pleased but surprised by Ernest's appearance. Ernest was relieved, but counted the steps the minutes, what if Mrs Cunliffe found her son sprawled out on his bed? "Thank god!" Ernest said when Christopher slumped down the stairs, batting his mother away, he looked very different without his rubber helmet

on.
"Oh hello, Ernest! Is Janet not with you?"
Christopher looked over the top of Ernest's head
like he was searching for someone, Janet in the
shadows of the driveway.
"What? Janet? Why .. Huh? Why would she be
here? Anyway, there's a downhill on the way to
 your house!" Ernest joked to his friend, puzzled
and regretful he had not even thought to invite
Janet to visit Christopher. It was a spur of the
moment visit anyway.
"Erm, I missed you on the club run"
"Right" Christopher did not know what to say but
wanted to stand his ground.
"I just wanted to know that you're alright really,"
Ernest said.
"I'm OK" Christopher hesitated. Ernest had been
his only friend, he now doubted that Ernest was
anything to do with Janet's feelings, but he was
the reason for them. After a pause, he said "I'd
invite you in, but"
"Well, I've homework to do, so long as I know
you're alright Christopher, not had one of your
funny turns" Ernest rode off towards his home, but
that was it for Christopher. 'Funny turn' he said to
himself 'who does he think he is? Funny turn?
"Christopher!" his mother's voice floated down the
hallway "Has Ernest gone?"
Christopher had never spoken about Janet or
anything really to his mother before...

Chapter 29: Mr Cooley.

Mr Michael Cooley age thirty-six had always dreamed of becoming famous. His talents plentiful from a young age. Piano, amateur dramatics, painting and most of all writing. He would dream of readers, washed up on desert islands surviving only because they had a copy of the best-selling stand-alone masterpiece written by Mr Michael Cooley. Providing hope in a hopeless situation. He had planned only ever to write one novel because one would be *enough.*

But it was1962 now, and Mr Cooley had to accept that it was too late for celebrity status. He was married to Mrs Cooley and father to the Cooley twins, his saviours. But he was always left with the nagging sensation of what-could-have-been. Because those who can, do; those who can't teach. When Mr Michael Cooley had been a teenager; just as his life started to take shape on that dinky portable Imperial Good Companion typewriter, things started to fall apart. It had never really been his ambition to become a teacher, despite what he said in assembly. The WWII had conspired against him. His mother putting the fear of God into him as a thirteen-year-old when war broke out... praying and obsessing daily that the war would not last until Michael Cooley was eighteen years old.

"You ought to take more water with it!"
"Pardon? I mean, what?!" Mr Cooley addressed the headmaster, Mr Byrne tucking his shirt in like

a naughty boy on uniform inspection day.
"Mrs Ogle has erm... well she has made a
complaint about you"
"Mrs Ogle?" Mr Cooley wiped escaping drool from
the corners of his mouth with his shirt cuff.
"Yes, Mrs Ogle. Said she is refusing to play piano
in assembly unless you start acting
professionally"
"Piano? I can play the piano myself!"
"Listen, Mr Cooley, Michael... your mind has not
been on the job since you've ... since the twins
were born. I turned a blind eye on your rants
about World War III, but there are standards...
you can't jump out of your skin at the slightest
bang during class time! ... It's 1962 now" Mr
Byrne the headmaster despaired of Mr Cooley
sometimes.
"Mrs Ogle?" Mr Cooley despaired of Mr Byrne
sometimes.
"It's the governors, they'll want to investigate, they
didn't take the dinner ladies' complaint seriously
but two complaints..." Mr Byrne dodged blame,
his left hand moving from side to side, tipping
imaginary scales "I'll have to put you on
gardener's leave on full pay... take the family out,
though... have a rest"
"It's the start of term!" Said Mr Cooley.
"Why don't you have a think about a change of
career? Have you ever thought of doing
something else, Michael?"
Mr Cooley had of course. He opened his mouth to
tell the Headmaster that he was going to write a
bestselling novel when Mr Byrne said:
"You know what they say, Michael? Those

who can't teach, teach teachers how to teach..."
And if I can't do that, I can always write policy, Mr
Cooley thought as Mr Byrne escorted him off
school premises.

For the first time, Ernest felt lacklustre about
this evening's club run. He had spent all of his
energies on his cycling fund, and all of his funds
on the green Viking. Ruminations about his
friendship with Christopher overwhelmed him. At
least he knew where he stood with Mark Crosby.
"Hello Ernest," Brenda Towers said, interrupting
her conversation with a man in a waterproof cape.
"Hellow" Said Ernest, adjusting the lamp on his
bicycle.
"Hey lad, are you related to Norm Schofield?"
Said the man in the waterproof cape.
"Uncle Norman? Yes, he's married to Auntie
Marigold. I've not seen them for a couple of
weeks, I've been competing"
"Aye, I know. Brian can't stop talking about you. I
know your uncle from t'pub. How's his dog?"
"Rusty? Well he's a red setter"
"Aye, he didn't take your uncle for a walk last
Sunday, said he'd hurt his paw I think.
 Anyway, lad, I hear you're going to go after my
record!" The man in the cape tried to lighten the
mood, with an assertive grin and a friendly
warning.

Ernest could not concentrate on the club run. He
had known Rusty since he was a puppy. A ball of
ginger fluff with teeth as sharp as
needles... Hurt his paw? In the war, apparently,
there were special boots made for

dogs so that they would not hurt their paws Ernest
was sure of it. Uncle Norman should have bought
some of those little boots for Rusty, he can afford
it. Ernest was sure of that too. He was nearing the
corner for his aunt and uncle's house, hoping not
to be in trouble for not visiting for a few weeks...
I'll tell them I've been speaking to a man in a
waterproof cape about Rusty...Ernest slammed
his brakes on, the man in the cape asked if he
was going after his record. What if this means that
he thinks I'm going to attack his achievement?
Have I broken an unwritten rule? Ernest ghosted
his way out of the club run and took the turning for
Auntie Marigold's house.

*Time Trialling for Beginners, rule number 9:
Competitors must obey the law of the land.*

"He's dead Ernest!" Auntie Marigold sobbed in a
voice that was neither inside or out.
"Dead?" Ernest tried to sneak a glance down the
hall behind his aunt "Do you want me to cycle
back? Fetch me mother?"
Auntie Marigold stopped in her tracks, a tattered
tissue up around her nose.
"You could ring Mrs Bassett next door, she'll
knock on if you want to speak to her"
"No, oh Ernest you are such a sweet nephew, I
don't want to trouble your mother. I don't even
think she cared for him that much, she never had
time for him"

"Well I think she'd want to know Auntie, I know
she thinks he was a bit of a 'know it all' but I

think she'd want to know!"

"A know it all? Oh, you're a funny little thing, Ernest. Anyway, leave your bicycle here next to the porch, no one'll pinch it, don't worry" Auntie Marigold's outside voice had returned "And come in, won't you, I've no cordial but I'll make you some tea"

"What about me cousins? I can't believe they've left you on your own at a time like this!"

"Well, they're at work Ernest, they're all grown up and married, got their own lives! They won't be that interested that he's died" Said Auntie Marigold.

Ernest shuddered he could not imagine not clinging to his family should his Uncle Billy ... or worse his mother died. His cousins were callous.

"And besides, I've not been able to get hold of Thomas"

"Thomas doesn't know?!"

"No, well he didn't have much to do with him"

"No?"

"No!"

"Auntie Marigold, are you feeling alright? Do you want me to put the kettle on? I mean, you're on your own now!"

"I'm not on my own Ernest, oh you are a daft apeth" Inside voiced Auntie Marigold filled her new electric kettle up with water. Ernest, not knowing what to say, thought about his granddad, the only person he had known to have died. Ernest was eight then, and granddad definitely had a funeral... All of a sudden, Ernest knew exactly what to say."What about his funeral?" Ernest said, and all of a sudden, this was definitely not the right thing to say. Auntie

Marigold dropped the sugar bowl, the tattered tissue reappeared and her hands were on her face. She threw herself, sobbing towards Ernest. "Oh Ernest, your Uncle Norman!" At this point, there was wailing, mumbling and noise ending with "Buried in the back garden!"
As the conversation slipped into confusion, Uncle Norman appeared at the back door, sweat running down each temple. Ernest did not know whether to be relieved or worried. Auntie Marigold had just told him he was dead...   "I think if we get another dog, Marigold I don't want another setter. Too big. Took me ages to dig that hole! Hallo Ernest lad, where's your bike?"

Rusty is dead not Uncle Norman.

"Outside Norman!" Marigold recovered her voice to chastise her husband.
 "Are you alright, Marigold love? Listen it'll be me who misses him the most, I'll have no one to walk me to the Brown Cow now! Right, I'm just popping to the allotment, fetch some celery from the greenhouse, fingers crossed" Uncle Norman said. Whilst some things stayed consistent in Ernest's world, some things were starting to fall apart. Rusty the red setter, the dog he had known since he was three, now deceased. Auntie Marigold still sounds the same and despite her grief always likes to have a supply of celery in her fridge. Uncle Norman popped his head back round the door.
"Oh I meant to say, Ernest, your hero Harry Hill will miss Rusty, I was talking to him the other day

in't pub, told him you're going in for t'Olympics!"
...

Chapter 30: No One Ever Got Sacked in Those days.

"*Cynthia!*"
"Oh don't you start on me *lady,*" Said Cynthia
Crosby as she bundled fresh produce and apathy
into her launderette bag.
"Have you been crying? Are you ok Cynthia?
Look put that down, have your break early. I'll put
the kettle on" Rose said, both cautious and caring
about Cynthia.
"Pah! No one ever cries these days Rose, make
yourself useful and pass me one of those bottles
of sherry before Potts gets back from the pub"
Cynthia wiped her face on her tabard.
"No! I'm not helping you *steal*" Rose whispered
the word 'steal'
Cynthia stopped in her tracks, she put the
launderette bag down, and folded her overcoat,
tucking in her loot with purpose. She sighed, she
folded her arms, she cornered Rose.
"Listen. If you can take your matching hat from
over your ears for once. You have got no idea
what it's like to be me. No idea. I've not been
crying, and I've not been stealing either. You're
not telling me that Old Potts can't afford to
 spare a few spuds here and there?"
"What about the sherry?"

"What about it? It's not meant to be here anyway! Potts' Greens is a flamin' greengrocer, not an off-licence!"

Cynthia Crosby was making Rose Bradshaw's life hell. That is how it works; Cynthia's life actually was hell, so unconsciously she dispersed her unhappiness to those all around her. Rose should not take it so personally.

"I'm sorry Rose, I didn't mean anything by it. It's just that I've just found out" Cynthia hesitated "I've just had some bad news, that's all"

Rose looked around the storage area. Cynthia Crosby could not keep her in this uncomfortable conversation *forever*. She had
floors to scrub, she had Mr Potts to annoy.

And Rose had customers to sort out, she did not wish to know Cynthia's bad news, she had worries of her own, and yet here it came :

"See I've just found out my husband has managed to lengthen his stretch... He only got sent down for a misunderstanding about the pub's garden furniture!" Cynthia huffed.

Rose remembered Mr Crosby had stolen and sold on the benches from the Brown Cow's beer garden earlier in the year.

"He got into a ... *disagreement...* shall we say with a screw. " Cynthia eyed Rose "That's a prison guard to you... and... well, they'll fit you up, give a dog a bad name, so to speak. Soon eighteen months for a petty offence becomes a five-year stretch!"

Cynthia's wrists were facing outwards, hands

palm face down on the window ledge, imprisoned in the storage area, looking out into the grey autumn sky, acting out the starring role in her own kitchen sink drama. Rose edged out of the storage room.

"I'm sorry Cynthia, I don't know what to say."
Rose did not know what to say, that was true, but then all of a sudden she said something she should not have "If there's anything I can do, just let me know!"

Bingo! Thought Cynthia Crosby.

"Well don't let Old Potts' know about today will you love? And if there's anything you need, just let *me* know. Want me to sneak a bottle of sherry for yourself?"

"NO! No, Cynthia, I do not! I don't drink and Uncle Billy doesn't either!"

"What about your Ernest?" Cynthia said, pointing the business end of a bunch of carrots generously towards Rose.

"Ernest is too young! And so is your Mark, for that matter!" Rose's hand clenched the neckline of her grocer's overall.

"Suit yourself, Rose, though the last time my Mark got in trouble over drinking he'd started his night out with your Ernest!"

"I'd better get back to work, Cynthia!" Rose excused herself from the oppressive storage area.

Common as muck! Rose thought.
Stuck up cow! Cynthia said to herself.

Cecil Potts had treated himself to a pint in the pub and a read of the newspaper.
'PRESIDENT KENNEDY ADMITTED TO

HOSPITAL DUE TO A RESPIRATORY CONDITION'

Who cares? Potts thought to himself. He's nowt to do with us; We've got our own Prime Minister!

"It's all a conspiracy you know! Chest infection? Pah! That's convenient!" The Rose and Crown's landlord had nothing to do all day except polish his glassware and think the worst "Keep your hands off that newspaper, anyhow, Potts!" He said in grumpy tones, wiping down his bar.

Cecil Potts looked round, he was the only living customer of the Rose and Crown.

"I thought this paper belonged to the pub!"

"It does! But the crossword belongs to ME!" The landlord tinkled pint glasses around under the counter.

"Any luck on shifting the rest of that sherry?"

"Any luck with seven down?" Potts defended "Got a few good customers, don't worry Mrs Smith up on the hill will finish them all off, plus she won't be taking any business from this place, she never makes it down to the high street anymore"

"Good, we've got to stick together us high street traders it's all going to change in these modern times y'know. New decade, new era. Anyway, that Mrs Smith... She's a widow you know. You ever ... y'know, been there?"

"Nah! Anyway, a new era? Another conspiracy?"

"Never mind that, only Cynthia Crosby said..."

"Mrs Crosby?! That woman is making my life a misery!"

"Haha, well she was only saying, no need to get so touchy Cecil!"

"I'm not interested in her. I've still got my eye on
..."

"Don't tell me you're still sweet on Rose flamin'
Bradshaw? It's not natural!"

"Not natural?"

"Cynthia Crosby told me, well what did she say?
It's going back a few years...
your father Old Potts took a shine to Rose, took
her under his wing after her sweetheart died in
the war. They reckon her lad is *his* lad, so you
couldn't court her, surely?" The landlord
whispered the words 'his lad' and had now taken
ownership of the crossword puzzle. Cecil Potts
had taken leave of his senses. Where was he
fifteen- sixteen years ago? He returned home
after the war and his father, *even* Older Potts had
promoted him to the delivery boy. But Cecil Potts
was a man now, he had been to war. He should
be a man with a van, not a delivery boy without a
clue. And so, with no wife, no mouths to feed,
Cecil Potts left that one horse town and tried to
make a life for himself elsewhere, only to return,
unsuccessful when his father retired. And to think!
He had employed Ernest Bradshaw into that
same delivery boy job his own father tried to palm
off on him! Surely not! Not Rose! But wait...
flamin' Cynthia Crosby! Only last week she was
whispering to me outside on the wall, implying
that Mr Alfred Smith... Mrs Smith's dead husband
was Ernest's father! That woman is making my life
a misery! He supped the remainder of his pint and
returned to work.

The sound of smashing glass masked the sound of Cynthia Crosby's foul mouthed response.
"Mr Potts!" She defended herself with sherry dripping down the shelves and pooling around their toes. If only Rose Bradshaw had reached it down for her when she had asked... "Fancy creeping up on me like that... err when I'm dusting the top shelf! You gave me a fright!"
"Dusting the top shelf?" Cecil Potts assessed the situation, his eyes scanned all around him in the back storage area. Noticing the bulging launderette bag, he would not have to keep Cynthia Crosby there too long in this uncomfortable situation.
"Just go! Get out of my grocers Mrs Crosby! You're fired!"
"Fired! Ha! No one gets the sack these days Mr Potts!" Indignant, Cynthia Crosby buttoned the side of her tabard one popper closer to her voluptuous frame "Suit yourself! I'll just go and get another job... There's plenty who'd hire me... Mr Brown the butcher said I'm the fastest cleaner on one mop!"
"He said no such thing, Mrs Crosby! And should you seek employment elsewhere on this high street, I'll be letting them know about your laundry bag trick, how you bring it in folded up in your overcoat pocket in the morning, then even before your lunch break it's full to bursting, with my potatoes!"

Rose Bradshaw, outside the back storage area door, was not really listening in, but could not help hear the almighty din that was coming from Mr Potts and Cynthia Crosby. Some of the customers were raising their eyebrows too,Father Dunn particularly taking extra time to pick a pear. She turned on the radio to drown out the noise, praying for a bit of Edith Piaf but instead was greeted by a radio drama, on BBC's light programme. The door to the back storage area swung open the wrong way, followed by an angry Cynthia Crosby.

"Where is she?!"

Rose darted behind the door, which swung shut into Mr Potts' face.

"Oh, there you are! You little tell tale tit!"

"Rose didn't say a thing! She didn't have to! I've got eyes!"

Cynthia Crosby buttoned her overcoat, pulled the grey woollen hat (previously stolen from Ernest) down over her ears and sashayed out of the grocery shop, almost knocking the nosy vicar over.

"Have you sacked her?" Rose asked whilst Father Dunn hid behind her.

"Yes, but no one really gets the sack these days do they?"

Later that same evening when remaining stolen sherry bottles had been drained and early retirement was contemplated, Cynthia Crosby decided to confess all to her reprobate son.

"That's it now for me at Potts' Greens. He went crazy, accusing me of all kinds! Of stealing!" Cynthia said.

Mark Crosby looked at his mother.

"Well, you have been, perks of the job you always said!"
"I tell you how it is son, my face doesn't fit. That Rose Bradshaw's does, though, and it's all her fault I got caught! Yeah. So next time you see your little friend Ernest, next time he tries to get you in trouble for drinking stolen sherry" Cynthia took a swig of her own acquired bottle "You tell him, his mother is messing around with her boss... *again!* He doesn't care who he gives his potatoes out to that one!"

It was true, Mark Crosby could not wait to see Ernest, his mate Bradders and share
this new and important information.

Chapter 31: Duck and Cover

"Anyone seen Bradders today?" Mark Crosby shouted out at school at anyone in the vicinity. "No? Anyone? Bradders!" He shouted, cupping the side of his face with his fat hand. "Bradders! Bradders! I've got a bone to pick with you about my mum's job! I've been looking forward to seeing you all weekend!"
'*Not if I see you first,*' Thought Ernest, who had, indeed spotted Mark Crosby crashing through the school doors like a bumbling bee trapped in a foxglove flute. Ernest had managed to duck and cover, protecting himself from Mark Crosby's

inquisition. He had heard all about Mrs Crosby's non-sacking incident at Potts' Greens (several times, his mother kept going on about it). Ernest, quite frankly was not interested in Mark Crosby's side of the story. He was sure it would result in him being persuaded to steal more sherry from Mrs Smith. Fortunately for some, Mark Crosby spotted Harold Goatshead tottering along on his crutches. Poor Harold, his invalidity meant nothing to Mark Crosby, who soon had Harold in a headlock, his crutches clattering on the school parquet floor. And neither Mark or Ernest knew that Mrs Crosby had turned up to work that morning, refusing to be dismissed, trapping Rose with her graceless moves, like a spider in its web. In a parallel universe, somewhere in the local vicinity, inside Mr Cooley's mind, thinking of school, but not at school, Mr Cooley was preparing for war.

"Duck and cover. That's it children" Mr Cooley said, whilst gently pushing his twin toddlers over, on top of the cushion display he had fashioned in the under stairs cupboard. Both infants giggled, the eldest one, favoured by Mr Cooley, reached up with his baby fingers to pull the mattress on top of the family.

"That's it! Look, Mrs Cooley! My son's a genius! Covering us with the mattress!"

"Michael, they are not even two years old yet, they cannot say my name, never mind their own names, they have no idea what you are talking about" Mrs Cooley had despaired of her husband since he had been suspended from duties.

"Forewarned is forearmed, wife, we all need to be prepared"

"Yes, I mean, no, I don't think we need to take it this far? Do we?"

"Yes, we do!"

"No one else has taped up their windows, or made hats out of tinfoil for their family, not around here anyway"

"Well, more fool them, these are actions that can be taken in the first few crucial seconds after the nuclear blast. Duck and cover!"

"What if we're not at home? What if the blast does not happen? What if it does happen, but it is in America? Not here! Not in the Northwest of England? They're not interested in us!"

"Oh yes they are, and anyway, have you not been reading the newspapers? The detonation of a single nuclear weapon could quickly escalate into global nuclear devastation!"

"Michael! I've got enough on my plate" Mrs Cooley suddenly stopped talking and put her left hand on her upper chest and swallowed, she started shuffling out of the under stairs cupboard, her mouth filled with water.

"Where do you think you're going, young lady?" Mr Cooley had an awful habit of speaking to his wife as though she was one of his pupils. Mrs Cooley did not answer, she ran to the bathroom, to call God on the big white telephone, so to speak. Mr Cooley was oblivious to his wife's recent condition, he had enough on his plate with all the fear of nuclear bombs, which he carried on talking to the twins about. "Now, the first sign of trouble will be a bright flash, brighter than anything you have ever seen!"

The youngest twin lifted his arms up in the air.

Seemingly, they were both geniuses. Mrs Cooley returned to the door of the under stairs cupboard. "Oh, are you feeling alright, Valerie?" Mr Cooley only ever used Mrs Cooley's first name when he needed to show concern for her and today her appearance was very concerning.

"Actually husband, I've got something to tell you... I'm pregnant again, and yes, this time I hope it isn't twins"

Mr Cooley said nothing, imaginary bomb sirens sounded in his head. He stood up (taking care not to drop the mattress on top of the twins) and put his arms around his wife. It was as though a switch had been flicked. "Right, well I'd better pull myself together and go back to work then"

Mrs Cooley sighed, looked around their new build house, at the piles of newspapers and bomb shelter paraphernalia.

"Yes Michael, pull yourself together," Mrs Cooley said, it was 1962, after all.

Chapter 32: Ernest, The Triumphant.

Harry Hill, the bronze winning Olympian cyclist was a well-known character in those parts. Well known, and quoted as saying that he :"*Would not have been successful, if it wasn't for his team*" The Manchester and District Time Trial Association Autumn Race was a grandiose and excitingly titled day out for a very excited bunch of bonkers cyclists. Very exciting for Ernest, being offered the chance to compete after the last time trial. He was not on his own, however, and the whittled down numbers had been whittled down further, due to a number of riders that had come a cropper by the same fate that Christopher had (falling into the stream at the bottom of that hill). Ernest, of course, was not aware of this, Garth Pratt had not publicised the fault in the time trial course. He had simply published the time trial time results in the local paper, and written to each club to let them know which of their members were invited to the autumn Race.

"Mother! Mother! Bri... Mr Towers says I'm in the race on Sunday!"

"That's nice Ernest, is that another Sunday you won't be going to church, or visiting Uncle Norman and Auntie Marigold?"

"Well, err I could cycle up after"

"I think your Auntie has persuaded him, Uncle Norman, to give Rusty a proper funeral, rather than just dumping him in the back garden under the rhododendrons "

"Well, it's important!"

"Important?"

"Yes, it's the Autumn race!"

"What about your friends? Are they going ?"

"Err no, I don't know, Christopher isn't, and Janet, well Janet's a girl so no I don't think so"

"Janet's a girl?" Rose looked quizzical.

"Yes, how many boys do you know called Janet? Haha, mother! Well, you can't tell really under that bobble hat she's always got on"

Rose turned, one eyebrow raised, please do not

tell me that my son cannot tell that Janet is a girl.
"Yes, I know! I just didn't know that girls were not
allowed to enter a cycling race! It is 1962 you
know!"
"Well, it's oh it's a long story Mother, this race is
something big, though, do you think you and
Uncle Billy would come and watch, and maybe
even, err Auntie Marigold and Uncle Norman?"
Ernest felt a bit shy about asking after his aunt
and uncle.
"Well, what about your friends? Won't they want
to watch you, I'll telephone Auntie Marigold
tonight, on my way home, but you know what
she'll say... 'she'll only get to see you go round
once' !"
"Mr and Mrs Towers will be there, but I don't think
Christopher will be" Ernest looked sad, and his
mother never liked seeing him look sad.

Mr Cooley thought he had heard a snippet of
news, a nugget something about a Russian
diplomat having meetings with the American
President. He had to get the full story, he had a
wife and twin toddlers to look after, he wanted to
know if he needed to be prepared. More prepared
than he was already. The best way that Mr
Cooley could think of to get the full story was to
look at the weekend newspapers. He was getting
up earlier and earlier. Mrs Cooley was getting
more and more tired. She had not had a lie in for
over eighteen months. Mr Cooley was rather loud
when he woke up. He had promised to lift the
carpet on the landing, and fix the creaky
floorboard at the top of the stairs. That was a year
ago.

"Why would there be a creaky floorboard on the stairs of a new build?" he had said.
Mrs Cooley had forgiven him at the time, his skills lie in teaching; and obviously not carpentry. Carpets and floorboards can be tricky things. That was at the time, however. And as Mr Cooley's giraffe-like frame shot across the landing at the top of the stairs when he realised it was morning, Mrs Cooley woke up also. And this meant that the twins would now be awake. The nights and mornings were drawing in, but that did not stop the news. The papers were ready at the crack of dawn at Mr Cooley's nearest newsagent. Nearest not being walking distance, that was the trouble with living in a new-build. Rows and rows of identical houses built to house the booming population. A maze of 'closes' and 'cul-de-sacs' all identical. Ginnels and paths are hidden behind panelled fences and difficult to find your way around. The Cooley's had been living there just over twenty-six months, and Mr Cooley had just identified a new shortcut to the newsagent. So he had been hopping on his yellow Vespa and rushing off to get the morning Sunday newspaper. He woke the twins, of course before setting off, thus making life even more difficult for Mrs Cooley. This week, Mr Cooley had efficiently and expertly got under his wife's feet. She had put him in charge of looking after their youngest twin, the snottiest and most snivelling of the two. Who, had expertly and efficiently passed on the germs to his sibling, and in turn, on this Sunday morning, to their father (Mr Cooley). Desperate to leave the house to buy his newspaper, twin babies are a

 hotbed of sickness. Changed and cleaned, Mr Cooley was late now for going to the newsagent on his yellow Vespa for the newspaper. The Russian diplomat would not be forgotten by Mr Cooley.

The day that Mr Cooley was seriously late buying his Sunday newspaper was the day that Ernest and the cyclists had been waiting for. This Sunday was the day of the Autumn time trial. A twenty-five-mile course along Pilsworth Road, he would be representing the East Lancashire International Cycling Club. The riders were set to cycle the twenty-five-mile course. Mr Cooley was actually on Pilsworth road himself on this Sunday morning, searching for his full complement of Sunday papers, sold out at his local newsagent by the time he was baby vomit free.

Mr and Mrs Towers rode with Ernest to the meeting point, equipped of course with their flask of sweet tea. Three lonely little plastic cups, as Ernest was the only junior rider from their club competing. Brenda still only wearing a waterproof cagoule, it was not big coat weather as yet.
"Morning" Garth Pratt sailed by them, too busy and important to say anything more to Mr and Mrs Towers.
"Now come on Ernest, if you get a good time on this one, it's your chance lad. It's getting your name out there it is" Brian Towers said, his wife behind him, nodding over the top of her glasses. The two Towers stood either side of Ernest. It was all very official. As with all time trials, the riders set off one minute apart.

"Number thirty seveeeeen five-four-three-two-one... GO!"
Brian pushed Ernest's bike in an encouraging motion, and so did Brenda. But Brenda kept running alongside.
"Brenda, what are you doing, love?"
"I'm stuck! I can't stop"
"Can't stop?
"Ernest, stop!"
"What?" said Brian
"Eh?" said Ernest
"Stop! I can't stop" Brenda was getting out of breath and further away from Brian, who instinctively started running himself. Brenda's elastic fastener off the bottom of her cagoule had got caught in Ernest's bicycle spokes. She was not lying, she could not stop. Ernest skidded, it was touch and was getting ready to set off. Ernest screeched his brakes on, and Brenda yanked her cagoule elastic free.
"OH Ernest! Go all out!" Brenda narrowly escaped being shoved off the road by the next rider and fell dramatically into the arms of Brian.
"Must be an omen!" Brian said as Ernest and his bicycle disappeared into the distance.

One day, earlier that same week, when excitement loomed but tests of friendship doomed; Rose Bradshaw had tried to get in touch with Christopher Cunliffe. She knew that Sunday was a 'big' race. She hated the thought of Ernest being without his counterparts, Christopher and Janet. Ernest had been convinced that Christopher would not be cheering him along.

1962

Albeit a quiet person, Rose had a little speech prepared. Firstly, she tried to get through to the telephone box that Christopher and Ernest always met at. The operator was unable to connect Rose to the telephone box. When Rose was finally put through, the ringing rang out, a hopeless cause ringing out alone on a road, with no recipient to answer.

"Hello?" The voice said down Rose's telephone line.

"OH Hello! Who's that? I was expecting a boy to answer" Rose was shocked to hear the little voice.

"It's the operator, madam I've been unable to connect you, is there another line you would like me to try?"

"Oh! Yes, I would like to be connected to the Cunliffe household on Harwood road" Rose had adopted a telephone voice, as she had heard her sister do. She stood up straight, her posture greatly improved. Rose was just about to put the telephone handset down when she heard another telephone voice piercing her own eardrum.

"Harwood 36 double 1"

"Oh! Hello, erm am I speaking with Mrs Cunliffe?"

"Am, yeees"

"Well, I am telephoning about your son"

"Yeeees"

"It's about the race on Sunday"

"Yeeeees" Mrs Cunliffe answered the stranger on the other end of her telephone, without even thinking.

"Well the thing is lo" Rose stopped herself from calling Mrs Cunliffe 'love' "Mrs Cunliffe, my son is

 Ernest Bradshaw, and I think he will benefit from a bit of support on Sunday"

 "Ohhhh!" That broke the ice, and the two women spoke mother to mother on the telephone about their sons, resulting in Christopher's appearance at the Manchester and District Time Trial Association Autumn race this Sunday, appearing, but on the sidelines. Janet, however, was not present. After the lengthy telephone conversation with Mrs Cunliffe, Rose had run out of silver to put in the telephone box and had not contacted the Dootson household. Christopher stayed on the sidelines and kept watch. Christopher had his bicycle with him, along with a huge chip on his shoulder. He had a speech prepared about Ernest, breaking his heart and therefore causing an injury. But the lack of Janet, present in the crowd made him say something else.

"No Janet? Where's Janet? I thought she'd be cheering Ernest on!"

"She's not here, remember the to-do with Garth... Mr Pratt" Brenda Towers suddenly adopted hushed tones "She can't compete unless it's an all girl's race, and she didn't want to come and stand in the crowd. Said her mother does women's circle or something, so she was making fairy cakes or something. Why?"

Christopher did not answer her, the thought of Janet making fairy cakes rendered her ever more endearing to Christopher.

"Anyway Christopher, you've missed Ernest setting off! He won't know you're here! I thought you and him were big mates, time trialling is a solitary sport you know, makes all the difference

to have someone shouting you along!" Brian
Towers chipped in, without asking his wife's
permission to speak.
"Yes Christopher, don't be selfish, lad, just
because you didn't get the chance to ride today,
you've had many a time at the junior races. It's all
about Ernest today" Brenda told Christopher off.
And that did it. *All about Ernest today!*
Christopher hopped on his bicycle and rode off at
the side of the race route, and without telling the
Towers' where he was going.
" 'appen he's gone the short way to the finish, to
cheer Ernest on, we should be making a move
too, Brenda"
"Hold your horses, Brian I'm just finishing this
sweet tea"
"Just pour it back in the flask"
"Don't be disgusting, Brian! When Ernest finishes
his race, he won't want sweet tea and saliva,
slops from the flask? Don't be disgusting!"
Brian wished he had never spoken, the draining
of Brenda's orange plastic cup and the arrival at
the finish line were taking too long. What if his
protégé, Ernest got there before him? Cameras
would flash, Garth Pratt would probably fling his
arm around Ernest and get his picture in the
paper instead of Brian, whilst Brenda, his wife
who also loved cycling had been busy supping
her tea and examining her cagoule string. It would
be a different story if Janet was there!
"Come on Brian!" Brenda had placed herself in
her spot, the back seat of the tandem, they set off
on the shortcut to the finish line of the time trial.
Brenda was speaking into her husband's ear "I
hope that doesn't mean you've been spitting in my

 tea all these years, Brian! You *ARE* disgusting!"
They thought that they were following
Christopher, but when they reached the finish
line, they could not see him.
"Where's he got to?"
"He won't be here yet, Brenda it's not been an
hour"
"I meant Christopher! Not Ernest!"
"By the 'eck!" Brian clutched on to Brenda's
cagoule sleeve, taking some of her skin with him
"It's Ernest! He's got the hour!" Brian let go, and
ran towards the finish line, almost pushing other
cycling folk and families out of the way. He rushed
towards Ernest, who was now off his bike, being
congratulated by the timekeeper, and the time
trial officials. Brian felt a female pair of fingers on
the nook of his inner elbow holding him back. He
thought it was Brenda, and turned around to
prevent his wife from pushing him out of the way,
only to be met face to face with a woman in a
tweed coat and fake fur collar, and matching hat.
"Sorry love! I'm trying to get through so I can see
my boy. Ernest! Ernest!"
"Mum! Mum! I didn't know if you could make it!"
Brian's advance towards Ernest was thwarted by
the advance of Ernest's family. Uncle Norman had
driven them in their Morris Cowley car. Brian's
view was blocked by an older man, who appeared
to be ignoring him
"Excuse me!"
Where was Brenda, his bossy wife when he
needed her? Brian tapped the man on the
shoulder, who turned around and said
"WRRR"

Brian stood back, shocked. Ernest's family were laughing at Brian, and Ernest pushed his way through.

"Mr Towers, this is my Uncle Billy, he can't say much. Err he can't say anything"

"Norman Schofield, I'm Ernest's other uncle" Uncle Norman pushed in front of Ernest, shaking Brian's hand and nearly dislocating his shoulder.

"Err you've met me Mother, err Mrs Bradshaw"

"It's Rose, and this is my sister, Marigold"

"Mrs Schofield" Auntie Marigold nodded, knowingly at Brian, just as his wife Brenda came into view.

All of this introduction and explanation had stolen Ernest's moment, the moment he had been waiting for, a result! Getting the hour, making his mark, before it was too late. Ernest had done it! The time trial impossibility! Twenty-five miles in less than an hour! Ernest Bradshaw the junior East Lancashire international cycling club junior rider!

"Well done Ernest" Brenda enthused.

"Yes, well-done lad! You're a smasher, told you didn't I told you you'd do it! Didn't I? " Brian Towers was caught up with the adrenalin and excitement. Ernest was speechless and shaking, Brenda Towers had failed to supply him with his usual sweet tea after a race.

"Well done Ernest, my little soldier! What did I tell you? Well done! Oooooh!" Rose squeezed her son, who was too exhausted to push her away.

"Twenty-five miles in less than the hour!"

"I've no idea what that means, but well done," said Uncle Norman.

"WRRRRRPpppp" Said Uncle Billy, hugging

Ernest and squeezing the last bit of breath out of him. They did not understand the significance of Ernest's achievement but why would they? They were not cycling folk like the Towers' were. Christopher stepped forward, beholding in his rubber helmet. Ernest gushed with the pleasure of seeing him, his friend Christopher who had been strange towards him in the past few weeks. He reached out to embrace Christopher, who just put his right hand out to shake Ernest's hand.

"Well done," He said almost begrudgingly.

Brenda Towers clutched her husband in the crook of his elbow, Brian wished people would stop doing that! In hushed tones she said:

"Brian, I need to speak with you about something, urgent, like!"

Chapter 33: Ernest The Accused

"On the bend near the Three Arrows, he reckons he saw it"

"Well, that doesn't mean bloody anything! Why can't you just be happy for me? I mean for Ernest!" Brian was finding it difficult to understand why Brenda was not rejoicing in Ernest's unbelievable achievement. Unbelievable, that word was hanging in the air.

"I hope this is not because it was Ernest, not Janet!" said Brian.

"No! What's that supposed to mean! No. Listen"

Brenda Towers slammed her forearms on the kitchen table. Brian was in trouble. Deep trouble. "Listen, we know Christopher is trustworthy, and he said he saw that yellow scooter hanging around the bend at the Three Arrows pub. On the same day, that Ernest managed to do the unbelievable. Twenty-five miles in less than an hour"

"Well, that doesn't mean owt, what are you trying to say?" Brian flabbergasted at his wife.

"It is probable, possible that the yellow scooter picked Ernest up somehow and dropped him off half a mile down the road, improving his time to ... Less than an hour!"

"Don't be ridiculous! How on earth can a yellow scooter pick up a teenage boy, and a bicycle... besides, Ernest is nearly fully grown! And escort him half a mile down the road!" Brian defended himself against his wife's powerful assertions.

"He thinks he's seen it before" Brenda put her case forward.

"Who? What?" Brian hated it when Brenda spoke in 'he's' and 'it's' especially when she had a blazing scowl on her face.

"Yes, he's not sure, Christopher that is but he thinks he saw, he had a flashback. That yellow scooter was involved with his accident" the end of Brenda's sentence was whispered, which Brian hated.

"I think I'm going to have to report it to the British Cycling Federation," Brenda said out of the corner of her mouth, and now it was her turn to be in deep trouble with her husband, as Brian slammed his forearms on the kitchen table.

"You keep them... I mean Garth Pratt might get to

know about it!" Brian was away, not listening to Brenda, who was concerned that it should be them, Mr and Mrs Towers that consulted with the officials, not Christopher Cunliffe, who was threatening to report his friend Ernest, for cheating getting a lift, being towed by; the horror of all horrors: a motorised scooter! And for causing an injury breaking his heart. Of course, Brenda Towers did not know about the latter complaint, and that is why she believed Christopher's story about the yellow scooter, why wouldn't she? In her eyes, Christopher had no beef with Ernest.

Later that same day, when the actual yellow scooter had been tucked up away under an easy rain apron, Mrs Cooley was as silent as her husband's two-wheeled friend. The ride Mr Cooley had been on this morning had been the longest he had been absent on a Sunday.
It was late Sunday afternoon now. Mrs Cooley looked at the newspapers folded and unfolded on the glass-topped table. The twins were safely carolled in their playpen. She unfolded one of the newspapers and found the horoscopes. Mrs Cooley is a Pisces, much the same as Christopher Cunliffe.
Pisces: Sunday, October 7th, 1962
"Be careful Pisces, someone who previously appeared trustworthy will be accused of cheating today. A good day for needlecraft and catching up on correspondence "
Should that have read 'appeared previously' or does 'previously appeared' make sense? And

cheating is a funny word. Cheating at what? The crossword? Oh! It suddenly hit her. Mrs Cooley's husband, Mr Cooley had been cheating this morning by shunning his fatherly duties and spending too much time looking for newspapers. Or maybe the newspapers were a cover. Maybe that was why there were so many of them. Folded and unfolded to make it look as if they had been read, and then re-read. Mrs Cooley would test Mr Cooley when he came downstairs after his trip to the toilet. Why hadn't he taken one of the newspapers upstairs with him? And then there was a knock at the door.

"Hello love, is your husband at home?" A man with a bicycle said.

"Err yes, err could you wait here please, he's just upstairs, and I don't want to " Mrs Cooley looked over at the twins who appeared to be poking each other in the eyes and then giggling. The man, she could see out of the corner of her eye was now putting one foot into the door, leaning his bicycle against the front half window. Surely not! How rude! This is a cul-de-sac! When one of the twins started crying, Mr Cooley appeared behind her like a hero. "Can I help you?" Mr Cooley did not mean to shoo his wife away as such, but she was, on this occasion grateful for her husband's officious nature. "Garth Pratt, Manchester and District Time Trial Association" Garth held out his hand by way of introduction, Mr Cooley frowned and put his head on one side by way of blank dismissal. Garth retracted his un-shook hand and stood up straighter. Although he could not match Mr Cooley's stature, filled with his own self-importance, Garth got straight to the point. "Own a yellow Vespa?"

Mr Cooley's eyes flicked to the side at his two-wheeled motorised friend, giving it away under its rain apron.

"What is this?" Mr Cooley did something he had never done before and shut the frosted glass door behind him.

"I'm just trying to investigate an accusation of race cheating"

"What is this? Are you the police? What did you say? Cheating?"

"See the time trial bicycle race this morning?"

"Yes"

"Who were you supporting?"

"What? ... Pardon?"

"Which young lad had you come to watch ride? Do this often do you? We start at a conspicuous time to avoid traffic, so who were you watching?"

"No one! What are you accusing me of? I only wanted to go and get a newspaper!" Mr Cooley momentarily opened the front door thus indicating proof, that he had indeed been out shopping for several newspapers. Mr Cooley was met by one of the twins toddling towards the front door with a face full of mucus, swiftly scooped up by Mrs Cooley.

"Right, but you were there, you were seen... Do you know Ernest Bradshaw?"

Mr Cooley's face did indicate that he did indeed know Ernest Bradshaw, one of his pupils. Mr Cooley never forgot a pupil.

"No! I do not, you haven't even answered what this is about!"

"Look" Garth Pratt put his clipboard under his arms, and held out his arms and hands in front of him in the universal gesture of peace and patronisation "This afternoon, I've had a complaint about one of our junior riders. He has been accused of getting a 'lift' from a man driving a yellow Vespa, such as yours" Garth nodded at the accused scooter, under the rain apron. Mr Cooley bristled "And I just need to clear things up, that's what I've come about you see"

"Hold on" Mr Cooley put his right hand out in front of him, in the universal gesture of quieting the accuser "What time was the race?"

"Well. We started the first one off at the crack of dawn, prompt, time trialling is strictly one minute start time apa...." Garth's voice trailed off due to Mr Cooley's interruption

"When did you get this complaint then? Hmm?" Mr Cooley adopted the blank dismissal, using his strength not to ask Garth to call him 'sir'

"Oh, straight away, the lad who made the complaint cycled straight round and knocked on my door! I got a shock, actually. He said he had told his club leader, but it seemed to him they weren't going to do anything about that, and I can believe it of the Towers, trust me" Garth nodded at Mr Cooley, thus adopting him on his side.

"Hold on, you say the complaint was from a lad? Not a responsible adult?" Mr Cooley's teaching experience raised his suspicions further.

"Well yes, but like I say I couldn't trust Brian Towers to stick to the rules, and as for his wife.."

"You're a bit quick off the mark aren't you? Couldn't you wait?"

"Well the Manchester Evening News want the

times in first thing, or they won't print them, and if one's been disqualified... I can't put my name to it" Garth revealed his true intention "So did you do it then, or not?"

The door was shut in Garth's face. He cycled off awkwardly, with his clipboard under his arm. Mrs Cooley watched him as he disappeared, with one twin in her arms.

"What was all that about?"

"Oh, some nincompoop with a bee in his bonnet. Said I gave one of the lads from school a lift on my scooter, so he could win a bike race! Ridiculous! It's not physically possible! He liked the sound of his own voice, though, I can't see why a man would be like that... after one cause, like a dog with a bone!" Mr Cooley shook out one of the newspapers to read again, this week's article about threatened nuclear war, the one cause that was under his bonnet.

Mrs Cooley did something that she hadn't done since before the twins were born. It might have been the word 'nincompoop' it might have been the realisation that her husband could see in other men, what he could not see in himself, but most likely her horoscope had come true. Her husband had been accused of cheating, Mrs Cooley started laughing. She laughed long and loud at her husband, who of course put this silliness down to hormones and sleep deprivation.

The following week, when time trial officials had come to their senses, Rose Bradshaw saw her son's name in the newspaper. Her eyes filled with tears; tears of joy. It was inexplicable, her eyes were drawn to the familiar outline of the letters that made up the words. The name 'ERNEST BRADSHAW' on the newspaper page in front of her, as if they were the only letters on the page. Her Ernest! His rightful place in the paper, with no knowledge of the unfounded accusations of cheating.

"Ernest is in the cycling news! I've memorised it, listen! 'Ernest Bradshaw, twenty-five miles in under the hour!"

"Oh! What does that mean!"

"I've no idea! But it's wonderful isn't it!" Rose was beaming, her hair had trailed down a little at the side, her face was red, her eyes were blue, what was most attractive was that she had allowed Mr Potts into a little of her private life. Rose had a thought, she was about to say something else to Mr Potts, but changed her tune when she caught a glimpse of Cynthia Crosby. She could not ask Mr Potts not to say anything, maybe if she changed the subject, then Mr Potts would forget about it, and not mention Ernest's fame in black and white.

Please do not say anything to Mrs Crosby! Please! Rose was caught on the hop. The pressure was on. Cynthia Crosby was edging nearer and nearer. Rose need not have worried, it was Mr Potts who had to avoid all confrontation.

"Everything alright love?" Cynthia Crosby, having decided that there were no alternative job opportunities for her turned up at Potts' Greens as though nothing had happened.

"What are you doing here?"

"Mopping!"

"What! Can't you remember what happened last

week?" Said Mr Potts, the boss of Potts' Greens in name only.

"Ha! I've slept since then, cock! I've been here all week! Tell me another!" Cynthia Crosby made her way to the back storage area for her morning cigarette. She had walked to work and needed a break now that she had arrived.

"What's that you're reading Rose? Oh The paper, well some of us have got work to do no time for reading newspapers!"

Rose could not win, she folded the newspaper up to protect Ernest from the potential bullying of the Crosby family. Cecil Potts could not win. He had sacked Cynthia Crosby the previous week and here she was, refusing to accept it. Still, no one really got sacked in 1962.

Later that same day, when bullying in the workplace and Cynthia's P45 had been swept away, Ernest returned home from school. He could tell that Uncle Billy was pleased to see him, he was at the window waving the local newspaper at Ernest.

"Hello, Uncle!" Ernest waved, and walked past Uncle Billy.

"WRRR" Uncle Billy was trying to explain to Ernest that his name was in the paper. He jumped up and down and did a sort of dance trying to prevent Ernest from sitting down, going upstairs, or do anything other than look at the newspaper. Ernest was getting quite irritated at Uncle Billy, he had just come home from school, and was free because tonight was not a delivery night. He just wanted to get changed so that he could go straight out on his bike after tea. Uncle Billy was still blocking Ernest's way. He had seen Rose pointing and gesticulating at the cycling report in the local news, and he knew it was of the utmost importance to tell Ernest this news.

Ernest just needed the loo, and to get changed for his next bike ride. Wednesday night was the club run night.

"WRRR" Uncle Billy protested.

"Oh, what is it?" Ernest almost snatched the paper out of his uncle's hand and glanced at the cycling news. He had seen
this before and was taking his talent for granted. It did not excite him in the same
way it had his mother that same morning. Ernest folded the newspaper back over, he was on to his next race now. Uncle Billy, however,
 had been tasked by Rose to do just one job on that day, and that was to tell Ernest that he was in the paper. Ernest, unfortunately, did not
seem bothered. Taking his talent for granted,
 he dismissed his poor uncle, who watched him disappear on his green Viking bicycle.

"Hello!" Ernest hopped off his bike, the huddle of riders belonging to the East Lancashire International Cycling Club fell silent. After growing up with Uncle Billy, Ernest was trained in body language, which he read as follows :

Mrs Towers flickered her eyes, put her lips together and sympathetically put her head on one side.

Christopher Cunliffe's face turned bright red, ashamedly hid his face inside his scarf.

Paranoid Percy, having sold his best bicycle to
Ernest some months ago but had not been
recalled to the army, spat on the floor and turned
his back in disgust on Ernest. Colin Sidebottom
appeared to be in agreement with Paranoid
Percy. Mr Towers moved his hands from his hips,
folded his arms, and blew out a huge puff
of questions. He then put his lips together,
pushed his way through the others in order to
embrace Ernest.

Janet was missing again from the club. Ernest did
not usually notice Janet. Why would he? She has
now been assigned to race with the girls, but she
was coming up behind him.

"Sorry, I'm late!" She hopped off her bike, as a
loner, she had not adopted the full knowledge of
body language, everyone was silent "Are we
all alright then?!" She said chirpily.

The silence was broken. Percy and Colin were
shaking their heads and muttering to each
other. Christopher hid his deeper reddened
face further. Mr Brian Towers was about to
 speak in public without asking his wife.

"Ernest... There's something ... There's something
I need to ask you, to tell.." Brian was pushed
away at the inner elbow by Brenda

"Hello, Janet love, Ernest there's something I
need to talk to you about" Brenda's voice lowered
towards the end of the sentence.

It was now Ernest's turn to be ushered away by
the elbow, observed carefully by Janet.

"What's that about?"

This was the first time that Janet had
spoken to Christopher and Christopher

alone. But unfortunately, she was asking about Ernest, who had been pulled to one side, most probably yes definitely about Christopher's accusation that he is cheating. This was the first time that Janet had spoken to Christopher and Christopher alone. And would probably be the last time she would want to when she finds out "What's that about?" Janet nudged Christopher. Christopher's heart was in his mouth.
"Erm!"
"I'll tell you what that's about" Paranoid Percy interjected, "The golden boy Ernest has been caught cheating!"
Christopher relieved, he was off the hook, Paranoid Percy had not mentioned that Christopher was the tell-tale.
"What!" Janet found it hard to believe anything bad of Ernest, and she was not sure she cared for Percy's tone. Golden boy? Who did he think he was?
"Seen, would you believe it? Seen, getting a lift off some bloke on a yellow scooter, of all things!" Percy almost spat the words 'motorised scooter' Christopher cringed, willing his rubber helmet to melt over his entire self and hide him from view. The problem was, he had not actually *seen* Ernest getting a lift from the yellow scooter, the story was getting exaggerated from the Towers to Paranoid Percy and Colin Sidebottom. Ernest, the accused was now in discussion with Mr and Mrs Towers, on the other side of the fence.
"I don't believe it, no! I don't, don't be ridiculous, even I know that a scooter cannot give a person, an Ernest a lift!" Janet could not fathom why the

club members would believe this of Ernest, most likely they were jealous. And who would say such a thing? It was as if Paranoid Percy was reading her thoughts.

"It was Christopher of course who spotted it!" Percy said.

And then it happened. Janet looked at Christopher and Christopher alone. Her mouth opened, her freckles lost in a crinkled adored button nose.

"Anyhow, they're coming back now, I want to get a bloody ride in! Sorry, Janet didn't mean to swear in front of you" Colin Sidebottom rescued

Christopher, whose life had fallen apart right then when his report of Ernest's perceived wrong doing backfired spectacularly. Janet now knew who Christopher was. A blaming telltale.

Mr and Mrs Towers could be heard having an argument under their collective breath. Ernest was walking behind, head held low.

"Look, if he says he didn't do it, then he didn't"

"Well, why would Christopher lie? "

"Brenda. I'm putting my foot down! If he says he didn't do it, he didn't!"

"Shh!"

The Towers resumed their normal voices.

"Hello, let's start our club run, we're a bit thin on the ground tonight" Brian pushed off on his racer bike, Brenda set off last divided from Brian, not on their tandem tonight. Janet, Colin and Percy in solitary silence. Ernest too. Christopher tried to get his attention.

"Ernest! Ernest"

But Ernest was deaf to Christopher's plea. He

wasn't even ignoring Christopher, he just wasn't listening. Up and down, round and round the wheels of his green Viking's revolutions carried him. Ernest had turned up to tonight's club run, exuberant in his own success, name in the paper. Oh, sadness and guilt hit him, he had shunned away his uncle and felt shame. Is this why this had happened? Why had Christopher said this? He had not even noticed Christopher on that Sunday morning. The guilt, the shame. Had his friend Christopher turned up especially to see him? Had he? Up and down, round and round. Ernest remembered that he had visited Christopher, to ask him to come that Sunday, he had to go round especially. Up and down, round and round. Surely not? Was Christopher just as bad as Mark Crosby and his cronies? Up and down round and round. Ernest was at the end of the club ride. He did not even stop for Brenda Towers' sweet lukewarm tea.

He cycled home, Ernest the accused; his mother had been right. The world was about to end.

Rusty the Red Setter was buried in Auntie Marigold and Uncle Norman's back garden, on a Friday evening in October. It was the last Friday before the clocks change. Ernest did not pay attention in school that day, remembering back to how the clocks had changed all the way back in March when he had just realised that his destiny was to become a trophy carrying cyclist. How things had changed since then, how things were different since the yellow scooter scandal.

Rusty was not a religious dog, and so Father

Dunn was not required to send him to his resting
place. Ernest had a reason to complete his
delivery round in double quick time, no time for
Mrs Smith's nonsense, he had Rusty's funeral to
get to. He hoped that Rusty's doggy heaven
included plenty of furniture and furnishings in a
wipe clean damask, for Rusty to jump on with his
heavenly red, muddy paws.
Uncle Norman fiddled about in the shed. As they
had to wait for Ernest to finish his rounds, it was
now getting dark. The sky was turning purple. He
tried to find his spade with the flashing, obnoxious
torchlight.
"Where's me bloody garden hoe, Marigold?!"
The flashing light had made Uncle Norman forget
that the garden hoe had been given to Ernest, on
the day that he found a cycling club
advertisement. On the day that Ernest had walked
with him and Rusty to the Brown Cow pub. And
now it was Rusty's funeral, despite her grief,
Auntie Marigold did not forget to remind Uncle
Norman. Through sniffs, she chastised "Outside
voices, please Norman"
Ernest did not know where to put himself. His
mother and Uncle Billy were looking very sad.
Auntie Marigold was almost inconsolable. Then
Ernest's cousins started to arrive, Thomas and
Richard; the older two, at least. They had been
summoned by Uncle Norman, for Auntie
Marigold's sake.
Up and down, up and down the spade went. Over
Uncle Norman's shoulder part of the garden.
Despite her grief, Auntie Marigold did not forget to
remind Uncle Norman about the roses. And in

their ignorance, neither of Ernest's grown up cousins offered to help Uncle Norman bury poor Rusty.

The world was about to end. Christopher had betrayed Ernest. Rusty was dead. Ernest was the accused.

Chapter 34: Stuck between two worlds and one of them is about to blow up.

October 26th '*Soviet Premier Nikita Khrushchev proposes removing Soviet missiles if President Kennedy publicly announces U.S. would never invade Cuba'*

"That's enough of that thank you!" Rose snapped off the radio and put on her hat in one swift move. She went to leave but noticed Ernest's bikes propped up against the wall.

"I thought Ernest said he was leaving?"

Uncle Billy could not hear Rose but shrugged at his niece... But Ernest had already set off for the day.

"Bradders!" Shouted Mark Crosby, he was everywhere "Where's your bike?"

"I didn't feel like riding it to school today, thought I'd get stuck in, start thinking about getting a job"

"I'm leaving this old place as soon as I can. I think I'm goin' in for plumbing, Bradders. Sorting out old ladies pipes, that sort of thing..." Mark Crosby had a way of delivering everything crudely.

"Plumbing? My Uncle Norman said it's all about building these days plenty of new builds going up"

"Uncle? I thought he was deaf?"

"No that's Uncle Billy. He didn't say anything, he can't speak. He used to be a carpenter's assistant. Hey! Maybe it runs in the family, I might go in for that then!"

"It's like brass monkeys out here!" Mark Crosby said, blowing into his hands as the two boys approached school on foot.

"That reminds me" Crosby reached into his inside blazer pocket and pulled out a pair of grey recognisable gloves "A bit fairy like to wear woollens, but I don't want to get frostbite eh Bradders?"

Ernest could clearly see the initials 'E.B.' sewn on the cuffs of Mark's gloves. They were his gloves, not Mark Crosby's. Maybe it was the walk rather than the bike ride, but Ernest was freezing! "Don't look at me like that Bradders! Ok, tell you what, I'll let you borrow them!" Mark Crosby took Ernest's gloves off and handed them back to him, shaking his head in mock disbelief. The sky clouded over as two identical figures appeared over the bump in the road. Mark Crosby winked and nudged Ernest. "At least these two's birthdays aren't until the end of the year, and they can't leave school like what you and me can! Gawd knows what they'll do for a living! Is there a circus in town? Eh, Bradders?" Mark Crosby chuckled at his own joke.

One Benson twin pinched the other's school bag, but tripped over a kerb and fell flat on his face. "Dear oh dear" Mark Crosby shook his head and signalled to the front door of the school. Ernest noticed it first. A yellow Vespa parked in the school car park. Mr Cooley must be back!

Mr Michael Cooley had returned to Ernest's high school, no questions asked but to perform light duties. His job today was to interview all the fifth formers whose birthdays were before a certain date to identify a career path for them.
Mr Byrnes had instructed Mr Cooley on the use of a newfangled flow chart, which could then easily be correlated with a local apprenticeship directory. This was secondary modern school... it really was.
The pupils lined up alphabetically. Ernest Bradshaw would see Mr Cooley before Mark Crosby.
"Wait for me!" He had said.
Inside Mr Cooley's office, Ernest sat opposite his favourite teacher once again. The room smelt even mustier, Mr Cooley's stubble had started to develop into a beard. His shirt was untucked. Some of the books on the shelf and a photograph frame had been wrapped in tin foil. Mr Cooley was positioning bits of paper in rows, that would not stick to his desk and fluttered about every time one of them breathed. "When is someone going to invent a solution to this?!" He said to himself, and out loud at the same time.
"Are you alright Mr Cooley?" Ernest innocently asked. Mr Cooley's ears pricked up. It was his first day back on the job. He had not seen Mrs Ogle yet, the teacher who had complained that his mind was not on it, but it was certainly not the school children's business to ask...
"Erm ... we're not here to talk about me, we're here to talk about you... erm Ernest Bradshaw"
 Mr Cooley ruffled his papers, and found the first

name on his list "Right, what we're going to do is look at your results from your last few papers, and put them together with... with erm whatever suggestions you have about your future. I want to know about your ambitions, and then we can see what we can put together. See if we can make a career out of it"

Ernest sniffed. There was a lot of dust in Mr Cooley's office.

"Well"

"Well, what's your erm yes you live with your mother don't you"

"Yes and Uncle Billy, why?"

Mr Cooley ignored him.

"Hmmm says your best subject is physics here. And you are punctual. And you've never been in trouble, apart from one..." Mr Cooley looked at his own unfinished sentence in his own unhinged handwriting "You've never been in trouble. Right. Any ambitions lad?"

Ernest sighed a deep sigh, breathing in dust that caught in his throat. He started coughing. Another sharp intake of breath in a dusty room made him splutter. His words were stuck in his throat. Mr Cooley panicked. Papers fluttered, human giraffe limbs flung themselves onto Ernest's side of the teacher's desk. Mr Cooley searched his teacher's mind to remember first aid, he thought about slapping Ernest on the back, but Ernest had helped himself to a glass or water which was resting on the table.

"Are you alright lad?"

Embarrassed at stealing a teacher's drink, but with plenty to say about his spoilt ambition, Ernest answered "Yes thank you err ambitions, well err I like cyc- err chemistry sir" "Right, let's have a look. Good at physics, hard working... let's have a look.." With paper's fluttering, and apprenticeship directory thumbing Mr Cooley drew his conclusions about Ernest's future "Right.. here we are... coming right up... Ernest Bradshaw... you're going to be an electrician!"

Ernest waited around for Mark Crosby to have an identical conversation with Mr Cooley, although he was neither good at physics, or trouble free. "I'm going to be a sparky, Bradders!" He boomed excitedly, waving an identical slip of paper with an identical instruction to contact the same electrician's firm to inquire regarding an apprenticeship. Life is not meant to be fair, success is not possible without a certain amount of hard work and determination. Ernest Bradshaw and Mark Crosby were about to embark on an electrician apprenticeship together. The world was about to end because Mark Crosby was about to blow them both up with dodgy wiring. Ernest would be without his teammate, Christopher, without his two-wheeled friend the green Viking. Without being able to follow his Uncle Norman's advice about getting into the building trade. Without going in for the Tour de France, or the Great British Olympic cycling team. In that school corridor that smelled of vomit and sawdust, Ernest wondered when the Russians were coming.

Later that day, when hopes and dreams had been washed away, Ernest caught his mother singing Edith Piaf songs to Uncle Billy.

Billy could not hear of course, and perhaps it was just as well. Rose Bradshaw's impression of Edith Piaf would have provoked a different kind of response, had Billy not been deaf. She held both his hands, and he copied her hands, waving in time to the music. Both Rose and Billy put the palm of their hands dramatically, in the centre of their chests, their eyes half closed. And when the performance was over, Billy laughed and clapped and said the only sound he could get his mouth to form, in muffled tones "WRRR". Ernest's mother had always insisted that when Billy was a child, attempts to teach him sign language had failed; 'who needs sign language when you've got singing?'
 "Mr Cooley says I'm going to be an electrician" Ernest shattered the jubilation.
"A sparky! Well, there's nowt wrong with that I suppose" Rose turned the record player off, its automatic arm saluted goodbye. "What's up, Ernest? You'll still be able to ride your bike won't you?"
His bicycles... The Hercules Low Gravity carrier would, of course, be returning to Mr Potts. Waiting for another sucker to deliver to Lever Brew, although there had been rumours of tarmac, so Ernest would not be needed anyway. Things were changing. The Tour de France, the Milk race, the Great British Olympic cycling team were becoming a childish fantasy to

grown up Ernest. If only Mr Cooley had sprung this intrusive interview on him about the rest of his life *before* Sunday. If Ernest could not talk to God, could not talk to anyone associated with cycling, and could not talk to Mother or Uncle Billy, then the next best thing would have to be Uncle Norman.

It was the first time that Ernest had taken the green Viking racer out for a spin since the scooter accusation incident. He knew he was in the clear because his time had appeared in the newspaper, taunting him in printer's ink, here is your record, the challenge being cycle faster next time. Garth Pratt had been unable to prove the accusation.

Article 7. Rule 2: Where an individual or club is alleged to have infringed the regulations for the conduct of Time Trials, an enquiry will be held within 72 hours. Any disqualification or reprimand must be put in writing within 14 days.

So there it was, Ernest had been accused but received a letter informing him he was in the clear. He had never been so insulted in all his fifteen years. He wanted to tell the world that he would never cheat. His good name had been tarnished, though, but all he could do was sit tight, time would heal his wound. Or would it? The way Ernest saw it, he had two roads to go down now. He could give up cycling, give up his dreams, go in for an apprenticeship and risk getting electrocuted by Mark Crosby, risk even becoming Mark Crosby's best friend. Or he could carry on cycling, and the only way he could really and truly prove his innocence would be to carry on winning. He needed advice. Uncle Norman would have to do.

Ernest rang the doorbell. Without the accompanying barking, Ernest felt the need to check he was at the right house. His mother accepted visitors at the back door, but not Auntie Marigold, she would only answer the front door. And here she was on the porch, in the same black funeral dress, not in a good way.

"Ernest, love what's the matter? It's so sad, isn't it? So very, very sad"

"What is?" Ernest said alarmed. Had Uncle Norman found something out in his broadsheet newspaper? Had America started blowing Cuba up?

"Oh! You're just like your Uncle! He's gone to see a man about a dog, well he's gone to the pub anyway"

"Oh Rusty, yeah I still miss him. Auntie Marigold, I'd come to ask Uncle Norman for a job"

"Oh!" Auntie Marigold had no say over what happened at Uncle Norman's business. If she was honest, she did not even know what her husband actually did. Two of her grown up sons worked there, but they had nothing to do with the heavy manual work load. And there was only so much room for executive type manoeuvring, in the offices. That is why only two of her sons had been employed.

"I thought you were going to cycle for a living?"

"It's not a proper job, Auntie. Anyway, there's been a fall out in the club"

"A fallout?"

1962

"Yes, a fall out"

Those words hung in the air like a nuclear aftermath.

"Please can you tell Uncle Norman I called, only Mr Cooley said that I've got to sign up for an electrician apprenticeship, but Uncle Norman told me to go in for building, but then I thought, he could just give me a job at his works" Ernest got back on his bicycle and turned away from the awkward doorstep conversation with his auntie.

Auntie Marigold scrambled around her porch for a pen to write down Ernest's message, her three boys had all been to the grammar school she reminded herself.

Four doors down from Auntie Marigold and Uncle Norman's, a bobble hat concealed mousy brown hair, and an anorak encapsulated a thudding heart.

"Ernest"   She   shouted.

"Oh, Hellow Janet" Ernest stopped his bicycle and mounted   the   pavement   near   Janet's   drive.

"Why did you not come on the club run the other day?"

Ernest replied with a lot of hot air that sounded like "Ohh eww.. y'know!"

"Ernest! I hope you have not been put off by that silly scooter business! *No one* could possibly think that a scooter could have given you a lift! It was just jealousy, Ernest! They all wanted to get the hour, and you actually did it"

"Yeah, but I was accused of *cheating*. Have you not read the 'Rules and Regulations of Time Trialling'?" Ernest despaired of Janet sometimes. It was the first time he had spoken to Janet and Janet alone. Teenage girls

sometimes get over excited. Especially if they have some new and exciting information they can share with someone they view as less intelligent than themselves. That's how it worked. Even more so if this less intelligent person is a *boy.*
Her eyes widened, her fingers splayed out, and her hand flew up and down.
"Wait there, Ernest! Wait there! I've got something to show you that I read in the newspaper!" Janet ran back inside, leaving Ernest stood outside one of the posh houses on Brandlesholme Road for the second time that evening. Janet's heart was pumping, the newspaper article had been there, but then it *just was not!*
"Who are you talking to out there sweetheart?" Her mother asked, whilst scrunching up newspaper pages to keep her suede effect boot's shape.
"The newspaper!" Janet grabbed it, and returned to Ernest, followed by her nosy mother.
"Oh... Do you want to invite your... friend in? Are you Mrs Cunliffe's boy?"
"No! Mother, this is Ernest!" Janet said proudly.
"Hellow Mrs," Ernest said.
"Here! Here it is Ernest!" Janet forced the newspaper into Ernest's hands. Under her front door porch light, he read the article about a French cyclist who had refused to be drug tested, thus proving his guilt.
Janet had folded her arms in triumph.
"What's that got to do with me!" Ernest handed back the newspaper.
"Drug taking is proper cheating Ernest! That cyclist is a professional, and besides, you didn't

do anything!"

Ernest thought about it.

"Drug taking, Janet? What's that got to do with you?" Mrs Dootson clasped her hands over Janet's ears.

"Don't fuss Mother! The women's circle can't hear you at our front doorstep! This is about performance enhancing drugs, to make cyclists go faster. Everyone thinks it's cheating and that they should be banned!"

"Well, they ought to be! It's 1962 for goodness sake!"

Janet's mother swished herself back inside.

"Sorry about that Ernest"

"No! She's right! It is cheating! And besides, I didn't do anything!"

"I know Ernest, that's why I'm showing you, even professional French cyclists get accused of cheating, and he hasn't given up!"

"Yeah, it's not just that" Ernest hesitated, it was the first time he had spoken to Janet and Janet alone, a late starter, he did not know how to work girls "Have you seen Christopher recently?"

"He wasn't at the club run either Ernest. Look I don't think he meant to report you, he said he was just following the rules"

"Christopher reported me?"

"Well, he just said what he saw"

"I was just about to tell you that I've ... " Ernest suddenly felt silly, his disappointment made him say something sillier "Well Christopher's not like my friends from school, well I just wanted to tell him that I'm thinking of starting an electrician's apprenticeship with my mate Mark Crosby. He's my new best mate"

"Oh"

"Yes, well goodbye then, Janet, I'm still going in for that Time Trial though that Mr and Mrs Towers have set up. I've already paid my fee!"

Uncle Norman had not been in to ask advice, to find out which road he should go down. Ernest had to make do with his grieving auntie and Janet with her newspapers and opinions. But they had helped him make a decision. Nothing was more important now to Ernest than cycling, he pushed those pedals like he was just in reach of the yellow jersey, the milk trophy, and the gold medal all at once on his way home. It would be every man for himself from now on, even if he was wishing he could tell Christopher.

On this day in 1962, President Kennedy resolved that the U.S. would never invade Cuba. And Janet, who had never spoken to anyone really about Ernest, put her head on her mother's shoulder and told her all about him...

Chapter 35: Harry Hill.

Uncle Norman did not have what a man might call friends. Married to Auntie Marigold for almost all his adult life, he knew all about his
 own faults and flaws. A successful business man, three grown up sons, none of them he
could call his friend. Two of which worked at his factory; they definitely were not his friends. It had been one man and his dog since the end

of the second war for Norman Schofield. Walking Rusty the red setter down to the brown cow, his only escape from Marigold and their lengthy garden in their bay fronted house. Menfolk would flock to the Brown Cow, some of them from their own prefabricated houses were indeed employed by Norman Schofield of 'Schofield and Sons'. This was not a 'works do' this was the quiet supping of pints after a hard day's work; Uncle Norman did not have many friends. That is until a car mechanic moved to the area and started frequenting the same pub. He never stayed long, but long enough for Uncle Norman to bend his ear. It was one man and his bike for Uncle Norman's new friend, not the usual type of chap that Marigold would be alright withNorman befriending, but soon it appeared that everyone wanted to befriend the cycling car mechanic. Especially when they found out he had an Olympic medal.

"How's your lad getting on then with the Towers' club?" Harry Hill said.

"Oh, my nephew?" Norman reached down to stroke the invisible Rusty, a habit he could not shake when starting a new conversation "Aye, I think he is getting on alreet. We went to cheer him the other Sunday, lot of your type there all into their cycling. I drove, of course"

"What time has he got?"

"Time? Let me think, it was twenty-five minutes... no wait it was twenty-five miles... hmm I'll get back to you on that one, Harry" Uncle Norman reached down to the space where Rusty would have been at his ankles as though Rusty could have reminded him of Ernest's times.

"Ha! You want to take more water with it Norm! I don't even drink me, well not much. This pub just happens to be on route home when I'm out cycling, I just wet my whistle, use the facilities and I'm off again"

"Well it's always good to see you, Harry, I see you on your cycle and I think to myself, I think I *do* need to get another dog. It's early days since Rusty left us, but I feel a fool walking about on my own"

"That neighbour of mine, it turned out to be kittens they want rid of not puppies, but I'll keep my eye out" Harry Hill knew everyone "I've got to know Brian Towers and his missus. They seem like they'll set your lad out on the right track"

"Well his mother's on her own so he'll have to make sure he gets a job"

"Ha! Well there's no flippin' war on, he can keep riding, nothing to stop him competing"

"Don't talk to me about war. The newspapers, President Kennedy and these Russians have got my Marigold and her sister in a right flap!"

"Hmm the last war stopped my professional career"

"You've got your own car repair shop?"

"Cycling career I meant! Look tell your Ernest that if he wants to be a professional cyclist, he needs to carry on the way he's going. Do not let anything get in his way. He needs to go all out, enter as many races as he can, and win them of course! Get a good time recorded and make his mark. That's the most important thing, tell him. Make his mark"

And with that, Harry Hill was away, lemonade

drained, and rain cape secured. What did he say? Make his mark? Did he say how? I'll have to remember to tell our Ernest that, I'll write it on a beer mat for him... Uncle Norman tore a piece of cardboard in half to make a note for Ernest... Still, he seems too busy cycling on a Sunday these days. And it's not as if I ever get a word in with Marigold and her sister. That Uncle Billy, he's got the right idea. He cannot hear a word they are saying, and he doesn't speak either.

"Is he talking to himself again?" The landlord of the Brown Cow asked his barmaid.
"Yeah, I think he forgets that his dog has died after a few pints, although his dog could never answer him back either!"
"Time Gents please!" The landlord woke Uncle Norman up; Ernest was never going to get Harry Hill's advice.

Chapter 36: Even Older Potts.

"Aww did you ever meet him, Cynthia?" Rose asked.

"Erm I think so, I can't remember. The likes of me don't have owt to do with the likes of management. Oh, shush! Here he is!" Cynthia Crosby, the lowest paid and most uncouth member of staff at Potts' Greens was unsympathetic to Cecil Potts' loss.

"Oh Mr Potts, you've no need to come to work today! You've just lost your father!"

"I've been awake all night Ros... Mrs Bradshaw. I just thought I would come in and do a bit. Y'know take my mind off things until the funeral. All welcome" Cecil Potts looked over his shoulder at Cynthia Crosby who of course was listening in "Even you, Mrs Crosby"

"Aww I remember when I first started here, I was only a girl" Rose Bradshaw took her mind back, she could not even remember which year it was that she had started work. Everything else had been measured in 'before the war' or 'after the war'.

"And then, of course, he took me under his wing when I had our Ernest. He said, 'don't worry about the baby, your job will still be here when you're ready to come back' ..."

"Ha!" Cynthia Crosby volunteered from behind her mop.

"Any road, it's a sad time Mr Potts, and your father has done well to live so long, what with his weak heart, I thought he was going to die of a broken heart when your mother passed on. Of course, I was in the same boat at the time"

"What d'you mean?"

"Oh, broken hearted. It's nothing, I'm sorry I said anything" Rose excused herself.

"When did your mother die then, Mr Potts?"
Cynthia Crosby could not help herself.
"Oh it would've been erm, well getting on for
fifteen, sixteen years ago now"
"Aww, I remember that year, pregnant with our
Mark I was, same as Rose would've been with her
Ernest!"
"Erm yes, 'appen I'll go home after all. Will you
ask Rose to telephone me at home from the box if
we get a rush on?"
"Will do Potts, I mean, Mr Potts!"
The shop door tinkled on Mr Potts' way out of the
shop.
Telephone if we get a rush on? Even Rose
Bradshaw can't do two things at once... eee,
he'll be asking me to shove a brush up my
backside next news! Cynthia Crosby chatted
away to herself, whilst hiding oranges in the
gap of her tabard.   Potts' Greens closed for the
afternoon, whilst Cecil Potts and all of his
employees attended his father's funeral. It was a
small village, so although this had never
happened before, everyone knew that Cyril Potts,
even older Potts had passed on, and Father Dunn
had agreed to an afternoon funeral on account of
the big morning delivery on the distribution side of
the business.
There was only Mrs Dootson who fell afoul of the
special closing time. Potts' Greens' 'closed' sign
slapped her in the face, after a mad dash to the
high street shops to procure an orange or two.
She had found a recipe in her deluxe recipe card
box for 'speedy orange cake' orange juice and the
rind was needed. Perfect for a surprise visit, she
had thought because someone from the women's

circle had telephoned her earlier. Time for a little run-around, she decided as she tried to think of the next nearest greengrocer... Or maybe I just should not answer the telephone and hide behind the couch?

The Potts' family was tiny. Mrs Potts had died donkey's years ago. Cecil Potts was an only child. But the thirty-six members of staff from Potts' Greens made up for it. Mrs Smith had even managed to make an appearance, standing behind a tree like an unwelcome mistress.

"Come and stand over here with us, love, oh your mascara's smudged, did you know?"

Cynthia Crosby beckoned Mrs Smith over, her tabard visible under her coat. "What? I've no funeral frock!" Cynthia defended.

"How are you feeling now, Mr Potts? Did you manage to have a lie-down?" Rose had to think of something to say.

There were much whispering and nudging amongst the fruit and vegetable staff. They were in the warehouse and market side of the business, where heavy palettes full of potatoes were sorted, packaged and prepared ready for delivery by Potts' delivery vans. Dispatching to other nearby grocery conveniences. The Palette handlers and delivery van drivers all welcome at Mr Potts' funeral, invited by his son, who was now welcome to his business, being the only son and heir.

"I see she's started cosying up to Mr Potts now that his father's dead!" Ron the van

driver said to Ian the palette handler. Over
the years, they had made Rose Bradshaw's life
hell. Especially after Mr Potts had promoted her.
Truth was, they did not like being bossed about
by a woman. As if Rose was ever bossy!
"You two are bigger gossips than I am! Shame on
you, at a funeral!" Cynthia Crosby was able to
listen in to every conversation.
"It was you that told us! Hey look, Ron, Mrs
Smith's on her own over there, now's your
chance!"
The crowd dispersed, and poor Cynthia did not
know who to listen in on next.

Later that same day, when sausage rolls and
salmon mouse had been nibbled away, Mr Potts
senior, Cecil's Father was saying his final
goodbyes, in secret from the other side.

"Come on you daft bugger ask her out!"

There was a scene in the Rose and Crown pub,
where Mr Potts senior's wake had been held, of
Cecil Potts and Rose Bradshaw sat together in a
dusty corner of the pub. Sunlight streamed in
through the window, and fluff and crumbs were
everywhere. Rose had plated up the remains of
the buffet for her boss.
"You've got to eat something" she had said.
"You put it in a box and take it home for your
Ernest and Billy" Cecil had insisted. Of course,
Cynthia Crosby had already seen to it that no
good food was going to waste.
There had been a silence, a pause.
Mr Potts senior had never been so frustrated at

not being able to say his piece.

*"I'm off now son, but think on, I didn't work hard
through two world wars to build that business up
just so that you could squander it away now that
I'm gone. It's not too late to start a family of your
own, Rose Bradshaw is perfect, she's already got
a son, Ernest, it's all ready-made for you, don't be
a fool, she's perfect"*

"You're perfect" Cecil Potts whispered,
interrupting the silence.
"Pardon?"
"Oh, I said I'm just going to settle the bill. Do you
want a lift home, Rose?"
"No, it's fine Mr Potts, I'll get the next bus, I've got
Ernest to sort out. You shouldn't be driving
anyhow you've had too many"
Cecil Potts thought of telling Rose that Ernest was
more than old enough to sort himself out, he had
seen him grow up during 1962 himself. Then he
imagined what his father would say.
"Do you want a lift? Just ask her out!" but his
father was gone.

Mr Potts settled the bill for his father's wake. The
landlord of the Rose and Crown gave him a
discount, of course, because 'high street traders
should stick together'.

Chapter 37: Belief in one's team

"I've always thought of you as a son, Ernest,"
Said Mrs Smith as she carefully placed each item
of her delivery from Mr Potts on her kitchen table.
Ernest, meanwhile was just getting on with his
round, carefully completing each delivery "Why
don't you stay for a cuppa? Hey! how are you
getting on in that Olympic team?"
"Oh! Well, it's not as simple as that, Mrs Smith.
Anyway, I've decided I'm going to get a proper
job when I leave school. I'm going in for an
apprenticeship"
Mrs Smith sat down, and so Ernest sat down too,
just like that, she had persuaded him to keep her
company. There were photographs and
newspaper cuttings scattered on the coffee table
like an empty nest in Autumn.
"Look at this picture, Ernest" Mrs Smith was now
about to show him each and every picture. Oh
well, thought Ernest, I've got time now, I suppose.
Ernest had been slacking with his cycle training
since the business with the yellow scooter. Mrs
Smith carefully put a faded newspaper cutting in
Ernest's hands. The photograph was a proud
groom and wow! A very beautiful young bride, it
was Mrs Smith, thirty something years ago on her
wedding day! She was smiling and crying a bit on
the couch. Ernest flipped the cutting over and he

 saw a black and white photograph of a man he recognised... Wow! It was Harry Hill! An article about his Olympic glory in 1936. *'I'd be nothing without my team mates'* the words spoke to Ernest, all these years later. Ernest was finally getting the advice from Harry Hill, no thanks to Uncle Norman. Mrs Smith was still talking about her dead husband.

"Of course we had girls, all grown up and sodded off now, but I would've liked a son.

Between you and me, Ernest, I wish my girls had been boys!" Mrs Smith whispered the last few words, and Ernest was sure he had heard this story before. Mrs Smith liked nothing better than to talk about her dead husband and her aloof daughters.

"So, I'll be leaving you, Mrs Smith"

"Right you are then Ernest. Cup of tea next time"

"No, I'll be leaving the delivery boy job. Not yet, but eventually I will, in a few weeks or months at the most"

"You're leaving me!"

"Well, I'm getting on an apprenticeship, I'm going to be an electrician. That's if the Russians don't get us"

"What? What Russians? Oh... An electrician you say? Well I've some lamps that want re-wiring if you could Ernest"

"Well I've not started yet, Mrs Smith, still at school for the time being"

Ernest did not know how he got onto the subject of his career choice, maybe it was Mrs Smith asking him about the Olympics or maybe, admitting his choices out loud made it

sound real. He was not one for lying. So if he said
he was going to do it, he would have to do it. Just
like when he said he was going to win a cycling
race. He said he was going to get the hour, and
then he got the hour. But at what cost? Maybe
Ernest was over dramatising things. Maybe he
was growing up.
"I am still going in for that time trial race at the end
of the month though Mrs Smith. I think it starts on
Lumb Carr Road if you wanted to come and
watch. I've already paid me entrance fee"
"Right you are then, lad"
And with that, Ernest was gone.

The sweet-smelling freesias plunged into Rose
Bradshaw's very being as she stepped through
the back door. The washing up had been finished
and put away, the laundry had been folded,
everything was tidy and the back room seemed
empty.
"Ernest? Ernest love! I've come home to sort your
tea out"
"Hallo Mother!" Ernest shouted from upstairs
"Uncle Billy has gone for a lie down"
"Oh, he does that if anything changes, what's all
this anyway?"
"I just felt like buying you some flowers, Mother"
Ernest did not know how he got on to the subject
of flowers. It might have been his new career
path, it might have been Mrs Smith's odd
comments about wishing he was her son, or it
might have been that he was growing up, but
Ernest felt like doing something adult for his
mother. And as Rose Bradshaw watched her son
walk downstairs in the autumn light, the fluff

on his face, his deep voice and filled out
shoulders, she realised that Ernest had grown up.
Her little boy was not a boy. He was a man. A
young man, Mr E Bradshaw of Bolton grown up
and soon to take on the world, take on his own life
 maybe find a wife, and soon he would no longer
be living at home. Rose Bradshaw had given
everything for her son. She had looked after
Uncle Billy, and her own father until he had died.
Rose Bradshaw had spent her life looking after
men, she had even made one herself now, her
own son. And not one of these men was her
husband.

Chapter 38: The East Lancashire International Cycling Club (Maiden) Time Trial Event

Brenda Towers was a woman with ambition,
cycling ambition. Her husband, Brian Towers was
a man with dreams. Road Race dreams.

Founding and forming their own cycling club had
proved a massive commitment.
And along the way, the reason for founding such
a club had fallen by the wayside. Brian had
wanted to get away from the stuck in the mud
members of their previous cycling club and start
 getting into road racing. It was the stuff dreams

are made of. All clubs need ambition, even amateurs can dream of the Tour de France and its multiple stages. Even novices can dream of the Isle of Man cycling festival. And even the Ernest's of this world can dream of the Olympics.

Then of course, along came Brenda and her ambitions. It was 1962, and women simply did not participate in hill climbs or road races. A compromise was met, and despite what had been said, the first event organised and marshalled officially by the East Lancashire International Cycling Club was going to be... A Time Trial.

This meant that Ernest, Christopher and the rest of the club would participate in one leg, and then Janet Dootson, Brenda's project could compete in the women's time trial event, straight after. They had applied to the proper channels, they had organised the race to be at an inconspicuous time, thus avoiding traffic. They had quarrelled about it. Initially, Brenda wanted to stick to the Pilsworth route as Janet had trained around there. "No, Brenda! How about incorporating some of Holcombe Brook to Edenfield?" Brian knew this included some hill work. Ernest was good at hills. "Besides, that way we get to go through Ramsbottom, don't forget about their sport's committee!" "Brian!" Brenda screeched "Bury Sports Week is during the summer! It's October now! We've missed our chance of flirtation with the Ramsbottom sports committee!" Brenda loved being right.

"This year, maybe, Brenda. But if they notice us now, we might get recognition next year!"

"Recognition?" Brenda's tone softened

"Recognition? Next year? 1963?" She had no doubt that 1962 would turn into 1963, the threatened nuclear war was between America and Russia. Brenda had not thought any further than that.

"Yes, Brenda, recognition from the Ramsbottom sports committee. And while we're on the subject, I happen to think the course which turns at Edenfield is very *SPORTY!"* Brian persuaded his wife, who stopped in her tracks.

"Sporty? I like the sound of that. Sporty! That fits in with the East Lancashire International Cycling Club! Sporty!" Brenda loved thinking of new words and ways to describe her club. And Brian loved persuading his wife. Just like that, Brian had got his own way and made Brenda think it was her idea. The event had been advertised in the local and regional press, and by several telephone calls from several telephone boxes to the club leaders around the North West. Even Garth Pratt received a telephone call. They had administered the finer details with receipt books, postal orders and envelopes. Applications had been filed via elastic bands. This was going to be a professional and prestigious event. Brenda had not slept a wink in the run up to it. Brian's bald patch was getting bigger. Ernest had nothing to lose now. He still wanted to win a cycling event before the world blew up, but he had the hour under his belt and a potential electrician's apprenticeship in the real world to look forward to.

"I've told you much and more not to put soup into these flasks!" Brenda Towers was trying to salvage the dusty old hot drink receptacles from the creaky old garden lean to.

"Soup? Soup! I've not a clue what you are talking about woman" Brian said, moments before the lip of a steel flask was shoved under his nose by Brenda.

"Vegetable soup, that's all I can smell. Imagine completing a time trial, only to be given a cup of sweet tea that smells of vegetable soup!"

"They can cater for their own cups of tea! We don't have to quench all thirty-six thirsts!" Brian despaired of Brenda sometimes "More importantly, I think my stopwatch has stopped" Brian shook his time keeper's piece up in his ear "No, nothing"

Brenda despaired of Brian sometimes, and if looks could kill when she whipped the watch out of her husband's hands, well, she would be up for murder.

"You-just-need-to-wind-it-up-you-fool!" Every syllable wound an angry few seconds on to the ancient stopwatch.

"Pass me that newspaper, Brian I want to know the weather report for tomorrow"

"You can't go off what they say in the papers, Brenda"

"Shhh, here we are" Said Brenda as she licked the top of her forefinger and thumb to gain purchase on the newspaper sheets. "Mostly dry at first Sunday, though turning windy in the Northwest with a chance of heavy rain. Further

South largely dry with unseasonal warmth."
"You might as well've sung me a lullaby Brenda,
I've no idea what it's going to be like tomorrow. I
told you. Can't go off what they say in the
papers."
"Oh, how awful! Look at this Brian, some
American, some U.S. Major has been shot down
over Cuba! Oh, I hope this doesn't mean war,
Brian!" Changing her tune, Brenda snuggled up to
Brian.
"They are at war Brenda! It's not a flaming
disagreement!"
"Nope, look says here, calling it the 'Cuban
Missile Crisis' oh" Brenda's eyes could not scan it
quickly enough. Brian took the newspaper off his
wife and folded it away.
"I think we've done enough preparation for today,
so we should go to bed, make sure we're up
bright and early for our first East Lancashire
International Cycling Club Event"
"Club Time Trial, Brian, men's and women's"
Brenda corrected.

Not much later that same day, when fears of
Armageddon had been folded away, Brenda
Towers shot out of bed during a hypnagogic
slumber.
"What if they blow us up tonight? Retaliation for
shooting down that plane? Where's that
stopwatch Brian, I want to work out what time it is
in Russia!"
"Ahhhtishooo!" Said Brian.
"Bless you, but cover your mouth will you, you
dirty dog!" Said Brenda.

Chapter 39: The Cuban Missile Crisis.

"You know what they say about 'know it all's' don't you lads?" Brian Towers came up behind his time trial riders in matching jerseys.

"No?" Christopher was always the first to respond to a rhetorical question.

"Coughs and sneezes spread diseases... And laryngitis!..." Brian's eyebrows and forehead nodded towards his wife.

"Can you hear me?" Brenda rasped. She coughed, the rasping sound of her inflamed tonsils grated on her husband's ears. The sight of Brenda touched Garth Pratt's last nerve. The crowd was loud, a hubbub of riders strutting and performing. Garth's pleas of 'let me through' fell on deaf cycling ears.

"Excuse me! Excuse me, young man!" He finally managed to push his way through "Mrs Towers! Mrs Towers, allow me to err" He stopped a few feet in front of Brenda Towers as though her germs were a visible wall of disgust, and prized the start sheet out of her hands.

"OH NO! Flamin' Garth Pratt, he's not going to start us off, is he? He's saying summat to Brenda! Let me through! Let me through lad!" Brian had felt quite smug when he woke to discover that his wife had a terrible sore throat.

She could hardly speak. What a wonderful life.

But Brian had spoken too soon because now his nemesis was about to take over. Garth Pratt will get where water could not, he thought, too loudly.

"Pardon? Did you say something, Brian?" Garth Pratt passed the start sheet over to Brian as though it was a bubble about to burst. He then batted his hands against one another to get rid of Brenda's germs. There were no congratulations, no 'job well done' Garth Pratt excused himself, and Brian turned around to meet a sea of expectant riders anticipating the Time Trial. The sun had not yet risen, the extra hour in bed had done Brenda no good, and in the dawn, the inconspicuous time, no traffic about, Brian knew this was going to be a success. He just knew that out of these riders, Ernest was going to be the one!

Ernest, aged fifteen, soon to leave school and become an electrician's apprentice was experiencing an altogether new set of emotions. At every event, and most club runs up until recently, his friend Christopher had met him at that same red telephone box, their beacon of ambition. This morning, however, his mother had been the one to wake him, but he was already awake. She made him toast, and a cup of tea but he could not eat anything. The moment he had been waiting for was about to arrive.

"Aren't you coming to watch mother?" He had said, but she had protested it was too cold, the spreading westerly breeze had put her off; "Maybe next time son" She had said. And now Ernest was stood in line with his teammates.

His friendship with Christopher tested, he was
feeling rather awkward. Mr and Mrs Cunliffe had
parked their mini at the bottom of Lumb Carr
Road, it was a spectacle for the gathered crowd
to observe all six foot five of Mr Cunliffe getting
out of the driver's seat.
"It's a bit tight around here isn't it dear?"
Christopher's Father said to Christopher's Mother,
but it was Garth Pratt who answered.
"I don't know what they're playing at! An incline
like this is no starting place for a time trial. It's not
a flamin' hill climb, fancy using the Holcombe
circuit! They should have advertised this as a
mountain climb! Have they not read the
regulations!"
"Mountains? Where? I've not got my stout shoes
on" Christopher's Mother said.
Brenda Towers, of course, opened her mouth to
explain that the race was going to start a bit
further down Bolton Road West, Lumb Carr Road
was just a meeting point, but nothing came out of
Brenda's mouth, her voice was completely lost.
Mrs Cunliffe spotted her son in his rubber helmet,
and waved, he was lined up and ready for the off.
But then it was Brian Towers' turn to speak.
"Thank you all for turning out at this hour for the
first official East Lancashire International Cycling
Club Time Trial. We will be pushing off shortly to
my left onto Bolton Road West, you'll see the
route for those of you that don't know,
through Stubbins, continue through Edenfield,
turn at Rawtenstall and back. The finish is
opposite to the start. We've measured it on a
revolution counter, it's exactly ten miles. Lads...
erm Gents event first, you know the

drill, one minute apart" Brian then addressed each rider individually, reminding them to obey the rules of the road at all times, to keep their head up at all times. Brian put his particularly officious voice on when he spoke to Kenneth McKenzie, Garth Pratt's lad "Any rider who does not comply will be disqualified." Brian wished. As Kenneth McKenzie was now otherwise occupied in the line, Garth Pratt desperately started looking around for an ally, so that he could say what he thought about today's event;

"I know the drill, and that route will have to include a few twists and turns to get ten miles in, and a few inclines! It's not a bloody hill climb! He should've stuck to the flats of the East Lancs Road. Amateurs!" People had started to ignore him, and Garth Pratt was now talking to himself.

"Excuse me," Said a lady wearing a satin scarf "What time are the girls setting off?"

"Oh the ladies event will follow the men's, I saw to that... I believe there are thirty male riders, so it won't be for over half an hour yet"

"I told you, mummy, what if I..." Janet spied Garth Pratt making his presence known "What if I need to use the facilities?" She whispered.

"Very well Janet, we will wave your friends off, and then I will run you back here in half an hour. But only because I need to change my lipstick, I'm not quite sure if this shade goes with dawn" Janet's mother said, touching her make-up drenched face.

"Eee there's an awful lot of young men here, do you know what time young Ernest will be

1962

setting off?" Mrs Smith bustled her way forwards, Garth Pratt was in his element, making himself useful, and it wasn't even his race! "Will we get to see him go round more than once?" Mrs Smith always wore bright red lipstick. It could be the day, night or otherwise, there was always time for radiant red. Garth Pratt despaired of Mrs Smith.

A few moments later that same morning, when supportive mothers were planning to surprise, and Uncle Billy was having a problem getting dressed, there was a knock on Rose's door.
"Mr Potts! What are you doing here!" Rose Blushed, guiding Mr Potts into her back room and hoping amongst all hopes that her undergarments were not the first thing to greet him on the laundry pulley.
"It is this morning isn't it? Your Ernest's race? You mentioned it at Father's funeral"
"Yes, yes it is, but you've no need to turn out at this time, it's your only day off!"
Uncle Billy sat coughing in his chair, trying to manipulate his elastic braces.
"Oh, you know my cousin, Billy"
"HELLO BILLY!" Mr Potts shouted
"ACHOOO" sneezed Billy.
"He's completely deaf Mr Potts, and he doesn't say much either, but don't think piteously, he's a very talented man is our
Billy" Rose was fussing around with Billy's stretched braces. Billy was chuckling away to himself.
"I'm sorry, how do you do Mr, erm Mr Bradshaw?" Cecil Potts held out his business hand to shake a greeting to Billy. Uncle Billy coughed loudly into

his hands, and then shook hands firmly with Old Potts, with an accompanying wink, because that was all he could say.

"Ernest doesn't know I'm coming to cheer him on, I'm going to surprise him, Mr Potts! Do you want a cup of tea? Although, I don't know if there's time. It's all about time this Time Trial thingy. I've no idea what it means, and he's done one before so I don't know why this one's so special, Oh yes I do. I remember what he said now. 'Cycling clubs from around the region have been invited to participate' I memorised that!" Rose said a lot of words all at once.

"Call me Cecil, Rose" Mr Potts said, he put his newspaper down on the table.

"I'm just excited for Ernest, Mr Cecil... Ooooh!" Rose was distracted by the headline of the Sunday newspaper "Cuban Missile Crisis! Oh, Mr Potts, there's going to be a war, I knew it!"

"Trust me, Rose, this newspaper will be tomorrow's rubbish, I promise you, Mrs Crosby will be folding that newspaper into those little boxes she makes to cradle the citrus fruits, it will be fine, trust me..." Cecil Potts gently held on to Rose Bradshaw's wrists, before she could reach for her hat "Trust me"

"Rrr," Uncle Billy said having noticed two figures walking up towards the door.

"I didn't know that Sundays had six o'clock twice, so much for an extra hour in bed Marigold, and whose is that car outside?"

"Norman, outside voices, please! Oh! Hello Rose, Oh, sorry we're late... erm hello there" Marigold said to Mr Potts.

1962

"Hello, Cecil! Been a long time, you know the wife" Uncle Norman was at it already, speaking without his wife's permission.

Mr Potts and Uncle Norman shook hands, Uncle Norman looked down at his sticky palm.

"Right, come on then Lumb Carr Road did you say the meeting place is, oh I can't wait to see Ernest's face when he sees we've come to cheer him on. Do we only get to see him go round once, though?" Auntie Marigold was expertly arranging Uncle Billy into his braces, coat and flat cap. "He feels clammy, Rose, he feels clammy, have you felt him? Oh, are you alright Billy love? You look absolutely terrible!"

Uncle Billy expertly sneezed Marigold Schofield's Sunday hat right off her head.

"Oh I'm not sure we should take him, it's parky out there as it is"

"Oh, he's been looking forward to seeing Ernest ride a cycling event, though, aww Billy love!"

Uncle Norman sucked in a large amount of air, turned his head and raised his eyebrows at Mr Potts. "He can hardly say a bloody word, but Rose reckons he speaks to her"

"What's that you say, Norman?"

"I was just asking Mr Potts about his new car, dear"

Uncle Billy had been looking forward this day not quite, but nearly as much as Ernest that was true. Surreptitiously shining up the chrome on Ernest's Green Viking. Keeping the chain oiled in a clandestine manoeuvre, Uncle Billy could fix anything. Not only that, he had been shoving the biggest bits of meat from his own plate onto his dear nephew's. Athlete's need protein. Every fool knows that. Today, though, Uncle Billy had been coughing and spluttering all of the previous night. It must be going around, nasty it was. He looked at the clock and his two fussing nieces, eyes widened gesticulating and clucking like the little girls he had gone to live with when he was a teenager. Time was of the essence in a Time Trial race. Billy knew he had to do it. He took off his coat and hat and pretended he was falling asleep in the chair.

"Right well there's nothing else for it, Rose, he obviously needs his sleep, he'll be alright, but we'd best set off now otherwise we'll miss Ernest!"

Car doors made that neat shutting sound, engines were started and the two sisters were conveyed towards Lumb Carr Road.

Uncle Billy risked opening one eye, and when he could see car headlights had vanished, he expertly opened his other eye. He looked at the blank wall where Ernest's bicycle had been a short while before, and although he was not in church, it was a Sunday, he thought of Father Dunn, put his hands together and had a private word with God about Ernest.

Chapter 40: An Entanglement of Cyclists.

"Good luck Ernest" Christopher tried to shake hands with Ernest, but his wishes could not be heard against Brenda Towers' rasping instructions and Ernest's family's chatter.
"Ernest! Ernest love!" It was mainly his mother and auntie that were doing all the shouting.
Mrs Towers had hold of him by his elbow.
"You're up next" She mouthed.
Ernest had just enough time to hug his mother and auntie and give the thumbs up to Mr Potts and Uncle Norman... And was that Mrs Smith behind them, peering over shoulders to blow a bright red kiss at Ernest?
"What're they doing here?" He mouthed at his mother. He got in position on his bicycle, just as he saw the back of Christopher being pushed off.
There had been no rhyme or reason to the order of the East Lancashire International Cycling Club Time Trial race. It was as if Brenda Towers' ambitions had become jaded after all that organising and rearranging and list writing of the Heywood Flyers, the Salford Cycling Club, the Bury Clarion. She had decided it would be noble for her club to ride last in the Time Trial, as they had invited the others to compete. A sort of polite challenge, something that Garth Pratt disagreed with, of course.
"Ernest Bradshaw!"
Brian and Brenda held his handlebars and pushed him off, Ernest could have sworn that

Brenda patted the back of his saddle as he cycled away, and it might have been the wind that had started up but were those *tears* in Brian's eyes? "Finally," Said Garth Pratt, both hands on the small of his back "Don't forget to leave the adequate and prescribed gap between the men's and women's trials. Got to be separate, it's the rules! Rule number thirteen of time trialling for..." His voice trailed off into his own importance. Brenda Towers had never wished for anything so much than to be able to speak right then. Her throat was so painful every time she swallowed. She got a box of liquorice all sorts out of her saddle bag and shoved them in front of Garth Pratt. He took one of course. Hope you choke on it! She thought.

Ernest was battling away against the westerly wind. Up and down, round and round. This wasn't about a young man trying to get into the Olympics, this was about Ernest living his life just in case the news was right. Just in case it was all going to end, just like that. And then what would there be? Hurry up, Ernest!
"Bradders! Bradders! Woooooooo! Hahahahahahaha..." Mark Crosby really did get everywhere! Ernest must have told
him about the race today. Surely he had
not come out at this time just to cheer
Ernest on? He was probably up to no good and
 had just happened to spot him, on Bolton Road
 West... quite a distance from his house.

Sunday morning, a light flicked on in an upstairs

bedroom window in a vicarage slightly off the main road. Father Dunn opened his curtains to welcome another Sunday in, of 1962. Getting towards the end of the year now. The bedroom light caught Ernest's attention; just for that split second, he could have sworn that he saw the Vicar in his underpants and dog collar. Oh no! He noticed me! He waved! He probably thinks I'm not going to make it to church! Hurry up, Ernest.
Is that Harold Goatshead on the pavement? He's milking that ankle fracture! He'll be forever on those crutches if he's not careful.
Up down, round and round revolutions Ernest's powerful legs. He was taking it in his
stride. A professional. Surely he couldn't give this up for a life of electricity?
The morning light of October, is that the sun coming up? Or the smog setting in? No one ever knew; Ernest did not care. He was making a good time, trees, houses whizzing past. He was passing them by with speed. Exuberance, exhilaration, Ernest! He was leaving it all behind. Courageous and determined in whatever he was doing. How fast could he cycle today?! Clawing his way back to the finish line with each revolution, as he reached the end of Bolton Road West, Ernest caught sight of Christopher! He reckoned on a fifteen-second gap between them. Ernest was catching up,Christopher batted away the wind so that Ernest did not have to, giving him a twenty percent advantage.
"Christopher!" Ernest shouted. Christopher indicated he knew Ernest was behind him, the sun behind them, he had noticed Ernest's shadow at the back of his wheel. Push, push, up, down.

They had covered considerable ground, approaching the halfway mark, under the disused railway bridge at Stubbins when Christopher's eye was caught on the image of a waterproof cape. The figure of a man and his bicycle stood on top of the bridge.

"Ernest! Ernest! Look who's cheering us on!" Christopher turned his head around, his neck acting as an axle, his front handlebars acting as a see-saw.

"Y'what, Christopher?" Ernest could not hear Christopher or quite see the man on the bridge, or his waterproof cape. Maybe he's forgiven me, for whatever it is he thinks I did. Or maybe he's about to accuse me of cheating again! Ernest had never had to question a friendship before in all his fifteen years.

"Go all out, lads!" Harry Hill recognised Ernest and Christopher by their matching jerseys. He had had to wait for all the other cycling clubs to get through first of course, the Todmorden Flyers and so on, but it was worth the wait, Norm Schofield's nephew was certainly a talented young man. He could see something in Ernest that he thought he had seen in himself all those years ago. Now, the two lads should have appeared at the other side of the bridge by now like a couple of pooh sticks on bicycles. But there was a crashing sound, crashing and shouts of exclamation. It all happened so quickly, the two boys had collided.

"Oh! Christopher! Are you alright! Ernest ran to him, under the bridge and in the darkened morning light, their bicycles looked like a tangled web of fate, adding on to their time, yet renewing their friendships.

"By the 'eck!" Harry Hill had abandoned his own cycle and made it to the roadside "Are you alright to stand both of you? Christopher,
it's a good thing you're wearing that helmet.
Best thing, let's get into the light and assess the situation, then hurry up and get back on it!" Harry Hill knew what to do.

Ernest had a minor contusion on his elbow, the mud and grit from the road imprinted on his right forearm like a child's potato painting stamp.

Christopher was standing on his two feet, he had not even reached the ground, Ernest's bicycle forcing his bike into the bridge wall, that he had started careering into when he was trying to tell Ernest that Harry Hill had come out to cheer them on. The collision was Harry's fault really.

"I was trying to tell Ernest that you had come to cheer us on!"

"Yes, but how's your head?"

"The same as it was a few minutes ago!"

Ernest, despite his smarting elbow, was feeling great. Time was ticking on, he was aware of that, but Christopher was back to normal, he just knew it.

With a quick dusting down, both bicycles were wheeled on to the flat. No obvious signs of damage, just a few scrapes.

"Well come on then, get back on quick! Need me to push you off?"

"Should we carry on Christopher? I mean we won't get the time now that we've collided"

"You'll still get a time lads, just let Brian know what's happened. You're teammates aren't you?"

Ernest and Christopher looked at each other and nodded in agreement.

"Aye, of course, we are!" Christopher said. Four hands gripped two handlebars and they were ready for the off.

"Are you the last Ernest?" Harry said.

"Yes, but the women's event is starting just after the men's"

"Crikey, you'd best get going, hurry up! You don't want the girls chasing you!"

"No, I flamin' well don't!" Ernest said.

And with that, they were off.

"Go all out, lads!" Harry Hill shouted, his waterproof cape billowing in the wind.

Push, push, up down, absolutely gutted but hearts no longer were broken.

"Janet Dootson?" A familiar voice rang in Janet's ears like an alarm clock. She instinctively turned away in her bobble hat. Cycling was her thing, her solitary hobby, she

 didn't welcome any friends amongst the female
 riding crowd... this was her thing, how dare
 they.

"Janet Dootson? Is that you?" the alarm clock said.

Now, depriving the human body of one sense often enhances another. Today, of all days, Brenda Towers had not been able to speak due to laryngitis. Her foresight, however, had much improved. And from the other side of the group, the hubbub of cycling fans, as Brenda had predicted, she could clearly see that Janet was feeling uncomfortable; Brenda was right by her side like an anxious cat.

"Hello Janet, I had no idea that you were into team events!"

"Oh, hello Miss Little. Well I do like cycling, but I... well I have entered a cycling race before, and I joined this club, and..."

"Brenda Towers" she held out her hand to introduce herself, but her name rasped out of her throat, like a dying rattlesnake.

"This is Mrs Towers, Miss Little, she is the leader of my cycling club" Janet turned to Brenda "And Miss Little is just the games mistress at school" Brenda Towers opened her mouth to try and say 'oh a teacher, I'm a qualified teacher' and Miss Little opened her mouth to say 'what do you mean by *just* the games mistress?' but Brian stepped in. He shook Miss Little's hand.

"Our Janet is my wife's protégée. Saw her cycling down our brew and said, 'Brian, that young lass has got some athletic talent on her' and she's been part of our club ever since. The Grammar school is it? Well 'appen you should introduce a bit of cycling into your lessons!" Brenda Towers loved her husband very much, and Janet was glowing too.

As the last male riders arrived at the finish line, times shouted out and recorded, it was time for the female riders to line up ready for the off.

"Ernest! Ernest! What has happened, oh I knew it wasn't safe, the speed you go! You should slow down! Be more careful!"

Ernest laughed at his mother.

"We had a crash, Christopher and me!" Ernest's grin was beaming from ear to ear, despite a time of twenty-nine minutes.

"Blimey, we could have walked faster" Christopher slapped Ernest on the back. Rose Bradshaw's eyes were blazing at Christopher.

"Oh, it's not Christopher's fault! It was Harry Hill, the Olympic local hero! Christopher was so excited to tell me that he had come out to cheer us on, that we had a collision! The opposite of what he had set out to do!"

"Harry Hill! Well, I'll make sure I get a pint out of him later at the Brown Cow for that!" Uncle Norman lunged forward to hug Ernest, Auntie Marigold pushed him out of the way.

Janet could hear much clucking and fuss over by the men's crowd. Ernest' mother and auntie wrestling over who could spit on a tissue the quickest to wipe the mud off Ernest's arm "Ger-off!" he was shouting.

"Stop fussing, Mother, I didn't even bang my head!" Christopher joined in.

Then Brian Towers came over to assess the situation. At least they were friends again.

Chapter 41: Victorious.

Brenda Towers' knees were clamped together, her jaw was clenched, her fists were balled. If only she could shout! For the second time that day, Brian did the talking for Brenda.
"Come on Janet! Dig in! Dig into those reserves!" Janet was grinning from ear to ear, the sun had risen, and the wind had rescinded. The sweeping hand of the stopwatch counted for the thousandth or so time that day.
"Number five, twenty-seven minutes!.."
"I don't bloody believe it, she's the fastest female rider so far today!"
Brenda was exploding, not being able to speak. Janet hopped off her bike.
"Oh, come on, tell me what I got then? I had a bit of trouble, you know I'm not keen on going downhill!"
"You're winning Janet!" Brian said. Brenda's eyes were popping so far out of her spectacles, her eyeballs were nearly dusting the glass.
"Only two more riders to come in, so we'll see what they get, but if they're slower than you, we'll be able to crown you queen of the East Lancashire International Cycling Club!... Oh, well underneath Brenda that is" Brian said.
"Janet, Janet I knew you would be good at *something*. Oh Janet, wait until I tell your father he will be so embarrassed that he wasn't here! Oh, and wait until I tell the women's circle!" Mrs Dootson appeared to have more silk scarves on than usual, and yes, had changed her lipstick.

Brenda had been overwhelmed with lipstick marks on her plastic tea cups today with Janet's mother and Mrs Smith.

"Well done Janet, that's great," Christopher said, stepping out of the crowd. Janet looked around and behind him.

"Is Ernest not with you?"

"No, he's gone home, said his Uncle Billy is not well, his boss, Old Potts gave them a lift home in his new car"

"Oh"

Rose Bradshaw had received a complimentary knowing nod over the top of Brenda Towers' spectacles when she stepped into Mr Potts' Alpha Romeo after the race.

"What time did you two get then?" Janet asked, and Christopher explained the whole sorry story, as the remaining two female riders approached the finish close together.

"Oh looks like they've had a nasty collision, I hope that Harry Hill's not up on that bridge still cheering folk on!" Brian said.

Janet's mother was negotiating if Janet was to return home with her, somehow folding Janet's bicycle into her Ford Anglia 105 E car, or cycle home herself; When it was announced:

"Janet Dootson is the women's winner of the East Lancashire International Cycling Club's maiden Time Trial!"

Janet burst into tears. But they were not the tears of victory.

Chapter 42: The End of the World.

Because her mother was anxiously rearranging her headscarf, Janet clutched on to the nearest person she could, Christopher. Huge teeth in gigantic rows smiled a delighted smile. Janet's face was hidden in purple and lime green racing jersey and bobble hat. Ernest had a dramatic bow out of the Time Trial with his worst time ever, even the Hercules carrier had delivered a better time than today. And now here was Janet. Stealing Ernest's thunder. He would probably never forgive her. No wonder he had not hung around until the end. All that Janet could do was turn to Christopher for consolation, and Christopher was delighted.

"Would you like to come in for a cup of tea Mr Potts?" It was awkward, but Rose felt she should thank him for the car drive up to the Time Trial and back. There would be just enough time for a small cup of tea before setting out to church. Father Dunn's eleven o'clock service. It was awkward for Mr Potts,Ernest would be following them not long after on his bicycle, would they all be sat there with her deaf cousin drinking tea? This was Rose Bradshaw and this was the moment he had been waiting for, for nearly two decades, and he had left his newspaper inside her house.
"Do you know what? I would love a cup of tea"

Rose swung her legs out of Mr Potts car with its new car smell and dependable interior. She opened the back gate. No Uncle Billy stood at the window as he sometimes does when he can tell the back gate has been opened. She opened the back door.

"Billy! Oh, Billy!"

Uncle Billy was lying on the floor next to his chair. It was freezing cold in the back room, and of course, could not hear Rose.

"Quick! Do you have any blankets, Rose?" Cecil Potts dashed to Rose's side and to her rescue. He rolled Uncle Billy over, who appeared to be asleep, he was sort of softly snoring from his chest, but therefore breathing.

"Oh, do you think we should telephone for an ambulance? Oh, I've no change for the phone box!"

"I don't think you need any change to ring the emergency services"

Uncle Billy looked like he was starting to come round. He was not able to explain what had happened, and even if he could speak, he was not sure how he had ended up on the cold kitchen floor asleep. His head hurt, and his chest hurt every time he coughed. Uncle Billy felt so unwell, that it didn't dawn on him to wonder how Ernest had got on today.

"I think we should help him to get on his chair" With much pushing and shoving and tests of physical strength, Uncle Billy, who is heavier than he looks was helped back on to his chair. Rose put the fire, and the kettle on.

"Oh hello Ernest love, you're back, it's Uncle

Billy, we think he's had a fall, he's not well"
Rose explained the whole thing to Ernest as she
made a cup of tea. And Uncle Billy started
coughing.
"He looks in a lot of pain Rose, now that Ernest's
back, he can help me get Uncle Billy in my car
and we can take him to the infirmary.
"Your nice new car? Oh don't be silly Mr Potts you
don't want to be doing that, giving people lifts
here and there, we'll get the bus. I'm sure Father
Dunn can forgive us just this once."
Cecil Potts thought about what he could say, that
it was really no problem, that taking Uncle Billy to
the hospital would mean that he got to spend
more time with Rose, that his main reason for
spending his Father's money and buying that
extravagant car was simply to impress Rose. But
what he actually said was :
"Trust me, it's no problem"
"Yeah, and I get to have a ride in it too," Ernest
said, inviting himself along.

At the Time Trial finish line, the sun was shining
on Janet's victory. The crowd had dispersed,
parents in cars had driven away. Even Garth Pratt
had disappeared.
"Right you are then, well done you two, and
especially to you Janet. I'll make sure the
results get in next week's paper for your mother's
... what was it? Mother's union?"
"Women's circle. Thanks, Mr Towers" Janet said.
Mr and Mrs Towers set off home to Lever Brew
with a rucksack filled with empty sweet tea
flasks.
Then it was just Christopher and Janet left.

"Do you fancy an Icecream?" Christopher said, knowing there was a little newsagent shop next to the Hare and Hounds pub.

"Yes, I think I do," Janet said.

They sat together on the park bench, Janet's feet swinging as they could not reach the floor.

"Are you sure that Ernest will be alright about me getting the best time from our club?" Janet swung the conversation back to Ernest. Christopher thought about what he could say, that Ernest would not be giving Janet a second thought, but that he would, that he had been thinking about her a lot since the day they met on Blackburn Road, but what he actually said was :

"Trust me, Janet, he won't mind. Don't worry about it"

"Hmm"

"Christopher, did you know there are plenty of Italian ice cream shops about because miners started buying ice cream to soothe their throats of dust after they had finished work"

"Fancy that! Who knew eh?" Christopher looked at Janet's freckly button nose "Who cares Janet?!" Christopher went for it, and playfully blobbed a circle of ice cream on the end of Janet's nose.

"Hey!"

It worked, Janet was laughing! She did not have to think what to say to Christopher, her words just came out. It was just easy. And Christopher was thrilled to bits.

Later that same day, when dreams of glory had been postponed and worry had set in about dear Uncle Billy, a ward sister adjusted her nurse's hat. "Mr and Mrs Bradshaw?" All three of them sat up to pay attention, they did not correct her because it was 1962.

"Mr William Bradshaw is stable now, he's got a nasty chest infection, and a bit of grazing to his forehead" The nurse took a sideways glance at Rose. "We'll have to keep him in for a few weeks, so he'll need his overnight things. He's only fit for a short visit, so you can either see him now or when you drop his bag off" Ernest and his mother went in to see Uncle Billy. They were both thinking the same thing, how would they explain about Ernest's time in the time trial. He had fallen asleep, though, so exhausted, so there was no need for counting on fingers, and so on. Rose's eyes were red-rimmed when she came out of the hospital ward.

"Oh, Mr Potts! No need to keep waiting, I'm sorry we took a long time, I was just so worried about him"

"He will be alright Rose, trust me," Cecil Potts said, despite what he wanted to say.

The next few hours were a roller coaster of emotions, laced with guilt for missing Father Dunn's Sunday service. An emotional telephone box call to Marigold and Norman to let them know about Billy. Laughter when Ernest told his mother and Cecil Potts about Harry Hill waving to Christopher and himself. Fear from Rose when she worried she should have been out panic buying because of the bomb threat. More tears when they dropped an overnight bag at the hospital for Uncle Billy but were not allowed to visit for the second time.

"The patient needs his rest" they were told.

"Do they know how to communicate with him, Mam?" Ernest had said.

Followed by exhaustion, the most exhilarating and draining day of 1962 so far. Cecil Potts started the engine of his new car with its new car smell.

"How about I take you two out for tea? I know a lovely place, we don't need to make a reservation"

Rose looked down at her dress, her everyday shoes. She had her tweed coat with its fake fur collar on, though. No lipstick, she was not the type. Fortunately, Ernest had changed from his racing jersey despite all the excitement, though.

"Oh! You'll be sick of the sight of me Mr Potts! Work tomorrow!"

Cecil Potts thought about what he wanted to say to Rose Bradshaw, how he would never be sick of the sight of her.

"I promise you, I won't," Cecil Potts said, despite what he wanted to say. "Besides, I need to speak to Ernest about this apprenticeship he's going in for before he leaves me in the lurch with no delivery boy!" he winked at Ernest.

"I heard your sherry supply has dried up anyway Mr Potts!"

"Oh crikey, don't mention the flamin' sherry! I was only doing a favour for the pub landlord. I think he's got Russian blood in him!"

"What makes you say that?" said Rose.

"Because he wouldn't take no for a bloody

 answer! I mean, oh excuse my language"
He turned the radio on.

 *'The time is exactly six pm. The headlines this
Sunday evening... Soviet Prime Minister Nikita
Khrushchev has written to President Kennedy 'I
regard with great understanding your concern and
the concern of the United States people in
connection with the fact that the weapons you
describe as offensive are formidable weapons
indeed.*
The radio fizzed and crackled "Oh I want to
hear this. Oh!" Rose clutched on to Cecil Potts'
arm.   *'In order to eliminate as rapidly as
possible the conflict which endangers the cause
of peace, to give an assurance to all people who
crave peace, and to reassure the American
people, who, I am certain, also want peace, as do
the people of the Soviet Union, the Soviet
Government, in addition to earlier instructions
 on the discontinuation of further work on
weapons construction sites, has given a new
order to dismantle the arms which you
described as offensive, and to crate and return
 them to the Soviet Union."*
The Cuban missile crisis is over.

The news reporter went on to broadcast what
President Kennedy had said, and media
speculation about the past few weeks.
"It's over! See I told you Rose, today's news, is
tomorrow's chip paper"
"Oh shush, Cecil, I want to hear the rest of this
radio programme!" Rose said.

Ernest found it amusing that his mother was talking to Mr Potts in the same tone that Auntie Marigold spoke to Uncle Norman.

"Does that mean that we're not going to get blown up? That Russian bloke doesn't sound that bad, he's going to take all his weapons back"

"Don't worry Ernest, you've got your whole life ahead of you, there's always next year"

"Next year? What for the nuclear bombs to come back?" Rose said.

"Don't be daft Rose, I meant for Ernest to become a cycling champion" Cecil Potts turned the radio down, and his car's windscreen wipers on.

The end.

1962

Acknowledgments

1962 is a work of fiction, the texts of the radio and newspaper reports included in the book have been slightly altered. Although the Cuban Missile Crisis was a true event in history, the novel has been written mainly from the point of view of a teenage boy, who only knows what he overhears the adults say. I acknowledge the information widely available to the general public in the present day regarding the history of 1962. Both on television, such as the history channel, and the internet, such as the BBC website. No direct text has been lifted from any source, the words have been put together by the author.

Speaking as the author, I am extremely grateful to my parents, who not only gave me their personal accounts of what they remember about 1962, they interviewed their counterparts and fed information and attitudes back to myself.

It goes without saying, but I must mention here, I am so very grateful to my Dad, for introducing me to the world of cycling. A sport that has always appeared to have its own
language. Despite having a worse fear of downhill cycling than the character Janet, I used to
 enjoy rides out on the tandem with my Dad, before illness got the better of me. I would also like to say, that my Dad has answered numerous questions about

cycling in the 1960s but must not be held responsible for any mistakes or misquotes I may (or may not) have made when writing about cycling. Please see Bury Clarion on YouTube.

As stated in this book's disclaimer, any resemblance to any person living or dead is purely coincidental. That said, the character Uncle Billy was inspired by the real life story of one of my Dad's relatives. He died when my Dad was very young, he told me what he could remember. I spoke with one of my friend's who's child is deaf, she told me 'It's great you have included a deaf character and how things were back then, it helps people to understand.' The character Ernest Bradshaw is fictional.

Thanks as always to Lyndsey Prince for the cover... and for coping with my scatter-brain.
Thanks to the competition entering cheerleaders. Cake baking, naked, or otherwise!
I am continually grateful to my cake-eating, proof-reading, hard-of-hearing (at book launches) husband, Mark.
Thanks for reading.

More by the author:

Quirky Tales to Make Your day: A short story collection.
Three teenage girls find some sweets in a lift, aliens on the beach in Brighton, a washing machine's memoirs, a couple who do not like

their new neighbours, missing underwear, a witch hunt, Kurt Cobain's ghost, two crimes, and much more. This short story collection looks at the quirky side of life and is almost guaranteed to make your day.

Piccalilly: A remembrance day short story
Piccalilly is a short children's novel about Lillian, an eight-year-old girl who is missing her older brother, Joe. He has been serving in the army in World War One. When Lillian's parents receive a telegram informing them of the worst, Lillian discovers that Joe's spirit is living on in a series of comforting events.

Both available from Amazon.

Sharing is caring; like this book? Tell someone! (Please) Either word of mouth, or a review on Amazon. Thank you.

Watch this space: Future writings include a novel 'Curmudgeon Avenue' about the ill fated Harold and Edith. And another short story collection: 'Short Story Glory'. ©Samantha Henthorn 2017.

Get in touch on my Facebook page SamanthaHenthornAuthor.
Visit me on my blog
SamanthaHenthornfindstherightwords@WordPress.com.

19450897R00196

Printed in Poland
by Amazon Fulfillment
Poland Sp. z o.o., Wrocław